Shannon Kirk is a practicing attorney and a law professor. She attended West Virginia Wesleyan and St John's Universities, is a graduate of Suffolk Law School, and was a trial lawyer in Chicago prior to moving to Massachusetts. She has been honored three times by the Faulkner Society in the William Faulkner–William Wisdom Creative Writing Competition. She lives in Massachusetts with her husband, a physicist, and their son.

The Method won the 2015 National Indie Excellence Award for best suspense, has been optioned for a major motion film by Next Wednesday productions and will be translated into several languages.

THE
METHOD

SHANNON KIRK

sphere

SPHERE

First published in the United States in 2015 by
Oceanview Publishing, Longboat Keys, Florida
First published in Great Britain in 2016 by Sphere

1 3 5 7 9 10 8 6 4 2

A CIP catalogue record for this book
is available from the British Library.

ISBN 978-0-7515-6431-0

Typeset in Garamond by M Rules
Printed and bound in Great Britain by
Clays Ltd, St Ives plc

Papers used by Sphere are from well-managed forests
and other responsible sources.

MIX
Paper from
responsible sources
FSC® C104740

Sphere
An imprint of
Little, Brown Book Group
Carmelite House
50 Victoria Embankment
London EC4Y 0DZ

An Hachette UK Company
www.hachette.co.uk

www.littlebrown.co.uk

For Michael and Max, my loves.

ACKNOWLEDGEMENTS

Many thanks to my supportive family for giving me the time and encouragement to write. To my husband, Michael, who routinely brings coffee to my writing office, I could never have completed much of anything without you. You inspire me to never give up. To my son, Max, who, although so young, finds ways to prop me up and who unwittingly provided the emotion of "love" wherever it may be found in this tale. To my parents, Rich and Kathy, who read every draft of whatever I write and provide not only encouragement, but also excellent feedback. To my brothers, Adam, Brandt, and Mike, I feel bolstered in this world because I know you always have my back. To Beth Hoang, a cousin who is a sister, without your edits and tough love, there is absolutely no way I could ever have a final product. To all my friends and family, thank you for never leaving me alone in this. A special note of appreciation to my brother, Michael C. Capone, an accomplished rap/blues musician. *"Focus. Please. Focus. Breath,"* as used in this novel, is a line from his song "Hate What's New Get Screwed

By Change." Mike's music is a muse to my writing, and I thank him for all his lines.

As a lay person, I relied upon many sources to explain such complex topics as Cross-Modal Neuroplasticity, Altered Cross-Modal Processing, and other scientific topics that are far beyond my comprehension. The following publications provided invaluable background: "Super Powers for the Blind and Deaf," Mary Bates, *Scientific American*, September 18, 2012; "Altered Cross- Modal Processing in the Primary Auditory Cortex of Congenitally Deaf Adults: A Visual-Somatosensory MRI Study with a Double-Flash Illusion," Christina M. Karns, Mark W. Dow, and Helen J. Neville's, *The Journal of Neuroscience*, July 11, 2012.

To my agent, Kimberley Cameron, thank you for giving me a chance. Thank you for taking the time to see through the slush pile, making the call, and changing my life. You are a joy to work with, the definition of grace. To Oceanview Publishing, Bob and Pat Gussin, thank you for giving *15/33* a chance, and for your enthusiasm, invaluable guidance, and support. To the Oceanview team, Frank, David, Emily, Lee, Kirsten, thank you for all the support, thank you for accepting me into the Oceanview family.

~Carpe diem every day~

Brain development can be characterized as the gradual unfolding of a powerful, self-organizing network of processes with complex interactions between genes and environment.

Karns, et. al., July 11, 2012,
Journal of Neuroscience, Altered Cross-Modal
Processing [title truncated]

CHAPTER ONE

I lay there on the fourth day plotting his death. Compiling assets in a list in my mind, I found relief in the planning . . . *a loose floor board, a red knit blanket, a high window, exposed beams, a keyhole, my condition . . .*

I remember my thoughts then as though I am reliving them now, as though they are my present thoughts. *There he is outside the door again,* I think, even though it's been seventeen years. Perhaps those days will forever be my present because I survived so completely in the minutiae of each hour and each second of painstaking strategy. During that indelible time of torment, I was all on my own. And, I must say now, with no lack of pride, my result, my undeniable victory, was no less than a masterpiece.

On Day 4, I was well into a catalog of assets and a rough

outline of revenge, all without aid of pen or pencil, solely the mental sketchpad of piecing together potential solutions. A puzzle, I knew, but one I was determined to solve ... *a loose floorboard, a red knit blanket, a high window, exposed beams, a keyhole, my condition ... How do they fit together?*

Over and over I reconstituted this enigma and searched for more assets. *Ah yes, of course, the bucket. And yes, yes, yes, the box spring is new, he did not remove the plastic. Okay, again, go over it again, figure it out. Exposed beams, a bucket, the box spring, the plastic, a high window, a loose floorboard, a red knit blanket, the ...*

I assigned numbers to give a dose of science. *A loose floor-board (Asset #4), a red knit blanket (Asset #5), plastic ...* The collection seemed as complete as possible at the start of Day 4. I would need more, I figured.

The sound of the pine floor rattling outside my jail cell, a bedroom, interrupted me about midday. *He's definitely out there. Lunch.* The latch moved from left to right, the keyhole turned, and in he burst without the decency of even a pause at the threshold.

As he had at every other meal, he dropped on my bed a tray of now-familiar food, a white mug of milk, and a child-size cup of water. No utensils. The slice of egg and bacon quiche collided with the homemade bread on the plate, a disk of china with a rose-colored toile of a woman with a pot and a feather-hat-wearing man with a dog. I loathed that plate to such an unnatural depth, I shudder to remember. The backside said 'Wedgwood' and 'Salvator'. *This will be my fifth meal on this salvation. I hate this plate. I will kill this plate too.* The plate, the mug, and the cup looked to be the same ones I had used for breakfast, lunch, and dinner on Day 3 in captivity. The first two days I spent in a van.

'More water?' he asked, in his abrupt, dull and deep monotone.

'Yes, please.'

He started this pattern on Day 3, which, I believe, is what kicked off my plotting in earnest. The question became part of the routine, him bringing my meal and asking if I wanted more water. I decided to say 'yes' when he asked and steeled myself to say 'yes' each time, although this sequence made no sense. *Why not bring a larger cup of water to begin with? Why this inefficiency? He leaves, locks the door, pipes clang in the hall walls, a spit and then a burst of water from the sink, out of eyesight through the keyhole. He's back with a plastic cup of lukewarm water. Why?* I can tell you this – many things in this world are unsolved, as is the rationale behind many of my jailer's inexplicable actions.

'Thank you,' I said upon his return.

I had decided from Hour 2 of Day 1 that I'd try to feign a schoolgirl politeness, be thankful, for I soon discovered I could outwit my captor, a man in his forties. *Must be forty-something, he looks the same age as my dad.* I knew I had the wits to beat this horrible, disgusting thing, and I was just Sweet Sixteen.

Lunch on Day 4 tasted like lunch on Day 3. But perhaps the sustenance gave me what I needed because I realized I had many more assets: time, patience, undying hatred, and I noted, as I drank the milk from the thick restaurant mug, the bucket had a metal handle and the handle ends were sharp. *I need only remove the handle. It can be a separate asset from the bucket.* Also, I was high in the building, not below ground, as I had first anticipated, on Days 1 and 2, I would be. By the crown of the tree outside my window and the three flights of stairs it took to get here, I was most surely on a third floor. I considered height another asset.

Strange, right? I had not yet grown bored by Day 4. Some might think sitting alone in a locked room would cause a mind to give way to dementia or delusion. But I was lucky. My first two days were spent traveling, and by some colossal mistake or severe error in judgment, my captor used a van for his crime and this van had tinted side windows. Sure, no one could see in, but I could see out. I studied and committed our route to the logbook in my mind, details I never actually used, but the work of transcribing and burning the data to eternal memory occupied my thoughts for days.

If you asked me today, seventeen years later, what flowers were growing by the ramp of Exit 33, I'd tell you, wild daisies mixed with a healthy dose of devil's paintbrush. For you I'd paint the sky, a misty blue-gray rolling into a smudged mud. I'd re-enact the sudden action as well, such as the storm that erupted 2.4 minutes after passing the patch of flowers, when the black mass overhead opened in a fit of spring hail. You would see the pea-sized ice-balls, which forced my kidnapper to park under an overpass, say 'son-of-a-bitch' three times, smoke one cigarette, flick the spent butt, and begin our trek again, 3.1 minutes after the first hail ball crashed the hood of that criminal van. I morphed forty-eight hours of these transportation details into a movie I replayed every single day of my captivity, studying each minute, each second, each and every frame, for clues and assets and analysis.

The van's side window and how he left me, sitting and able to survey our progress, led to a quick conclusion: the harbinger of my incarceration was a witless monkey on autopilot, a soldier drone. But I was comfortable in an armchair he'd bolted to the floor of the van. Suffice it to say, despite his many protests about my sagging blindfold, he was either too lazy or too distracted to tie the oil cloth properly and I, therefore, ascertained our direction from the passing signs: west.

He slept 4.3 hours the first night. I slept 2.1. We took Exit 74 after two days and one night of driving. And don't even ask about the colossal embarrassment of bathroom breaks at deserted rest stops.

When our trail came to an end, the van rolled slowly down the exit ramp, and I decided to count sets of sixty. *One Mississippi, Two Mississippi, Three Mississippi . . .* 10.2 sets of Mississippi later, we parked, and the engine sputtered in a lurching stop. *10.2 minutes from the highway.* From the top-most corner of my drooping blindfold, I made out a field cast in a twilight gray and glazed with a swath of full-moon white. The wisp-scratch branches of a tree draped around the van. *A willow. Like Nana's. But this isn't Nana's house.*

He's at the side of the van. He's coming for me. I'll have to leave the van. I don't want to leave the van.

I jumped at the loud metal-on-metal scrape and bang of the van door sliding open. *We're here. I guess we're here. We're here.* My heart ticked to the beat of a hummingbird's wings. *We're here.* Sweat accumulated at my hairline. *We're here.* My arms lost all slack, and my shoulders stiffened to straight, forming a capital T with my spine. *We're here.* And my heart again, I might have trembled the earth to quake, I might have roiled the sea to tsunami, with that rhythm.

A country breeze whooshed in as though rushing past my captor to console me. For a quick second, I became washed in a cool caress, but his presence loomed and broke the spell almost as soon as it came. He was partially masked to me, of course, given the half-on, half-off blindfold, yet I felt him stall and stare. *What must I look like to you? Just a young girl, duct-taped to an armchair in the back of your shit van? Is this normal for you? You fucking imbecile.*

'You don't scream or cry or beg me like the others did,' he said, sounding like he'd grasped some epiphany he'd been struggling with for days.

I turned my head fast toward his voice, as though possessed, intending in my motion to un-nerve him. I'm not sure if I did, but I believe he shimmied backwards a fraction.

'Would that make you feel better?' I asked.

'Shut the fuck up, you crazy little bitch. I don't give a shit what you fucking sluts do,' he said loudly and fast, as though reminding himself of his position of control. From the high decibel of his agitation, I surmised we were alone, wherever we were. *This can't be good. He's safe yelling here. We're alone. Just the two of us.*

By the tilt of the van, I could tell he grabbed hold of the doorframe and hoisted himself in. He grunted from the exertion, and I took stock of his labored smoker's breathing. *Typical, worthless, fat slob.* Shadows and slices of his movement came toward me, and a silvery sharp object in his hand glistened under the overhead light. As soon as he got into my space, I smelled him, an old sweat, the stench of three-day-old body odor. His breath was like fetid soup on the air. I winced, turned toward the tinted window, and plugged my nostrils by holding my breath.

He cut the duct tape melding my arms to the bolted chair and put a paper bag over my head. *Ah shit-breath, so you realize the blindfold doesn't work.*

Comfortable in the evil I came to accept in that traveling armchair, I had no clue what was in store for me. Nevertheless, I did not protest our move into what must have been a farm. Given the aftermath scent of cows grazing all day and the high blades and stalks that slapped my legs, I reasoned we entered a field of hay or wheat.

The night air of Day 2 cooled my arms and chest, even through my lined, black raincoat. Despite the bag and the drooping cloth on my face, light from the moon illuminated our trek. With his gun on my spine, and me leading a blinded way with only the moon as my pull, we waded through knee-high stalks of America's grain for one set of sixty. I stepped high so as to punctuate my counting; he sloshed behind in a gunman's shuffle. And such was our two-person parade: *one, swish, two, swish, three, swish, four.*

I compared my sorrowful march to the watery death of mariners sentenced to the gangplank and considered my first asset: *terra firma*. Then the terrain changed, and I no longer sensed the moon's presence. The ground gave a bit with my unnecessarily forced and heavy steps, and, by the sprinkle of dry dust around my exposed ankles, I supposed I was on a loose dirt path. Tree limbs scratched my arms on both sides.

No light + no grass + dirt path + trees = Forest. This is not good.

My neck pulse and my heartbeat seemed to catch separate rhythms, as I remembered the Nightly News' account of another teen, who they found in the woods in some other state, far from me. How distant her tragedy seemed to me then, so displaced from reality. Her hands were severed, her innocence taken, her carcass dumped in a shallow grave. The worst part was the evidence of coyotes and mountain lions, who took their share under the evil winks of devil-eyed bats and the mournful glare of night owls. *Stop this . . . count . . . remember to count . . . keep the count . . . focus . . .*

These dreadful thoughts caused me to lose my place. *I've lost count.* Pushing my horror aside, I steeled myself, swallowed a jug of air, and slowed the hummingbird in my chest, just like my dad taught me in our father-daughter Jiu-Jitsu and tai chi classes and just like the lessons in the medical school books, which I kept in my laboratory in our basement.

Given my quick blip of fear upon entering the forest, I recalibrated the count by three digits. After one set of sixty in the dense wood, we skidded into short grass and back under the unencumbered illumination of the moon. *This must be a clearing. This is not a clearing. Is this? This is pavement. Why didn't we park here? Terra firma, terra firma, terra firma.*

We hit another patch of short grass and stopped. Keys clattered; a door opened. Before I forgot the numbers, I calculated and logged the total time from the van to this door: *1.1 minutes, walking.*

I did not get the opportunity to inspect the exterior of the building we entered, but I pictured a white farmhouse. My captor led me immediately up stairs. *One flight, two flights . . .* Upon landing on the third floor, we turned 45 degrees left, walked three steps, and stopped again. The keys clanked. A bolt slid. A lock popped. A door creaked. He removed the bag and blindfold and pushed me into my confines, a 12' x 24' room, with no way out.

The space was lit by the moon through a high triangular window on the wall to the right of the door. To the front was a queen-sized mattress on a box spring, directly on the floor, but strangely surrounded by a wood frame with sides and slats and rungs and all. It seemed like someone ran out of energy or perhaps forgot the boards for the box spring and mattress to rest upon. Thus the bed was like a canvas that had not yet been secured, only rested crooked within its picture frame. A white cotton coverlet, one pillow, and a red knit blanket dressed the makeshift bed. Above spanned three exposed beams, parallel to the door: one over the threshold, the other cutting the rectangular room in two, and the third running over my bed. The ceiling was cathedral and so, with the exposed beams, one could surely hang – if they so chose. There was nothing else. Eerily clean, eerily sparse, a quiet hiss was the only decoration. Even a monk would have felt bare in this vacuum.

I went straight to the floor mattress, as he pointed out a bucket as a bathroom if I had 'to piss or shit' in the night. The moon pulsed upon his departure, as though it too let out the air it was holding in its galactic lungs. In a brighter room, I flopped backwards, exhausted, and schooled myself on my roller-coaster emotions. *From the van, you went from anxiety, to hatred, to relief, to fear, to nothing. Get even or you won't win this.* As with any of my experiments, I needed a constant, and the only constant I could have was steady detachment, which I endeavored to keep, along with copious doses of disdain and unfathomable hatred, if those ingredients were needed to maintain the constant. What with the things I heard and saw in my confinement, those additives were indeed necessary. And easy to come by.

If there is one talent I honed in captivity, whether seeded by divine design, by osmosis from having lived in my mother's steel world, by instruction from my father in the art of self-defense, or the natural instinct of my condition, it was akin to that of a great war general's: a steady, disaffected, calculating, revengeful, and even demeanor.

This level repose was not new to me. In fact, in grade school, a counselor insisted I be examined due to the administration's concern over my flat reactions and apparent failure to experience fear. My first-grade teacher was bothered because I didn't wail or jump, screech or scream – like everyone else did – when a gunman opened fire on our classroom. Instead, as the video surveillance showed, I inspected his jerky hysterics, slicks of sweat, pock-marked complexion, enlarged pupils, frantic eye movements, track-lined arms, and, thankfully, fruitless aim. I recall to this day, the answer was so clear, he was drugged, skittish, high on acid or heroin, or both – yes, I knew the symptoms. Behind the teacher's desk was her emergency bullhorn on a shelf under the fire alarm, so I walked over to both. Before pulling the alarm, I shouted 'AIR RAID' through the horn, in as deep a six-year-old voice I could muster. The meth-head dropped to the ground, cowering in a puddle of himself as he pissed his pants.

The video, which placed the issue of my evaluation on the front-burner, showed my classmates bawling in huddles, my teacher on her knees imploring God above her, and me atop a stool, trigger-fingering the bullhorn at my hip, and hovering as though directing the mayhem. My pig-tailed head was cocked to the side, my arm with the bullhorn across my baby-fat belly, the other up to my chin, and I had a subtle grin matching the almost wink in my eye, approving of the policemen who pounced upon the culprit.

Nevertheless, after a battery of tests, the child psychiatrist told my parents I was highly capable of emotion, but also exceptional at suppressing distraction and unproductive thoughts. 'A brain scan shows her frontal lobe, which supports reasoning and planning, is larger than normal. 99th percentile. Well actually, frankly, 101 percent, if you ask me,' he said. 'She is not a sociopath. She understands and can choose to feel emotion. But she might choose not to, too. Your daughter tells me she has an internal switch that she can turn off or on at any given moment to experience things such as joy, fear, love.' He coughed and said, 'ahem,' before continuing. 'Look, I've never had a patient like this before. But one need look no further than Einstein to understand how much we don't understand about the limits of the human brain. Some say we have harnessed only a fraction of our potential. Your daughter, well, she's harnessed something. Whether this is blessed news or a curse, I do not know.' They didn't know I was listening through the crack in his office door. I recorded every word to the hard drive in my mind.

The bit about the switch was mostly true. I might have simplified things. It's more a choice, but since mental choices are difficult to explain, I said switch. In the very least, I was lucky to have such a good doctor. He listened, without judgment. He believed, without skepticism. He had a true faith in medical mysteries. The day I left his care, I flipped a switch and hugged him.

They studied me a few weeks, wrote some papers, and my parents yanked me back into a somewhat normal world: I returned to first grade and built a lab in the basement.

* * *

Upon Day 3 in captivity – first day out of the van – we began the process of setting up a pattern. Three meals a day, served by him, on that stupid china plate, milk in a white mug, small cup of water, followed by a larger, lukewarm cup of water. After each meal, he would retrieve the tray with the empty plate, mug, and cups and remind me to knock only when I needed the bathroom. If I did not get a response in time, 'use the bucket.' I never used the bucket. I never used the bucket for relieving myself, that is.

From there, our developing process-setting was punctuated by a couple of visitors. Yes, I was blindfolded correctly for visits, so I did not then ascertain their full identities. But after what happened on Day 17, I set out to catalog all of the particulars so as to later exact revenge, not only on my captor, but also on my jail cell visitors. What to do with the people in the kitchen below, however, I did not know. But let me not get ahead of myself just yet.

My first visitor came on Day 3. Certainly medical, he had cold fingers. I labeled him 'The Doctor'. My second visitor came on Day 4, accompanied by The Doctor, who announced,

'She is doing well, considering.' In a hushed tone, the second visitor said, 'So this is her?' I labeled him 'Mr Obvious'.

When The Doctor and Mr Obvious left, The Doctor advised my jailer to keep me calm and to allow me tranquility. But nothing changed to afford me calm or tranquility until the end of Day 4 when I asked for Assets #14, 15, and 16.

And so, as the light began to fade on my fourth day in captivity, the floorboards again rattled. Through Asset #8, the keyhole, I noted the time, *dinner*. He opened the door and handed me the tray with the nonsensically-patterned plate, mug of milk, and cup of water. *Quiche and bread again.*

'Here.'

'Thank you.'

'More water?'

'Yes, please.'

Locks door, pipes clang, water runs, he returns: more water. *Why, why, why does he do this?*

He turned to leave.

With head to chest and in the most submissive, insipid voice I could tolerate, I said, 'Excuse me. I can't really sleep and I wonder if this hurts ... anyway, maybe if I watched TV, or listened to a radio, or read, or even drew, a pencil with some paper, would maybe ... help?'

I braced myself for a brutal, verbal tirade and even physical violence for my insolence.

He stared me down, grunted, and left without acknowledging my request.

About forty-five minutes later, I heard the now familiar floorboards rattle. I figured he was back, as was the established routine, to collect my plate, mug, and cups. However, when he opened the door, resting on his wide chest, he carried an old nineteen-inch television, a yard-sale radio about twelve inches long, a pad of paper tucked under his left arm, and a rather long, plastic school-kid case. The case, pink with two horses on the side, was the kind you buy for the first day of school and lose in a week. I wondered if I was in a schoolhouse. *Must be abandoned if I am.*

'Don't ask for any more shit,' he said, yanking my tray from the bed and causing the empty plate and cups to topple and clatter. On his departure, he slammed the door. Noises. Uncomfortable noises with him.

Tempering my expectations, I slid the zipper on the pink case, anticipating one dull and stubbed pencil.

No way. Not only two new pencils, but a twelve-inch ruler, and a pencil sharpener too. The black sharpener had the number '15' on the side. I took immediate stock of this valuable asset, which I labeled, Asset #15, specifically the razor within. *Asset #15 presents with its own label.* I smiled at the whimsical thought that the sharpener purposefully joined my plot, a faithful soldier reporting for duty, and determined '15' would form at least a portion of the name of my escape plan.

So as to make my captor feel appreciated for his effort, I plugged in Asset #14, the TV, and pretended to watch. Obviously, I didn't really care about his precious ego, but these ruses we engineer to trick our enemies, lull and rock them safely in their weak insecurities, until the time comes to spring the trap, pull the cord, and strike with the swift hand of death. Well, maybe not *so* swift, perhaps a tinge prolonged. *He needs to suffer, just a little bit.* I unhinged the bucket and used the sharp ends of the handle as a screwdriver.

Not one creature in the house or in the fields beyond surpassed my consciousness that night. Even the moon shrunk to a sliver of dawn while I worked the whole of Night 4.

He did not notice the subtle difference in my jail cell upon delivering my breakfast on Day 5, again on the offensive china plate. At lunch, I fought back a giggle when he asked if I wanted more water.

'Yes, please.'

He had no idea what lay ahead for him, nor the lengths I would go to impose my brand of justice.

* * *

I don't care what the news said at the time, I did not run away. Obviously. Why would I have run away? Sure, they were mad. They were furious, but they would support me. They were my parents, and I their only child.

'But you're an honor student. What are you going to do about school?' My father had asked.

They were even more baffled during the clinic visit when they learned I had hidden my condition for seven months.

'How can she be seven months pregnant?' Mother said to the obstetrician, even though her voice did not match the way her eyes accepted the undeniable sight of me.

In reality, I had not merely 'gained some weight,' but had grown a perfectly round globe beneath my then swelling breasts. Embarrassed with her own self-delusion, Mother hung her head and sobbed. My father put a tenuous hand on her back, not sure what to do with the woman who rarely shed a tear. The doctor looked at me and pursed his lips, kindly though, and he changed the subject to the near future. 'We'll need to see her again next week. I want to run some tests. Please stop at the receptionist for an appointment.'

If only I knew then what I know now, I would have been more perceptive and caught the clue in real time. Instead, I was too wrapped in my parents' disappointment to realize the duplicity behind the receptionist's glare or the chlorophyll fog surrounding her misplaced presence. But I remember now; I had subconsciously logged this information at the time. As we approached her, the white-haired, tight-bunned woman with green eyes and false pink cheeks addressed only my mother.

'When did the doctor say she should return?' the receptionist asked.

'He said next week,' my mother answered.

My father hovered over the scene, sticking his head into
my mother's space; his legs dovetailed hers – they appeared a
two-headed dragon.

Mother fidgeted with her purse with one hand and opened
and closed her other around a non-existent stress ball by her
thigh. The receptionist studied her appointment book.

'How about next Tuesday at two? Oh, wait, she'll be in
school, right? Prospect High?'

Mother hates unnecessary dialogue. Normally, she would
have ignored, even sneered, at the irrelevant question about
my high school. Normally, she might answer such a superfluous question with her own biting query, 'Does it really
matter where she goes?' She is volatile and has no patience
for stupidity or people wasting her time. Ill-tempered, highly
efficient, particular, methodical, and full of disdain, these are
her qualities: she is a trial lawyer. But on that day, she was just
a distressed mother, and she hastily answered the question as
she fumbled through her date book.

'Yes, yes, Prospect High. How about three-thirty?'

'Sure. Let's put her at three-thirty, next Tuesday.'

'Thank you.' Mother was only barely listening at this point,
and she quickly shuffled me and my father out of the clinic.

The receptionist, however, continued to eye us, and I eyed her eyeing us. At the time, I thought she was collecting town gossip about an 'unfortunate' teen pregnancy from a 'prominent family'.

She had our address from my records, of course, and just learned that I did not attend any of the local private schools, which meant she knew I lived a block from the public school, which, in turn, meant she could correctly conclude that I walked to school, down a heavily wooded and rural country road. Like a wrapped gift, I presented as the perfect target for this scout. Behind her squinting eyes of cold calculation and her curled hooked nose, she must have set things in motion the second we left the clinic. Perhaps my memory betrays me and makes me imagine this, but in the pictures in my mind, I see her pick up a phone and cover her pink-stained lips to speak. In this picture, her green eyes never lose sight of my return stare.

Mother most definitely would have noticed my developing condition much sooner, but for the fact that she'd been gone for most of the prior three months, on trial, in the Southern District of New York. She came home one weekend, and I made sure to be 'skiing with a friend in Vermont'. My father took the Amtrak once to visit her. I stayed at home, unattended but trusted, to do homework and complete lab experiments in the basement.

Don't get this wrong, my mother loves us. We knew, however, my father and I, we'd be better off leaving her be when she was in 'trial mode,' a state of war where she became consumed with tunnel vision in her one mission, winning the verdict, which she did 99.8 percent of the time. Good odds. Corporations loved her. Plaintiffs hated her. Investigative units of the DOJ, SEC, FTC, and the United States Attorney General's Office considered her 'the devil incarnate.' The liberal press routinely vilified her, which only served to increase her book of business and solidify her status as a rainmaker. 'Wicked', 'unrelenting', 'indefatigable', 'ruthless schemer', these were the words they used and which she blew up and framed as art for her office walls. Is she wicked? Personally, I find her rather soft.

My father would not have questioned my developing weight because he sees details only in miniscule and undetectable things, such as quarks and protons. A former Navy Seal-turned-physicist, he has a specialty in medical radiation. At that time in our lives, he worked feverishly on a book he was commissioned to write about the use of radiated balloons to treat breast cancer. As I recall, he, too, became consumed with tunnel vision. My mother in trial mode, my father with a publishing deadline. With this perfect storm of parental absence, my condition remained inconspicuous to their hurried lives. But, this is not about blame. It is about reality. I got myself into

21

my situation. I and another, of course, created my state. And I have never regretted what some might call a 'mistake'. I never would, but some might.

In the car ride home from the clinic, I sat silent in the backseat as long as I could. My parents held hands and consoled each other, without pointing fingers, in the front seat. I assumed Mother ached in her maternal guilt, and I tried to tell her that her career had nothing to do with my predicament. 'Mom, I didn't plan this, but trust me, it would have happened even if you stayed home and baked brownies every day. There is, on average, a .02 percent failure rate with the latex condom, and, well . . . ' I paused because my father audibly cringed, but I continued nonetheless; after all, science is objective. 'Biology will find a way, even with the smallest of odds. I'm still getting straight A's. I don't take drugs. I'm going to finish school. I just need your help.'

As expected, I received a litany of predictable lectures about disappointment, how unprepared I was for this responsibility, and how I had made my own life difficult at a time when I should be enjoying my childhood and focusing on finding a college.

'I just don't understand why you didn't come to me sooner – and how you chose to reveal yourself. I, I don't understand,' Mother said, her eyes weak and dark with a depression I'd never seen in her. It was true, the manner in which I showed her my pregnancy was a bit, well, stark. But let me not get ahead of myself here.

I didn't answer her anytime she asked why I hadn't told her sooner because, frankly, I didn't know how to answer in a way that would please her. When you often neglect to turn on emotions, you act on facts alone, on practicalities. And the bare truth was, I was factually pregnant and I did not think it practical to disrupt Mother's trial. I understand this may be hard to understand. Perhaps my story will help to explain, even to myself, my thoughts. My actions and inactions.

'We love you though, very much. We'll get through this. We'll get through this together,' she said. She repeated this mantra, 'We'll get through this,' in mumbles as she coached herself to action over the remainder of the week. And, as she calmed, she went to her safe harbor: scrupulous strategy. At some point, she called her office and said she wouldn't be back until the following Monday. She collected the appropriate prenatal vitamins and turned the library into a nursery. I did whatever she told me to, relieved and grateful for her support and, in spare moments when I released and tested my fear switch, scared out of my mind.

On the Monday following the clinic visit, the day before my scheduled follow-up OB/Gyn appointment, I slipped into my lined, black raincoat and grabbed an umbrella before leaving for school. My backpack was stuffed with books, a pair of stretch pants, sports bra, socks, and change of underwear – all needed for an after-school yoga class I had not signed up for. It was a tiny detail remaining from my months of unintentional deception, one I had neglected to tell my parents, for I was taking yoga on advice from a maternity book I had stolen from the library. Bottom line, to anyone else who didn't know, it appeared as though I'd left with a change of clothes.

Nevertheless, I slung my backpack over my shoulders and hunched out the front door, where I stopped. *Damn, I forgot the flat tacks and hair dye for art class. Lunch too. I better bring two lunches, so I don't pass out from exercising.* Without closing the front door, I went back to our butcher-block kitchen counter, grabbed the tacks – a mega-pack from my mother's law firm supply room – and dye and dropped them in my backpack, which I'd thrown on the counter. I then made four peanut butter and jelly sandwiches, threw them in too, and, because I didn't have time to parse everything, I also stuffed a whole canister of peanuts, a bunch of bananas, and a two-liter bottle of water. Look, you try being sixteen and pregnant. You get hungry, okay?

With the strained parcel on my back and my belly out in front, I looked like a terribly drawn circle with stick legs. I continued on my way, with poor balance given the weight on top, and stepped to our gravel driveway. At the mailbox, for some unknown reason, I was compelled to pause and look back at my house, a brown gambrel, shaded in a pine forest. Red front door. I believe I wanted to see if my parents' cars were both gone and to confirm they had returned to work – to their regular lives. Perhaps I found security in believing they'd continued their routines despite our familial upheaval.

At the end of the driveway, I had an equidistant choice of turning left or right: the back entrance of the school to my left and the front entrance to my right. I timed the distance once, going to the left took 3.5 minutes, and going right took 3.8 minutes, door to door. Really, the decision of going left or right landed upon my daily whim. My whim got it wrong on that Monday.

I turned right and continued under the canopy of my black umbrella in the direction of traffic. Fat raindrops pelted my cover and the ground around me, as though an airstrike began or the gunman had returned. Whenever I hear firing pounding like this, I think of first grade, so naturally, I thought of alarm bells and the blessed sight of policemen pig-piling a gunman. Distracted in this way and lost in macabre memory, I failed to notice the wet, hard, gray clay morning was a prelude, a herald of bad fortune.

Had I gone left, he would not have been able to pull the van alongside me to take me by surprise. He would have caused too much of a scene, for he had only about five seconds of roadway to haul me in, undetected. They had planned this out. Practiced, I believe. At first, I supposed they thought me worth their time. A healthy, young, blond girl with a healthy baby boy in her belly. An American girl with high honors, from a wealthy family, and the prospect of a startling career in science. I had received awards for my advanced experiments, demonstrations, models, and reports. Every summer since the age of six, I went to science camps, and all year I entered private contests. With the help of my parents, I built a lab in the basement with state-of-the-art equipment. A store-bought microscope had no place in my world. My equipment came from the same catalogs used by major universities and international pharma corporations. I studied, I measured, I counted, I calculated, everything. Be it physics, chemistry, medicine, microbiology, I loved all pursuits requiring order and comparison, calculations, and provable theories. I was coddled in this hobby of science and indulged by busy parents with a surplus of money. MIT was a foregone conclusion. *My baby and I are very valuable,* I thought as the abduction occurred. To my great dismay, however, I soon learned a hard lesson: we were not wanted for brains or ransom.

About twenty steps into my morning commute, a maroon van appeared upon a whisper, masked by a clap of thunder. The side door slid open, and a pot-bellied man pulled me in from my left. Simple as that. Quick as that. He threw me on an armchair, which was bolted to the corrugated metal floor of the van. He jammed a gun so close to my face, the steel hit my teeth, tasting of an inadvertent bite of the fork, the one that lingers in your mouth. One car whooshed by, splashing the quick puddles on the pavement, oblivious to my plight. Instinctively, I crossed my belly with my arms. His eyes followed my action; he moved the barrel of the gun to my navel.

'You fucking move and I'll put a bullet in that baby.'

Stunned to frozen stillness, I gasped and lost my breath. My heart even paused, despite the otherwise wild beating. I am not usually rocked so – only in times of serious shock might I be jolted, my heart set to race. For most of my confinement, I mastered this personal flaw. In the van, however, suffering the debilitation of a flash of emotion, I sat motionless as he pushed me forward, yanked the backpack from my shoulders, and threw it to the floor beside my open umbrella. He placed the gun on an olive-colored stove, held in place on the opposite wall of the van by a series of bungee cords. Then he ripped my arms from my stomach and wrapped duct tape around my wrists and the arms of the chair. For some inexplicable reason, which I have not quite figured out, he turned a green oil rag into a sloppy blindfold. *But I've already seen your face. Your beady black-eyed, puffy face of patchy stubbles and poor complexion.*

I was taken that fast. I was taken for turning right. I was attacked from my left.

He closed the umbrella, flung it to the back of the van, collected his gun, and hunched his way up to the driver's seat. All of which I did not see, but felt or heard, in the micro-filaments in the air, in the micro-decibels suspended on fractions of timing. It is these subatomic particles that now crowd my memory in cycles.

'Where are you taking me?' I yelled to him.

He said nothing.

'How much do you want? My parents will pay. Please let me go.'

'We don't want your money, bitch. You're going to deliver that baby for us, and I'm going to throw you in a quarry with the rest of you worthless girls. Now shut the fuck up or I swear I'll fucking kill you right now. I don't need any shit. Do you hear me?'

I didn't answer.

'Do you fucking hear me?!'

'Yes.'

And those were the facts. I put my foot on the backpack to prevent it from sliding away.

CHAPTER TWO

SPECIAL AGENT ROGER LIU

I was fifteen years with the FBI by the time they doled out case number 332578, the Dorothy M. Salucci case. Child abduction cases were my lot, and such a miserable life it made. As for Dorothy M. Salucci, her case remains the hardest case of my career to overcome. Ultimately, because of her, I quit the FBI. Fifteen years of hell is enough.

I may as well start from the start.

On March 1, 1993, I got a call about a pregnant teen, taken outside her school. This case fit a pattern of cases I had been working over the last year: pregnant teen, married parents, between six to eight months along, Caucasian. The difficulty with these cases is the initial misperception that the child has run away. Statistically speaking, a whopping 1.3 million teens run away each year, a high percentage of which are due to unwanted pregnancies. This statistic means critical evidence is squandered and resources flag in a matter of days, actually hours, worse, minutes, seconds.

In the Dorothy M. Salucci case, we had a boyfriend and two married and seemingly supportive parents insisting Dorothy had not run away. I profiled the picture of the blond girl, noted her high grades and honor student status, interviewed the family and boyfriend, and determined the case required my full attention.

On the first day of the investigation, I arrived around 10:00 a.m. to begin interviews and fieldwork. This was unfortunately not until the day after the kidnapping. The scenario: parents came home from work→ no child→ called police→ searched all night→ called all friends all night→ she didn't return by morning→ FBI alerted→ case lands on my desk. I, along with the local police and my partner, canvassed the entire school searching for anyone who might have seen anything on the morning she vanished. It was the morning, we knew, because her father stated that he woke Dorothy before leaving for work. The principal confirmed she had not shown for school, and due to a serious mix-up, no one called the parents. Fingers were pointed. There was evidence Dorothy had eaten breakfast, and her car was in the garage. Incidentally, the father's co-workers and videotape of his place of business confirmed his arrival at work at 7:32 a.m. He appeared unruffled and normal. I did not suspect the father.

The mother's firm confirmed her arrival as punctual as well; she arrived at 6:59 a.m., according to the security guard who logged all arrivals and departures. Video of the mother at McDonald's, where she stopped for coffee, showed nothing other than a normal drive-thru transaction and commute to work. My partner and I studied the tape of her humming a song to herself and fixing her lipstick in the rearview mirror, daydreaming and un-agitated. I did not suspect the mother.

Dorothy's boyfriend sobbed in the police station of his undying love for Dorothy and their unborn child. His mother insisted she dropped him at school right before 8:30 a.m., and the homeroom teacher recalled his prompt arrival, because he shut the door on the ring of the bell. I did not suspect the boyfriend, nor did I suspect his mother of lying. But, I put surveillance on them anyway.

In the course of our site investigation, we uncovered two clues. Police found one black, low-top All-Star Converse sneaker, which had rolled down an embankment and into a bush off the side of the road, about twenty yards from Dorothy's house. Her parents confirmed the shoe by wailing upon sight of the untied laces. The second clue came from a mother who had, on the morning of the abduction, dropped her daughter off at school. I'll never forget her exact words: 'I remember seeing a maroon van stop, definitely maroon ... Funny. I didn't think it was odd at the time, but, I did notice the Indiana plate. I noticed only because the frame said "Hoosier State", and I had talked the night before with my husband about the movie, *Hoosiers*. It's the only reason I remember. Divine coincidence, I guess.' She crossed herself.

Divine Coincidence echoed in my mind, so I copied the words in curling cursive along the margins of my typed report.

A day later, after we compiled dozens of pictorial options, this Hoosier woman identified a 1989 G20 Chevy Conversion Sportvan, the TransVista, with two tinted side windows. All of this work, finally notifying me, identifying the shoe, interviewing the parents and the boyfriend, checking their alibis, canvassing the school, interviewing the Hoosier woman, collecting pictures of possible vans, and returning to the Hoosier woman for identification, put us three days post-kidnap, in other words, three days behind.

Dorothy's parents went to every news source in the tri-state area and appealed to the national media. But, by the third day, the story no longer took top billing. The home office cut my resources for surveillance on the fifth day, and my partner, who remained on the case with me, got pressure to complete a backlog of paperwork on cold cases. The odds were against Dorothy M. Salucci.

CHAPTER THREE

Day 16 and there were the Kitchen People again. I imagined the kitchen a country kitchen, with yellow and green floral fabric tacked as skirts on wood worktables to hide pots and pans on makeshift shelves beneath. I imagined an old white country stove and a classic mixer in apple green. I imagined two women, of different generations, cooking my meals and wiping their flour-caked hands on red aprons lined with pink piping. I imagined very detailed things about their lives. One was the mother, the other her adult daughter. I imagined them doing this cooking routine for others in the area as part of their homespun business. I imagined they loved cooking for me in this kitchen with high ceilings. After all, most kitchens are on the first floor, yet we climbed three flights to get to my penitentiary, and I seemed to be directly above the kitchen.

All of these things I imagined, and what was so shocking to me was how right I was about some things, and how wrong about others. I choose now to remember the kitchen and those vaporous chefs as I had imagined, a sweet nursery rhyme, a cat on a braided rug lounging in the sun, cushiony women with wide smiles, holding wooden spoons and tossing the cat scraps. A folk song of acoustic guitar lulling the air into a working happiness. Perhaps even a bird chirping on the top of an opened door.

To recap, as I mentioned, my captor did not detect the subtle change in my room when he came to hurl breakfast at me on Day 5. I had worked all night and had not slept the night before. Since then, I had continued to work my plot to fruition.

As he had on Day 9, on Day 16, he arrived earlier than the other mornings, crept up to my bed and shook me until I 'woke'. Of course I'd been fake-sleeping, as if I hadn't been working all night again. He dropped the diabolical china plate by my chest and barked that if I had to 'use the shitter' I had to go 'right now'. He also said he'd come in and strangle me if I moved an inch or made 'even a ping of noise' before lunchtime. 'You girls are a dime a dozen. I'm not taking any chances with you, bitch.'

Good morning to you too, asshole.

I took his offer to go to the bathroom because I had

determined to take whatever he offered. I did not want to turn down any possibility to collect assets or knowledge. Also, I had taken the offer on Day 9, and I did not want any change to our established routine. The slightest deviation could be a serious threat to my list of ordered assets and might alter my forming Escape/Revenge Plan, which, as you know, I had named at that point, '15'. Any branch from the path I had set upon could have been fatal. And while fatality was surely in store, it was not I who would be death's prize.

After quick marching me to and from my morning relief, he returned me to detention and placed the bucket next to me, just as he had on Day 9.

Jabbing his finger in my face, he ordered, 'Use this, but use it on the bed if you have to piss. Do not get off this bed.'

Fortunately, I had returned the handle to the bucket only ten minutes before his arrival.

As the heat rose, the Kitchen People began with the electric mixer, as they had on Day 9. The sound whirred me into a state of near hypnosis for a full hour. I rubbed my growing stomach with the palms of my flat hands, mesmerized by a heel or fist that pushed back to meet me. *Baby, baby, I love you, baby.* Then my floor began to vibrate, which movement was accompanied by a low humming. I concluded this had to be a ceiling fan in the kitchen. With the fan came wafts of roasted chicken, bacon, brownies, rosemary, and most welcome, the scent of fresh bread.

Ladies, do you know your food is for me? Do you know I am a kidnapped girl? I didn't think so. Why else the early morning charade with my captor? Also, his phlegm-filled wheezing accompanied his agitated panther pacing outside my door; him there, my nervous warden. But only on the days they came. On the days the Kitchen People did not come, I don't know where he spent his time in between hurling food at me and collecting that damned plate. Still, certain factors led me to doubt the Kitchen People.

Only their muffled voices found a way to my straining ear. I caught some words, such as 'hand' and 'pan'. Their female tones, one raspy and old, one light and breezy, revealed a mini-hierarchy; one clearly bossed the other.

The Kitchen People's pattern, so far, was to come on the seventh day, which made sense. By studying the smells and the sequence of my meals, I could easily support a hypothesis that they came on Tuesdays to cook my meals for the coming week.

On the morning of Day 16, I almost shouted for help. But I needed more evidence to prove their innocence, and so with Asset #11, patience, I lay in wait to judge them. I had doubt about the level of their involvement because I didn't understand why he didn't bind and gag me on the days of their visits. *Could be, like with the van, he's stupid or lazy or both.* Still. I also had doubt because on Day 9, he greeted them by saying, 'We really like the food.' *We? So they know there is someone else? Here?* When I heard this, I realized they had cooked my meals for the first week in captivity. Seeing the timeline in thin air, I calculated the days between data points:

Day 2 = Kitchen People cook first week's food while I was in van
+ 7 days
Day 9 = Kitchen People
+ 7 days
Day 16 = Kitchen People

With this, it was easy to postulate their intervals at one week apart, and so, I could plan around this predictable cycle.

When he greeted them on Day 16, he said, 'Thanks so much, such great food for us.' This time he gave a false, fake laugh. *Phony.* I thought of my mother. Her disdain for phonies was even greater than her disdain for the lazy. When she encountered the PTO mothers at bake sales, done up in their thick-layered makeup and fried, dyed hair, clickety-clacketing across the gym in their kitten heels and capris and whispering to their fellow cougars about the hot phys-ed teacher's affairs with multiples of their kind, my mother would lean in and say, 'Never be like those vacant idiots. Use your brain productively. Don't waste your time on gossip.' And when they sing-songed a 'hellooo' to her, but soon enough shared looks of distasteful judgment about her, my mother never reacted, except to straighten her already cobra-straight posture and tailored Prada suit jacket. It was as if she and I had a world of our own, which not one unworthy person could penetrate. Shouldn't all little girls live as such? Raised on horse pills of self-esteem.

The Kitchen People tittered and sounded tickled in their womanly, higher octaves in response to the false charm and compliments about their prison food. *Fucking Prince Charming, you lying, piece of shit, asshole. I will kill you.* Although, to be honest, I had to agree; the quiche was delicious and the bread a sweet soft with a perfect mix of rosemary and salt.

But I digress.

So I had doubts, and I was not about to lead with haste by burning all my chances on the Kitchen People. No metrics, no data, no calculations, certainly no benchmarking, supported such an attempt.

Lending to my doubts were my concerns with acoustics. While their voices carried to me, my voice might not carry to them, especially over the mixer and the ceiling fan. If my voice did not carry, he would surely come in and shut me up. *I need not only judge them, I need also to test the soundproofing of this room.* Stomping on the floor might work, but they might believe it was only him and not take action quick enough. I could stomp and scream and make it impossible to ignore me, this captive. But, even if they heard me, I believed we were in a secluded area. So, they might have heard me and set out to help, but he might as easily, I imagined, shoot and throw them 'in the quarry'. I braced myself to get more facts. *Judge them, test acoustics, and insure he won't/can't kill them before help comes.*

All of these doubts led me to design '15' without involvement of the Kitchen People. Most people in my situation, I believe, would have taken the shot, would have yelled, screamed, pounded on the floor for help, and they very well may have been rescued sooner. But I would not allow for contingencies in my plan. *'15' will be foolproof and will have multiple layers of insurance. I am not going to rely on one elusive 'kill shot' or upon the potential that someone else might help, that someone else who invariably gets himself killed. This will not be a formula movie.*

* * *

On Day 17, the visitors returned, The Doctor, Mr Obvious, and this time, a new person. They arrived outside my door at exactly 1:03 p.m., according to Asset #16, my clock radio, which I set using the time given during the nightly news on Asset #14, the TV. Eight minutes before their arrival, my captor placed a pillowcase over my head, pinched the ends around my neck, and tied a long scarf to hold the contraption in place. The tassels met with my fingers, so I rolled them to steady my nerves. He ripped a gash in the case with scissors and his grubby fingers, I suppose as a breathing hole. And then, as though banding the claws of a lobster, he bound my arms over my head, tight, and my legs together as well, also tight.

'Stay still and don't move. Don't speak.'

He left.

When he returned only three sets of sixty later, he brought with him The Doctor and Mr Obvious. This time a woman accompanied them. She spoke first.

'This is her?' she asked.

Yes, 'this is her'. Was it the massive belly or the gigantic boobs giving away my gender, genius? I labeled her 'Mrs Obvious', even though it was hasty of me to so quickly conclude she was married to Mr Obvious. Regardless, had these miscreants not kidnapped me and intended to steal my baby, my mother still would have hated these people and their stupid, meaningless questions. I hated them for my own reasons.

'Let's see it,' she said.

My heart fluttered, the hummingbird returned, but I steadied myself in practiced tai chi breathing. And then I heard the most awful sound. The floor beyond the door creaked as if breaking, and metal wheels rolling on the wide pine boards announced the approach of something heavy. No one spoke.

The object slammed into the door jamb, and after shaking through the doorframe and rolling more, it came to rest at the head of my bed. The slither of a cord or rope scraped past me on the floor.

The song on the radio lost its momentum. A quick silence followed. Next came a scratching sound near the outlet at my feet. *They must need the outlet.* With a whoosh, whatever they'd brought in began to hum. *Must be a machine.*

'Let's give it a few minutes to warm up,' The Doctor said.

They left my prison-cum-hospital to whisper in the hallway. It was so hard to hear through the bag and above the drone of the mysterious machine, I got only fragments of what they said: ' . . . about seven-and-a-half months . . . too soon . . . blue . . . yes, blue . . . '

They spilled back into the clink. Footsteps approached the side and end of the bed. Masculine hands fished around my ankles and untied them, and, before this group of strangers to which I was blinded, my pants were removed, my underwear discarded, and my legs ripped apart. I fought with all my strength, kicking whoever was at my feet in his soft body. I can only hope I hit his groin.

'Relax those legs, young lady, or I'll have to sedate you. Ronald, come here, hold her legs down,' The Doctor said.

He can't sedate me. I need evidence. I loosened my grip, slightly. As soon as I did, without ceremony, warning, or apology, a hard plastic wand with a warm gel was inserted. It moved inside me.

The Doctor kept icicle spider fingers on my belly, pressing for movement and parts, just like I did all day in that cell, but for wholly different reasons. Black malice vs. pure love.

'Right here, this little curve, that's the penis. A boy for sure,' The Doctor instructed.

An ultrasound. I wanted to see my baby so badly, tears swelled up and wet the case on my face.

'Here is the heart. Very strong. Very, very strong. The boy is healthy. He's about three pounds now,' The Doctor said.

But the Obvious couple didn't seem to care about those details.

'And you're sure her parents also have blue eyes and blond hair?' Mr Obvious asked.

'Positive.'

'And, the father of this baby, him too?'

'We don't know who the father is for sure – but we believe the boyfriend is the father. If he's the one we saw her walking with a couple days before we took her, he, too, is blond, with blue eyes.'

'I'm taking it only if it comes out with blond hair and blue eyes. I don't want some ethnic-looking baby in my house,' Mrs Obvious said and laughed, although she most definitely was not joking.

'Your choice. We have a waiting list of customers, but you'll have the right of first refusal, especially given what happened with the last girl.'

'Just get me a blond baby with blue eyes,' Mrs Obvious said upon a hiss and a chortle.

Since my love switch was most certainly 'on' for my child, my heart broke. *He is healthy. He is strong. He weighs three pounds. They want to take him. Someone else will take him if they don't. His heartbeat is strong. He weighs three pounds. She doesn't want an ethnic baby. His heartbeat is strong.*

Hearing this conversation only gave me more resolution, more resolution I did not need. My fury was bolstered, solidified, garrisoned, and fortified. I believe God Himself would have lifted his heavenly palms in defeat upon meeting up with my otherworldly veneer of absolute hate. My commitment to escape and exact murderous revenge became a force unstoppable. With rage, I burned the tears from my eyes and set a course on these unsuspecting cretins that only the devil might have the audacity to attempt to rival, but he'd lose. I became the devil. If Satan were a mother, he, indeed, would be just like me.

The crowd dispersed in a trailing departure. The Doctor said, 'Ronald, leave this thing in here. Doesn't make any sense bringing it back and forth. This is the last you'll see of us for this patient – until her water breaks. Call only if there are problems.'

The room emptied, except for my jailer, *Ronald*.

There was an instant quiet, a moment of dead calm, until he lurched toward me and removed the case from my head.

Ronald, who I will try not to refer to in my re-telling by name out of disrespect, untied my bindings. For a split second, a boring familiarity tricked me, the kind like when Nana leaves after a visit and I'm left with only my parents again. The same-old. The blasé. But not to worry, the second passed quick enough, and unfathomable hate returned, just as I intended – the emotion necessary for me to plan, to plot, to escape, to seek revenge. I grabbed my underwear and pants and put them on.

He gathered the cord to the ultrasound machine, as I sat on the bed and stared at him, my arms crossed at the chest. When he met my eyes, I did not blink. *You are going to suffer, Ronald. That's right, I have your name now, motherfucker.* My pupils were not blue, but were red – crimson, bloody, rageful red.

'Don't fucking look at me like that, you crazy bitch.'

'Yes, sir.' I lowered my chin, but did not change the color of my eyes.

He left.

I went back to work. *Ultrasound machine (Asset #21), extension cord to ultrasound machine (Asset #22), scarf with tassels (Asset #23)* . . .

CHAPTER FOUR

SPECIAL AGENT ROGER LIU

I was in the drama club while attending St John's University in Queens, New York, and I acted for pennies at midnight showings of Off-Off-Off-Broadway-across-Soho-and-down-some-alley plays, which were written and directed by NYU grad students, who toiled in poorly lit theaters for the chance to present their work and the hope that someone, anyone, any late-night critic might stumble upon their masterpieces.

Amateur producers liked to cast me since I'm half-n-half: father's Vietnamese; mother's pure-bred Rochester, New Yorkean. I'm a perfect physical blend of the Asian and the American, although inside I'm 99 percent American – the 1 percent devoted to my father's insistence that we eat Pho once a month.

This is how I met my wife, Sandra. She was also in St John's drama club, and she did stand-up in Manhattan, also past midnight. We'd share a tuna fish sandwich after classes and club and then ride the rattler into the city. We were pretty happy, and we were in love. My major was criminal justice, which I picked only to please my parents. Or, maybe I subconsciously relented to a path set for me long ago.

On a lark or upon Sandra's dare or, perhaps, upon the realization that I'd need a job to support myself and my college-girlfriend-turned-fiancée, I applied to the FBI. Sure, let's go with that. Let's have this be the reason, and let's not pry further.

If only I hadn't scored so damn high on my SATs or inherited the burden of 'exceptional memory' – if anything, I may have a slight case of hyperthymesia – basically, really good memory, which the senior agents sensed from a mile away. If only my vision wasn't better than a fighter pilot's. If only I had half-assed my studies like other night entertainers and dramatists, maybe the Feds would have forgotten me. Maybe I wouldn't be so miserable. Maybe Sandra and I would have been happier living in comic, dramatic squalor.

So there I found myself, in the FBI, fifteen-sucked-away years later, as if on the day of admittance, I was placed into a time warp chamber. Laughter all but completely drained away.

When the lens through which you view the world invites the surreal perspective, you may see life as is: undoubtedly amusing. Sandra still had her surreal lens, and, God love her, she neither pitied nor cursed my loss of humorous sight. Instead, she'd try in vain to draw me from black moods by re-painting what I could no longer see. 'Actually, sweetheart, look closer, don't you see ...' Nevertheless, fifteen years into the thicket and once again I found myself holed up in a remote field office, scraping through miniscule leads about a kid-napped, pregnant teen. And Sandra wasn't the only woman in my life. I had a partner, who I'll refer to as 'Lola' to protect her identity for reasons I will later reveal.

Some cases have no leads at all, some cases have lots of leads, some cases have a couple of good leads upon which you can develop more leads, other cases have one good lead that requires tremendous effort to develop into anything else. The case of Dorothy M. Salucci had one good lead, the van, which required tremendous effort to develop into anything else. The black, low-top Converse sneaker was not evidence at all. How could I find a girl by having her missing shoe? There were no fingerprints or blood splatter on it from her assailant. The shoe was worthless to me. I devoted all of my efforts on finding a glimpse of the van, poring over, obsessing over, scouring each second of every last videotape from every last camera in her town and the surrounding towns and any tollbooth leading from ground zero.

On the eighth day of this effort, I finally caught the image of a 1989 maroon Chevy TransVista with Indiana plates, edging like a snake through a toll. The Hoosier woman confirmed my find: 'Exactly. This is definitely the one,' she said. I rummaged a two-person team back at headquarters to track the van's route from any highway videos they could acquire. Meanwhile, in checking Indiana motor vehicle records, my partner, who was two grades below me and therefore reported to me, uncovered fourteen registrations for late-eighties to early-nineties Chevy TransVistas fitting our lead.

I mention my seniority over my partner only for comic value, for she considered my rank un-considerable; she promoted herself above me and above the rank of God, I swear. As I mentioned, we'll call her 'Lola'.

Whether the registrations were cancelled or current, revoked, or expired, we set out to visit each address associated with each registration. This effort took us around the entire state of Indiana, parts of Illinois and Milwaukee, and a sliver of Ohio, where people were either on vacation or to where they had moved to or sold the vehicle altogether. Each one of these registrants and current owners had to be cleared, which meant interviewing them, profiling them, checking their property, reading their body language, and verifying alibis.

One registrant had died.

One registrant had wrecked his van the month before when he collided head-on with a car carrier full of Porsche 911s.

He showed us the newspaper clippings of the event and all, chuckling, 'Damn Porsches. I hate those little bugs. How can you make any dump runs or buy gravel for your driveway in one of those dinky things anyway?'

One registrant would not submit to a voluntary inspection of his ranch home, but who, upon better reasoning and advice of counsel, complied. He scurried to move a couple of pot plants as we walked through his house. *I don't give a shit about your Mary Jane. I'm here to find a kidnapped girl, idiot.*

Eight registrants were fairly normal, run-of-the-mill Chevy TransVista van owners, and by this I mean they were wholly unsuspicious and actually, were almost clones of each other. I suppose they each had their important distinctions, but in my investigator's mind, I lumped them all in one group: innocent, married retirees. Kind, too, nearly every one of the wives wept upon explanation of our mission, spanking or kicking the side of their van as if punishing it for being the brother of a kidnapper. During these interviews, Lola, who hung behind me and on the fringe, received sideways glances, which I took to mean, 'Does she really have to glare at us?'

As is the case in most instances, we could not find one registrant. He didn't appear to have a formal job anywhere, and not one of his neighbors knew where he'd gone off to. Small town, outside Notre Dame, that's where he was supposed to be. He lived in a fairly large, white Cape at the end of a two-hundred-foot, pine-lined, dirt driveway. A towering red barn loomed behind his home in a flat, grassy field, a spot hidden from roadside inspection. Naturally, this guy piqued my interest. Neighbors confirmed they'd seen him with a maroon van at one point, but they couldn't remember when. 'Takes off a lot. We don't know where he goes.'

I gave the neighbors my card and asked them to call me if he were to show up. Lola hunted down a local judge, knuckle-knocking on his country door while he ate his scrambled eggs. Although I wasn't with her, I can picture the scene. She hulked over His Honor as he signed the search warrant, and then she grabbed a piece of his buttered toast as retribution for having to go to the trouble of seeking permissions from persons she felt were below *Her Law*. 'We should be able to storm into whatever we damn well please to find these babies,' she said, and with this, I did agree. Right to privacy and due process of laws, my ass. Slowed us down. But leave the poor Judge's toast alone.

And, wouldn't you know it, as soon as we got our warrant, a neighbor called. 'He's back. But he has a black pickup. No van as far as I can tell.'

We sped down single lanes with low ditches and long fields on each border to return to our suspect. Along the way, Lola and I kept the windows down, taking in the cleansing odor of dewed grass and bubbling spring water. Indiana.

Indiana, Indiana, take me from her, leave me here, set me with the wheat and the moon and a wisp of a glimpse of her face. Indiana, Indiana. Several vacant swing sets squeaked out this haunt-rocking song to the rhythm of a lonely country breeze.

We greeted our mystery man in his driveway, where he was waiting for us. *Tipped off. Tight community.* Appearing as Paul Bunyan, he wore faded jean overalls, steel-toed work boots, and dangled a pipe from his crooked mouth. 'Name's Boyd,' he corrected when I asked if he was Robert McGuire. 'Robert's my Christian name, but Mama always calls me Boyd.' Boyd was a chicken farmer.

After introductions and the showing of badges, Boyd invited us inside. As we entered, he snuffed out his pipe and laid it on a birchwood card table on the porch. 'Only guests kin smoke in the house, so light her up, Mr Liu, if you got any, as I said, Mama always say, only guests kin smoke in your house.'

I noted, as did my square-jawed apprentice, that so far, Boyd had not once addressed her directly, nor had he suggested she too might smoke in his house. But Boyd wasn't being sexist, at least I didn't think so. I just think he was put off by Lola's no-blink stare and her regular intervals of spitting chewing tobacco beyond his bed of hostas. I didn't tell her to stop or even shoot her any incredulous looks; I had already tried so many times to get her to quit and failed. Her response was always the same: 'With what I got to see in basements and crawl spaces, Liu, spare me pleas about my packy. Now shut up and buy me a Guinness, boss.' I suppose she had a point, but let's add her wanting-to-get-mouth-cancer and her addiction to mud beers to the long list of reasons making my fifteenth year with the FBI pure hell. And also add this tidbit: Lola doused herself in Old Spice, which she reeked of morning, noon, and past midnight on all night stake-outs.

Boyd's place was moderately uncluttered but very dusty. Pans and plates were in the sink, and by the curdled milk smell and the fat, roaming flies, I guessed they'd been dirty awhile. On top of an open aluminum trashcan in the kitchen, a pile of unopened mail spilled over the rim and onto the floor. A dozen or more wet rolls of newspapers littered the linoleum counter. On a rag rug in front of a blue refrigerator, a mammoth Old English Sheepdog lounged, lolling her lazy eyes when we entered.

'Don't mind ol' Nicky. She's a farter, but a damn good dog to me,' Boyd informed, as he offered coffee by pantomiming drinking from a mug and pointing to a percolator. I declined. So did Lola.

Still within the kitchen, Boyd and I sat across from each other at a dandelion-yellow Formica table with thin chrome legs. Lola stood behind me like a sentry, staring Boyd into discomfort, her arms folded high atop the breasts she smashed down and in with who-knows-what – probably duct tape, I never asked.

Boyd bounced his furry eyebrows and pursed his lips, as if to say, *please begin, Mr Liu, you have my full attention now.* And thus began the interview of Mr Boyd L. McGuire. I memorized every word so as to later transcribe the exchange, which is what I did in motel rooms while Lola lurked around rural towns like a vampire, searching for loose-talking, drunk locals who 'might have seen or heard something' or perhaps 'suspect some pervert in town'; and so rumors and dark-alley whispers became her night-woman's probable cause.

Actually, I admire Lola. She was, still is, a good detective for countless reasons, which is why we'll have to obscure her identity. Many a child has been pulled from doom due to her questionable tactics. You never heard me ever once ask her to explain herself. Like a hungry dog, I took whatever intel she poured into my breakfast bowl. I had to feed a hole inside me, damage I'd carried within for decades.

'Boyd, you mind if my partner here looks around your barn while I ask you some questions?'

'Not at all. What ya'll lookin for anyway?'

'Don't know, Boyd. You got something to hide?'

'I ain't got nothin' to hide. Look evra-whar ya'll want. I'm an open book.'

'Thanks, Boyd. We appreciate you helping us out.'

Lola had already banged back out through the front door, having turned and left upon the cue.

'I understand you had a maroon Chevy van?'

'Sure did. Sold her 'bout three months ago.'

'That so? Who did you sell it to?'

'No idea, Mr Liu.'

'Yeah?'

'I parked the van on the curb with a sign, "For Sale". Had an ad in tha paper too. Guy shows up. Said he'd hitched a ride from the train station. Gives me cash, twenty-two hund-erd. Tha' end.'

'What about the registration? Did you talk to him about changing it?'

'Sure. He said he'd take care a 'dat. Don't know much about no paperwork since my Lucy died. She gone, three years ago come next month. God Rest Her Soul. She took care-a all that mumbo jumbo. What, I screw up bad with the law cuzathat, Mr Liu. This why you here? Don't the FBI got bigga fish ta' fry and all is what I mean, but mean no trouble, Mr Liu. Whatever you want. Like I said, I'm an open book, now.'

'No, no. Nothing like that, Boyd. What did the buyer look like?'

'Hard ta' say. Sorta' nondescript to me, yeah. Got him-self a belly, as I rememba. Not real handsome, no. I think he probably had brown, yeah, brown hair. Hmmph. Whole transaction took about ten minutes. I showed him she could start and all, showed him the manual tucked up in her glove box. Said I'd throw in the stove as well. I had an old stove in the back a' her. That was about it.'

'Did you have one of those specialty frames on the plate that says "Hoosier State"?'

'Sure as heck did. Cousin Bobby's boy useta play on the Indiana University basketball team. Proud of him. Proud of them. Proud of my state, Mr Liu.'

'I don't doubt you. This is real helpful, you confirming all this.'

'This guy who bought my van, he did something bad, didn't he?'

'You could say so, Boyd. A girl's gone missing. Trying to track him down as fast as possible to ask him about her. Anything else you can remember about him or the transaction?'

I studied Boyd's reaction and body language, as I was trained to do. Since I had just confirmed his vehicle played a part in a serious crime involving a child and this was no joke and we at the FBI were hot on the trail, if Boyd had something to hide, he likely would have crossed his arms, scrunched his eyes, averted mine, and looked up and to the left when he spoke again, all of which being the tell-tale signs of a liar *creating* answers. Boyd did none of this. He set his palms gently on the table, rounded his shoulders sad, and peeked into my eyes like a tired, old bear.

'I can't thinka one thing, Mr Liu. I'm real sorry. I want to help this girl. Ain't there ina-thang you can ask me 'bout I shoulda noticed? Maybe something will spark some kinda mem-ry.'

I surveyed the log of prior cases filed in my mind, thinking of past clues that led to past clues. I'd been in this situation before.

'How much gas was in the van? Do you remember?'

'Sure as heck I remember. Damn thing was damn near bone dry. I had just enuff gas in my shed to get her started.'

'What's the closest gas station?'

'R&K's Gas & Suds. End of the street. Matter a' fact, he asked the same thing, and I said the same thing to him, R&K's Gas & Suds. End of the street.'

Bingo.

'Did he sign anything? Touch anything in your home? Was he only ever outside or did he come in?'

Boyd turned to look behind him, swiveled back to face me, smiled, rocked his head, and pointed a finger in my direction, proud of me, his child-detective. 'Oh, you're good, Mr Liu, you're good. I never woulda thought of it, but you know what? You know damn what. He used my bathroom.'

Bingo, again.

'I don't mean to be rude, here, Boyd, but I have to ask. Have you cleaned the bathroom at all since then?'

Boyd laughed. 'Mr Liu, look at me, I'm a widower. Hell no, I ain't cleaned no bathroom. Don't even use 'er neither. I use 'er upstairs. Plus I been gone, visitin' my brother and Mama down in Lou-c-ana, where this Boyd was born, now. In fact, took off the night I sold the van. Jus' back ta-day.'

'Anyone used the bathroom since he did?'

'Not a soul.'

Bingo, bingo, bingo. Buyer used bathroom, hasn't been cleaned, no one else used it since.

'A couple of requests, Boyd. First, I'd like your permission to seal off the bathroom and dust the whole thing for finger-prints. Second, I'd like the name and addresses of your brother and mother down in Louisiana. Okay with you?'

'Sure as hell is, sir. But am I in trouble here?'

'Boyd, as long as your story checks out and my partner doesn't find anything suspicious in your barn, you are not in trouble. In fact, we really appreciate your cooperation. Incidentally, do you own any property anywhere other than this house?'

'No, sir. This here all I got.'

'You ever go by any aliases?'

'Boyd L. McGuire is what my mama calls me, and I don't have no right ta' go changin' it, now do I? Mama, she mad

57

enuff I came to live by my Daddy's side of the family in this here Indiana all those years ago. Can't be changin' my name now, can I, Mr Liu?'

'I suppose not, Boyd. I suppose not.'

I rose and walked to the bathroom and sized 'er' up. With Boyd's help, I roughly calculated the square footage for the forensics team, who would later in the afternoon dust for fingerprints. I sealed the entrance with the yellow tape we had in our field car.

In order to generate a thorough report, I inspected every micro-meter of Boyd's house, gun drawn, and with Boyd agreeably outside, leaning against a tree that I could check from nearly each one of Boyd's twelve, curtainless windows. This guy wasn't hiding a damn thing, except maybe the piles of laundry, which I assumed had been abandoned since his wife died. *This chicken-farming bachelor is as innocent as Land O' Lakes butter.*

My partner returned, sloshing through Boyd's side yard in her gait of choice: cowboy. She advised me – outside of Boyd's earshot – how she had walked the whole property, looked everywhere, high and low, and even pressed on walls in the red barn to make sure none were false. 'Nothing,' she reported. Nothing to indicate a crime within. 'Smells like endless whorehouse ass in his barn though – the cheap whore smell, the ones you find on the outskirts of Pittsburgh,' she complained, much like the man-woman she was and as if I would know whatever the hell she meant.

I didn't give one shit about the smell of Boyd's barn unless it was the odor of death, which I knew wasn't there because Lola's nose was trained to ferret out corpses upon even minor whiffs of rotting flesh. Despite my unwillingness to care, however, she complained for the next two days about chickens knee-deep in their own crap. 'I can't get the stench of those chubby, clucking, shitty chickens out of my damn nose,' she said, at least one hundred times. She even took to our emergency smelling salts to erase the malodorous memory. 'Better not harm my hunter nose,' she warned.

Although I didn't suspect Boyd of anything, one quandary sticks with me about him: Who cared for his livestock while he was in Louisiana? It doesn't matter, of course, but I've always wondered. By the time Lola had returned from her inspection, I had already cleared Boyd, so I thought it would be rude to inquire about the attention he did or did not give his chickens. So I didn't ask. And if this upsets you, too bad. I chase lost children, not neglected poultry. Go cry to PETA.

Boyd L. McGuire did, in fact, not own any other property. His brother and Mama in 'Lou-c-ana' checked out as well. But Boyd checking out clean was the best break of all, for elimination of suspects is just as important as finding them. Plus, I got two great clues from our Boyd visit. First, forensics lifted three matching, non-Boyd thumbprints off the doorknob and black rubber toilet plunger – of all things – in Boyd's bathroom. Second, down at R&K's gas station, 'at the end of the street', I was shocked to find that the owner actually changed the tapes in his three security cameras every night and kept them all. Most owners overwrite their tapes. Not this fantastic man. 'This way, here, I'll show you where they are,' he said.

Not only did he have the tapes, they were stored chronologically and labeled, down to the second. I wanted to kiss the man. And what we saw on one tape in particular, well, now this is why people become detectives, for moments like that.

On the night of our productive day with Boyd and the miraculous gas station owner, I called my wife Sandra after a brief celebratory dinner. I had ordered a well-done filet and a Bloomin' Onion at a not-so-nearby Outback Steakhouse – Lola insisted. Lola ordered two rare steaks, three Guinness, two loaded, baked potatoes the size of footballs, and extra rolls. 'Hold those darn veges,' she said to the waitress, 'and bring two slices of peanut butter pie too, please.'

'You know, someday this diet of yours is going to catch up with you,' I said, as I often said.

'With what I got to see in basements and crawl spaces, Liu, spare me the pleas about my food. Now shut up and buy me a Guinness, boss,' she replied, as she often replied. And then she burped.

What a charmer, that Lola.

Sandra was on an East Coast tour of comedy clubs and bars. I caught up with her after her last set at some watering hole in Hyannisport.

'Hey, darling, you make them laugh tonight?' I asked.

'Oh, you know. Same old stuff I always say. Old material. I'm getting old to me.'

'You don't ever get old to me. I miss you.'

'When you coming back? Where are you anyway?'

'Same place I always am, knocking on the devil's door, darling. One of these days, he's going to answer.'

'Don't be so sure he is a he. Could be a she.'

'Could be a she.'

CHAPTER FIVE

Day 20 In Captivity

It takes a long time to knit a full-size blanket. The red knit blanket, Asset #5. Now, mind you, I had a lot of assets. Some of them I did not even use. Some of them I used only partially. Some of them were prepped and ready for use on the Day Of, but became superfluous or irrelevant in the final moments. Like my makeshift slingshot. The red knit blanket, however, was a pure gem. I used every last fiber of that twisted cotton. If I ever had any blood on my hands, it was just the red lint of a beautiful, poetic, knitted piece of art. *Bellissimo, bravo to you, red knit blanket, I owe you my life. I love you.*

On Day 20, I awoke to our regular routine, with three days to go until the Kitchen People would return, and no apparent threat that The Doctor or The Obvious Couple would grace my room. I felt pretty secure in the routine at this point, so I did not expect any houseguests. I was wrong.

In any event, my captor arrived on Day 20, as scheduled, with my breakfast. 8:00 a.m. on the nose. The Kitchen People had made another quiche and, as I expected, that's what I had for breakfast, again, on the, you know it, toile china plate. As you are well aware, I had developed a severe hatred for that ridiculous plate.

Unable to withstand touching the plate for another meal, on Day 20, I picked up the quiche as though my fingers were tongs, unwilling to even brush the china with my skin. I set the slice on top of the television as a new place setting, and, using my sleeves as gloves, placed the plate on the floor where it belonged, with dust bunnies and mouse droppings, to await the hands of a villain, the only attention it deserved. Of course, I laughed at myself, for, rationally speaking, the china held no blame. Nevertheless, I needed some diversion and I did hate the toile.

In sitting on the floor with the quiche on the television, I had a changed perspective on the room. The vantage was only slightly different, yet still, the alteration in my eating routine and my stance caused a shift. Perhaps the vertical course of blood in my brain sparked the idea or maybe looking at the bed at a different angle jolted the solution that must have lain dormant from the moment I walked in and saw those three exposed beams. *The blanket can be turned into a rope.* Everything seemed so clear, finally, on Day 20, that I became disappointed with myself for failing to note the obvious earlier.

Sometimes, I think, we prevent ourselves from admitting inevitable conclusions because we are not yet ready for whatever task is at hand. Our vision becomes blocked to realized knowledge. For example, my mother, a woman who bore a child herself, neglected to admit her own daughter was a full seven-months' pregnant until the OB forced the truth upon her. Perhaps the mind holds us back from connecting the dots so we do not take conscious steps toward difficult changes until we are ready. I must have been ready on Day 20, because I finally achieved in a crystal vision, my entire plot. Until this point, I had put into place only pieces of the puzzle. I previously thought my resolve was hardened, but not until I envisioned the blanket as a weapon, did I realize just how far I was absolutely going to go to free myself and my baby and exact revenge.

You are kidnapped. They will steal your baby and sell him to monsters. They will throw you in a quarry. No one knows where you are. You must save yourself. This is the truth, accept it. Your only tools are the tools in this room. Figure this out. Execute the plan.

I finished the quiche with a smile on my face. Not one crumb cluttered the television top.

It takes a long time to knit a full-size blanket. It takes even longer to unravel. Somehow I knew this innately, and so I wanted to get started immediately. I waited until my jailer came for my breakfast tray and went through the whole bathroom routine. When that ordeal was complete, he left, and I thought I had three-and-a-half hours until lunch in which to un-knit and un-purl. I removed the bucket handle and began the de-knotting.

The air that morning had a yellowy tinge, the melancholic glow that both deflates and sedates you. The sky was an even overcast, which tricked the mind to think the day held no surprise, the blah, the drag-down type of day with no promise. I was wrong about this too.

I fought with a stubborn corner knot by jamming the bucket handle into its core and widening the gaps between strands of yarn, first with my pinky nail, then my whole pinky, and then ferreted the jumble out into a kinked, five-inch entrail. This took one hour, five minutes, and three seconds. At this rate, my projected timeline was already delayed. But before re-casting the completion projection, I figured I would collect de-knotting times over the course of the day to calculate an average. With one of the pencils from the two-horse, pink case, I plotted the first metric in a bar chart I designed.

With the chart started, I began the first row's deconstruction. *La Boheme* serenaded me from Asset #16, the yard-sale radio. Naturally, I chose the classical station: I needed passionate upheaval and eternal, unrequited longing – the kind of emotion you'd die trying to quell – as my motivation. Bubblegum pop-songs might have cost me the extra edge I required. Of course, the hard-core rap of Dr Dre and Sons of Kalal that I prefer today, seventeen years later, could have done the trick as well as any lovesick opera. Currently, as an adult, I crank gangsta rhymes during my daily Marine-level boot-camp workouts, especially when the retired sergeant I hired barks in my face that I'm 'slime.' But the grinding tunes work, because after a fifteen-mile sprint and on my nine-hundred-and-ninety-ninth stomach crunch, Sarge is hiding a reluctant smirk of pride from me. No one is ever going to take me again.

Sometimes I like to spit a wad of blood at ol' Sarge's feet. It is done with the utmost of respect, like a cat delivering a decapitated mouse on his owner's porch. Meow.

But enough with the present. Back to the past.

As Hour 2 set in on Day 20, a black butterfly slapped against the high triangular window and pasted itself in place, wings spread. Was he warning me? *Are you warning me about something?* The universe holds many unsolved secrets and invisible connections. So perhaps he was indeed warning me.

I studied him whole, placing my red dismantling on the bed and tip-toeing toward the window for closer inspection. But because he was so high, the best viewpoint was from about mid-room. *Are you visiting me? Sweet angel, fly to them, tell them I'm here.*

I slid closer, rubbing my belly, my baby, and stood beneath the window, leaning my face in until my cheek was flush against the wall. Due to my growing girth, I had to bend. With eyes closed, I tried to feel whatever vibration the butterfly's heart sent from above. *Is this loneliness? Am I lonely? Please shake this wall with your wings, tell me you hear me, black beauty, black friend. Please anything. Tell me anything. Save me. Help me. Shake this wall.*

Since I allowed the emotion in, I began to sob. I thought of my mother. I thought of my father. I thought of my boyfriend, the baby's father. What I would have given to have the touch of any one of their hands on my back or the brush of any one of their lips on my cheek.

But this wallow into deep sadness didn't last long. As though I had come to a right angle in the road, at the very height of my tears, the day, my plan, and the outlook took a sharp turn. While my shoulders slumped and my body heaved under the weight of depression and solitude, the stairs outside my room groaned under pounding footfall. A fast approach: I heard it. I ran back to the bed, the butterfly abandoned, folded the blanket, shoved my notebook with my chart into the mattress – which I had slit open about six inches on the side facing the wall – and with only one second to spare, lay the bucket handle atop the bucket as though it were attached. In he burst.

'Radio off. Follow me, now. And keep your fucking mouth shut.'

I detect fear in your voice, smell danger in your sweat, dear jailer. I wiped the tears with my sleeve in an exaggerated motion of confrontation, as though smearing blood in a heated street fight and in so doing, inviting the match to continue. *Bring it.*

I slowly walked to the radio and with the lethargy of an obstinate, maniacal child, turned the dial to off, unwilling in my movement to meet his agitation.

'Move your fucking ass. I will throw you down these stairs if you keep this shit up.'

Having fun with you, imbecile, you make this so easy.

I returned to the insipid, compliant captive I was supposed to play. With head bent and shaky voice, I delivered my catch phrase, 'Yes, sir.'

'Move.'

You are so predictable, dumb beast. Throw me? As if. You'd lose your cush job.

He gripped my forearm and pulled me so hard off balance I nearly collided with the bucket. Unfortunately, my foot brushed the side and for three heart-wrenching seconds, I watched the handle tilt and rock on the rim. *If it falls, he'll inspect closer. He'll find me out or he'll give me a different bucket, which might not have a metal handle. Don't fall. I need you. Don't fall. Don't, don't fall. Don't fall. Don't, don't fall.* Still it tilted and rocked. With head backwards as I was yanked forward through the doorway, I saw upon the butterfly's blessing that Godsend handle defy gravity to bend to my will and stay put. *It didn't fall. It didn't fall. It didn't fall.*

Out on the landing, where the walls were papered in a brown and dingy-pink floral print, he stalled. The cool, musty air and low lighting in this space reminded me we were in an old country house or building.

Twisting my wrist to near breaking, he peered over the railing to the steps leading down and then the narrow stairs leading up. Between these two choices, he shifted his gaze, seemingly unable to decide. A knock broke the stilted air. I presumed an unexpected visitor was at the door off the kitchen below. He froze. *A hare trapped by hunter.*

With the posture of a lizard who knows his camouflage has betrayed him, he hissed on low, 'If you make one bloody sound, I will find your parents and cut their hearts out with a dull knife.'

'Yes, sir.'

As though we were some derelict soldier team, chest crawling through high grass, he beckoned me with folded elbow forward, 'Move quietly. Go up these stairs now. Hustle, hustle, hustle.'

Yes, Captain.

I did as told, him at my heels, his head so close to my ass I felt like saying, *Get your head out of my ass,* but I didn't. He pushed me mid-spine to move faster.

'Faster,' he hissed.

At the top, I found myself in a long, steep attic. It was this view of open space, about three-quarters of a football field in length, when I realized I was in a colossal building. The sides jutted out in four spots, four wings, one of which was mine.

'Walk straight down the center to the closet at the end. Now!'

I practically skipped because he was pushing so hard. 'Faster,' he repeated, whispering madly. Unfortunately, there was nothing to see along the way – whatever may have been stored up there must have been moved and the floors swept clean. Not even a mousetrap remained.

When we got to a free-standing, double-door wardrobe with top vents, he stuffed me inside, shut the doors, and padlocked the handles from the outside. Through the slits in the door, he burned his droop-dog, jaundiced eyes.

'If even an itch comes from you, I will kill your parents. Understood?'

'Yes, sir.'

He left.

The only sound was him running down all four flights. I

may have heard a slight, slight talking as he opened the door to greet whoever was knocking, but I was so far up and closeted, I'm sure I only imagined whispers. *Cold silence, like in our house when Dad's sister died. Stillness of all, sound bleeding from your ears. Where did my butterfly go?*

I had not one clue who had arrived below. In a strained hope, I pictured a skeptical detective who wouldn't believe the imbecile at the door wasn't guilty of at least *something*. I contemplated blowing my vocal chords in blood-curdling screams and stomping and shaking and rattling my new cage. As it turns out, it's a good thing I chose not to take any chances on sound.

When reality sunk in, I turned lengthwise within the cabinet and slid to sitting. I had a finger-width margin on both sides to wiggle for comfort. My pupils took thirty to forty seconds to adjust to this dim light, but then everything was visible, and with night-scope vision, that's when I saw it. Like a diamond ring on a branch in the woods, an improbable fortune hung from a hook in the opposite corner: a one-inch-wide, three-foot-long segment of white elastic, the kind Nana would sew into the waistband of her homemade, polyester pants. *Nana.* I grabbed the elastic and placed it deep within my panties for safekeeping. *Asset #28, elastic band.*

Cat urine was the pervading scent of the closet, which triggered my gag reflex, but also made me think of my mother.

Mother is never wrong when she makes an affirmative statement. 'There is a cat in this house,' she said once.

'We own no cat,' my father said, laughing.

But to my father's assurances that her nose was only betraying her and to his suggestion that the rooms were simply stale having been sealed all winter, Mother protested, 'There is a cat in this house, as I am the mother of this child.' She pointed to me in her passing tirade, as though I were Exhibit A; her non-pointing arm was on her hip, her back erect, neck high, chin tipped. 'There is a cat in this house and I will prove it,' was her opening statement, delivered to her jurists: my father and me.

She grabbed my father's flashlight, which he kept in a tool box he hid from her, for reasons such as the one unfolding. She searched until three a.m., upturning every closet, crawlspace, attic, shadow, and basement crevice; she poked cracks in the garage and hollow logs in the yard, high, low, loose, and light; she flipped everything until the bulb dimmed from white, to yellow, to egg-yolk orange, to brown, to gray, to black.

She unearthed not one cat whisker, yet every hour she'd proclaim to her weary jurists – which actually was only me by midnight – 'There is a cat in this house and I will prove it.' The next morning, my father, the only soul permitted to reproach her, informed Mother she could not continue her 'effort to fly faster than the speed of light or prove the existence of a non-existent cat.'

Notably, I never once denied Mother's claim. I may also have guided her search.

While my father convinced my mother to stop, I slipped through our screen door and skated to a bald spot in a grove of white birch behind our house. Yellow dandelions carpeted this circular, open area, and so my hiding place was a yellow floor, white walls, and blue sky ceiling.

They didn't know where I was.

I returned quickly.

I said nothing.

Mother continued her relentless insistence about a cat in the house.

The odor dissipated over the course of the week.

Still, I said nothing.

With the waning smell, so waned Mother's interest. By the following Sunday, not a hint of cat vapor remained. Mother sat in her study in her pinched leather, Dracula's throne chair, editing a Motion for Summary Judgment with her silver Cross pen.

'Mom,' I said from the doorway.

Her eyes strained up, horn-rimmed glasses perched upon her nose, the legal brief unmoved in her hands. This was the most invitation to speak I would get. I cradled an old, scrappy cat in my arms.

'This is my cat,' I said. 'I got rid of the acidic odor with a mixture of vinegar, baking soda, dish detergent, hydrogen peroxide, and a layer of charcoal dust. I've been keeping her in a cage in the birch grove since she wet in the house, but she'll need to be indoors now.'

Mother plunked the brief on the coffee table in exaggerated drama. I'd seen this same motion of hers once when she reached the climax of a closing statement in a federal trial I was invited to attend. 'Son of a ... I told your father I smelled cat.'

'Yes,' I agreed stoically, as though confirming the Queen's dictate on a law of taxation.

'Why didn't you tell me?'

'I wanted to solve the problem before presenting her.' I had no emotions in her room. I didn't feel the need to allow them.

'Well.' She averted my gaze. I might have been the only person who could disarm her, which, I fear, unsettled her. It was as if I was an ever-growing thorn bush she was required to prune from ten feet away. But I didn't wish to trouble her; I only wanted to provide the facts.

'The cat is female. I've been testing a sonic collar for the purpose of dispelling fleas and ticks. She was roaming around the dumpsters at school. No tags. She's not feral though, definitely domestic and abandoned or lost. She likes humans. She only peed on the basement stairs because I didn't get a litter box until a day after I found her. I've hidden the box behind my sterilization unit, by the hydrogen chamber.'

I did not ask, as I think most children would have, if I could keep the cat. In my mind, she was not only my pet, she was also part of a lab project. I did not need permissions as far as the latter was concerned.

'Name?'

'Jackson Brown.'

'For a girl?'

'I thought you'd like the nod to your favorite musician.'

'How can I say no to Jackson Brown?'

I didn't ask for permission, just approval, which is different.

The psychiatrist later theorized that my mother's approval of my choice to tell her of the cat after I solved the urine problem, led me to hide my pregnancy – until I found a solution, I suppose the doctor supposed. But the only thing I solved in the first seven months of my hidden condition was my intention to name the baby Dylan, Mother's other favorite musician. This resolution, however, never materialized, since my baby's name changed in the course of captivity.

Indeed, on Day 20, lacking clear air in that casket of a closet in the attic, I began recalibrating my child's name, wanting to give him more meaning.

The closet-cage seemed doused in thick, acidic cat urine, and with little ventilation in that hot spring attic, I began to sweat and gasp for air. If I thought my room below was solitary confinement, the wardrobe was like being untethered to a spaceship and left to tumble through vacant space. *There goes my pod. There goes my planet. Gravity betrays me, lifts me hazardly beyond stars.*

Will he leave me here all day? Longer?

I believe an hour passed.

I blacked out from the heat.

I came to when he unlocked the closet and I sprawled to the floor, my head banging upon his boots.

'Son of a . . . ,' he screeched. He shimmied his feet out from under my skull as if I was a scurrying rat.

Hyperventilating, gasping for life, I lay like a fish flopping on the dock.

'Ah, she-it,' he said while stomping. 'Shit, shit, shit.'

He kicked lightly at my ribs as his method of checking my pulse, too bothered to bend and help me breathe. As he pigeon-pecked my chest with his steel-toed foot, I labored against practically collapsed lungs, wheezing, coughing, gagging along, until finally reaching a plateau and normalized rhythm. Not once during my struggle did I open my eyes or did he stoop to help.

When I could regulate the draw of air through my nose, I lay in a crescent position and cracked open my right eye, the one closest to the ceiling. Unfortunately, I met both his searing eyes, and thus a stalled moment of mutual hate suspended us in a dangerous stand-off.

He made the first move.

In a swift, downward swing, he swooped his right hand to grab a fistfull of my splayed hair. Upward he jerked my neck and torso to an involuntary and quick sitting, only to drag me bumping backwards along the floorboards, my tailbone taking the brunt of the hard wood planks.

Let me describe the pain. Imagine emptying ten tubes of superglue into a hat and placing the hat upon your head, allowing the inner rim and cotton skull to merge with every follicle in the spreading metastases of hardening adhesive. Now hook the top of the hat to a tree branch just slightly higher than your height. Stand. There is just enough room for the hat to yank each strand to within a micro fraction of snapping and the scalp skin to stretch to almost tearing. Rip, rip, slicing heat, rip.

Along he pulled me, while I flailed, skip sliding, seeking intermittent relief and traction with my hands upon his forearm and my searching feet that would catch and fail, catch and fail. My head felt like fire, burning, raging, crackling, white-hot fire. No foothold was secure enough to withstand the toppling force of his pull.

My body twisted left and right, a fighting tuna with raging fins being reeled out of the sea.

Naturally, with so much torque, the invaluable new asset – the elastic band – in my underpants slipped out and shimmied up to the bottom of my soaring waist. Its placement became so precarious, if I were to keep flailing my feet for traction, the angle and jostling would surely loosen the contraband further, off my rounded belly, and onto the floor. I had a choice: fight the pain or save the elastic. *Elastic*. I slackened my legs to straight, allowing him to freely pull my hair, and like a master pickpocketer, snaked within my pants, hooked the band, and squeezed the slithering life out of it.

He noticed nothing, immersed too deeply in his effort to harm me. When we came to the top of the stairs, he dropped me to the bare floor, my backside dotted with a hundred splinters, my tailbone bruised, possibly broken, but my resolve beyond a thousand mountaintops, beyond a billion billion galaxies, beyond God, His angels, His enemies, and beyond a million mothers of missing children. He would die in pain now.

'Stand up, bitch.'

I did, slowly, nursing my wounds, but with closed fists behind my back.

Again we stood in a standoff. I wanted him to go down the stairwell first so he couldn't see me slip the elastic to safety.

'Go, you moron,' he said.

You're commenting on my intelligence? Really?

A second slipped, two seconds. Tick. Tock. He ground his teeth and lifted his arms.

And then a phone I didn't know existed rang on the floor below.

'Oh, holy hell,' he said, as he slammed the stair treads on his way to the phone. 'If you're not down here in three seconds, I will drag your ass.'

'Yes, sir,' *moron, sir.*

I slid my prize into my waistband and smiled.

As I limped down the stairs, I strained to hear the conversation. I got his side, which was enough.

'I told you this place was too open. For damn sake, two Girl Scouts came to the door with their mother. The mother wouldn't freaking leave. I can't raise any damn suspicions, you say. Lay low, play the part, you say. Aren't I some guy caring for his elderly parents out here? Oh, isn't he the sweetest man, renovating the old building into a big home for his mother and father? Isn't that what you said they'd say? For fuck's sake! This is your dumbest idea yet, Brad. I had to give this Girl Scout bitch fucking tea, Brad. This is a shit idea of a cover. I fucking ... I fucking ... shut the fuck up, Brad. I fucking told you ... Of course I'd-a shot them all if this bitch had screamed.'

He winked at me when he said this, the kind of expression that says, *yes, I would have shot you all. I'm most definitely not on your side,* to which I thought: *Don't wink at me. If I get the chance, I will cut your eyes out for that gesture. I'll laminate your pupils in resin and carry them on a keychain.*

Back in my room, I allowed myself to rest on my side, what with the bruising and thin wood shards in my back. I lay on top of the white coverlet, the butterfly a distant phantom at this point, running through my ordered assets. ... *Asset #28, string for a bow, aka, elastic band. Thank you, black angel, for the warning and the gift.*

CHAPTER SIX

NUMEROUS DAYS, THE MONOTONY

The Shadow: And I hate the same thing you hate: the night; I love human beings, because they are devotees of light and I'm pleased when their eyes shine as they discern and discover knowledge – untiring knowers and discoverers that they are. That shadow, which all things cast, if the sunshine of perception falls upon them – that shadow am I as well.

Friedrich Nietzsche,
The Wanderer and his Shadow

Thales is generally accepted as the first Greek scientist. He invented what is known as 'Shadow Reckoning', an indirect method of measuring the height and width of an object that might otherwise be difficult to measure. Thales practiced this method on pyramids. My version of Shadow Reckoning not only calculated my captor's height and width, but also from there, his weight.

After the day in the attic, I already had enough assets to kill my captor five times over. What I needed, therefore, was to confirm a few things about him and also, like standing to the side of skipping ropes, calculate the precise time to enter the double-dutch and strike. *Not yet, soon, soon, soon, it's coming, wait, wait . . .*

I also needed to hone weapons, calculate and test my theories on his weight and gait, and practice again. So if you're wondering why I write only of the days someone visits or of the days I acquire something significant, it's because otherwise I'd be telling you hours and hours of repetition, such as was documented in the tiniest of script on several pieces of paper – my makeshift 'lab book' – which I buried within the cotton and feather stuffing of my top mattress. I've included an excerpt below, in which I refer to him, the subject captor, as this symbol: ⊙ the evil eye. The evil eye is universally considered in many cultures as an omen of misfortune on the person on whom it is cast. Oh, every single chance I got, I cast my hulking keeper the evil eye; I carried my wish of misfortune upon him even within my writing.

You might be wondering why I would include the evil eye

in a scientific lab book; isn't such a symbol mere myth and superstition? Perhaps. But let me illustrate my motivation with a bit of a side-story.

When I was eight years old, my Ecuadorian nanny picked me up from an after-school play rehearsal. She stood by the gym door with the other mothers. Naturally, she eavesdropped on their conversations. The play we rehearsed was *Our Town*, and I was the precocious child who yells a lot. In one scene, our director had me run down a ramp and shout my lines. I have no clue why. I did as I was told since play-acting was a prescription from the child psychiatrist.

'Perhaps some theater would assist her in overcoming the harsh reality of the school shooting,' he had told my mother after I made the mistake of informing her of several machine gun nightmares over the last month. Little did Mother realize, this was no bout. I had these dreams constantly, for I invited them. Having read much about the brain from age six to eight, I learned of the brain's work during sleep to heal itself. Grow stronger. So I forced the replay of the pop, pop shooting nearly every night to work a weaving magic and forge an even tighter coil of neurons in the folds of my amygdala. I'd lay in bed flipping through an ammo catalog and a deer-hunting magazine I'd found at the dentist office and hid in my underwear drawer, hurriedly burning the images to my hippocampus, like a teenage boy with *Penthouse*.

Still, the theater. I took the part in *Our Town* to calm my mother.

So there I was, running down the ramp, yelling my lines like the director told me to, and apparently, a gaggle of mothers started humming like bees. 'Tell her to shut up,' one whispered. 'She's the one. The freak who pulled the alarm when the shooter came,' another said. As my squat nanny turned to face them, a dainty woman with a helmet of blond hair cast me the ominous, slitted evil eye. 'I won't let Sara play with her. They should ship her off to a special school for weirdos,' so said the helmet queen.

My nanny gasped, which forced the pack to shut their claptraps quick. Before they could hurry a pitiful apology, my hired protector marched like a general announcing an act of war to the President, grabbed my arm, and whisked me out of the gym.

She drove without speaking, only muttering some prayer to herself, 'Dios Mio, Ad Te Domine,' she kept saying. At home, she propped me by the refrigerator while she fetched an egg, and then rubbed it up and down and all around my arms, legs, torso, and face. Mother stumbled in on this strange act and dropped her alligator briefcase on the kitchen floor.

'Gilma, what the hell are you doing?' she yelled.

Gilma didn't stop.

'Gilma, what on God's green earth are you doing?'

'Lady-Ma'am, no interrupt. Blond lady give baby evil eye. Egg is only cure.'

Mother would normally not tolerate superstitions, but Gilma's voice was firm, and if there's one true thing about my mother, if faced with an honest conviction, especially from a stout, tough-skinned, foreign woman with gold eyes, she will listen.

'Do not worry. I take care. I give blond devil evil eye back, and she don't know about the egg.' She winked, secure in her ancient myth.

I didn't mind Gilma rolling her egg around on me. I just didn't think it was very efficient. Why wait on the uncertainty of a curse? Why not take control and plot some tangible result?

A week later and it was opening night of *Our Town*. Before we took our spots, I went out to the audience to check where my mother and father sat. Gilma had a seat too, one row up, and I hadn't thought that she'd cared to come. I smiled, happy for her presence. Gilma nodded her head, motioning us to look across the aisle. We did. Mother flung both hands to her mouth, covering her audible awe. Gilma winked and mouthed, 'Evil eye. She don't have no egg.'

The object of our attention was the blond woman, but this time, her perfect hair held an uneven, shaved path from the base of her skull and up and over to the outskirts of what used to be full and curled bangs. The remainder of her helmet-like quaff was intact, but for that jagged scalp-road. She wore her hair disaster like a defiant badge, but her shaking, clenched fists betrayed her discomposure. I have no idea why she didn't cover her head wound with a scarf like any normal, self-respecting woman would have.

A woman in a conservative, blue sweater set leaned over to my mother and whispered, 'Her five-year-old did that to her with Daddy's electric razor. They say she was passed out drunk on her friggin' chaise lounge.'

Mother gave the sweater woman a warm cat smile while she winked at Gilma, my faithful governess, my hired knight, my evil-eye-curse-warding egg roller.

In any event, here is an excerpt from my jailhouse lab book:

Day 8: 8:00 a.m., arrives with breakfast. ⊙ places something on floor outside door. Sound of keys rattling. ⊙ takes 2.2 seconds to pull the latch and flip the lock, left to right. ⊙ opens door with right hand, places right foot in threshold, picks tray up off floor. When ⊙ stands, he hits 5'9" on the door jamb markings – which I had pre-marked with my twelve-inch ruler. Both of ⊙'s hands are full. ⊙ opens door further with right shoulder, walks in with left foot first. From deadbolt to left foot, time calculated is 4.1 seconds. ⊙ does not pause to check my placement; first step is on 3rd floorboard; walks the 8.2 feet from doorframe to edge of bed in 3 seconds and 4 steps: left foot, right foot, left foot, right foot meets left foot. Today's sunlight casts a shadow beyond ☉ to 3'3" above the uppermost edge of headboard and 3'1" beyond the side of bed, toward the door – I eye chalked the spots, which had been marked out in pre-gouged grooves in the floorboards, again with my twelve-inch ruler. ☉ *offers more water.* ☉ *leaves to collect water in the hall bathroom. This segment takes 38 seconds from offer to* ☉*'s return.*

8:01: ☉ *leaves.*

8:02–8:15: Eat breakfast: Cinnamon scone, banana, slice of rolled ham, milk.

8:15: Measure shadow contours, record height, and extrapolate width to be: 40" at waist; comparing my height and width to his shadow markings, and my weight – from last clinic visit plus 5–8 lbs, 135–143, with child – ☉*'s weight is 182 lbs. This finding is consistent with initial theory and prior measurements.*

8:20–8:30: Wait for ☉ *to return to take tray.*

8:30: ☉ *returns. Keys rattle. 2.1 seconds to pull the latch and flip the lock, left to right.* ☉ *opens door with right hand, places right foot in threshold, opens door with right shoulder, walks in with left foot first. From deadbolt to left foot, time calculated is 4.1 seconds – noted is* ☉*'s consistency whether carrying food or not.* ☉ *does not pause to check my placement; first step is on 3rd floorboard;* ☉ *walks the 8.2 feet from the doorframe to the edge of bed in 3 seconds and 4 steps: left foot, right foot, left foot, right foot meets left foot – consistency noted again. The sunlight casts a* shadow beyond ☉ to 3'2" above headboard, 3" beyond the side of bed, toward the door.

8:30–8:35: ☉ offers bathroom. Use bathroom, wash face, body, and teeth with cloth left on sink since Day 3, drink from faucet.

8:35: ☉ leaves.

8:36: Mark and measure the shadow I mind chalked and memorized. Vectors consistent at: 5'9" height, 40" at waist, 182 lbs. Will continue measurements for absolute certainty and to note fluctuations in ☉'s constitution.

8:40–12:00: Meditate, tai chi, practice placement of assets, evaluate inventory.

12:00: ☉ returns. Same observations as morning entry – everything consistent. Afternoon sunlight casts a shadow beyond him to a pool around his body, about 6" from his feet. His boots have rubber soles, but I don't think this will save him.

12:01: ☉ hands me plastic cup to collect more water while I use bathroom. Drink from faucet. I collect 7 oz. of water and return. ☉ leaves, locking door.

12:02–12:20: Eat lunch: egg-and-bacon quiche, homemade bread, milk.

12:20: Measure shadow, record vectors: 5'9", 40" at waist, 182 lbs. Findings are consistent. Will continue measurements.

12:20–12:45: Wait for ☉ to return to take tray.

12:45: ☉ returns. Keys rattle . . .

And so on. His patterns were punctual, timely, predictable. His vectors consistent. A clone trooper. A hypnotized soldier. In fact, based upon my Navy Seal father's militaristic ways, I queried whether my captor was ex-military. On Day 25, I confirmed almost as much. Odd, however, the discrepancy between his severe punctuality and his bedraggled physical appearance.

As you can tell from the above excerpt, I took repeated measurements. I wanted a bulletproof execution. But I soon determined that writing everything in longhand would be inefficient, so I switched to charts for metrics, calculations, and vector documentation and left new intel and acquisitions for longhand. So that my lab book was transformed to include mostly only charts.

CHAPTER SEVEN

SPECIAL AGENT ROGER LIU

Endless weeks into our investigation, Lola and I sat at a
corner booth in the famed Lou Mitchell's breakfast diner in
Chicago's West Loop. It was a late spring Wednesday, making
the crowd a thick mixture of tourists in tracksuits and business
persons in double-breasted power statements. My meal arrived
on a hot porcelain plate: two over-medium eggs with a sheen of
the butter they had fried in, white toast, home fries, and extra
bacon. Lola had the same, plus a stack of flapjacks and a side
of ham. Of course, there was a large pot of coffee between us.
I fell into the groove of cranky waitresses and busy patrons, all
of them with their Midwestern attitude and twang, as though
this morning were a nightclub and the work day or tour bus
was not imminent, but only a pit stop on the way to a chicken-
fried steak lunch and after-work beers with chicken wings.

Pulsing in this rhythm, I allowed myself an inward grin at the thought of enjoying an outdoor cocktail on Rush Street. But then my cell phone rang.

'Hello,' I said.

Lola lifted her nose, which seemed embedded in her steaming pile of pancakes. 'Hmm,' she said with her expression, as though she had answered my phone too.

The voice on the other end of the line caused me to leave the table and take the call on the sidewalk. Lola kept eating, unexcited. When I returned, I caught her picking toast off my plate.

'Boyd called,' I said. I loved dropping bombs like this on her.

She threw my toast on her plate and grabbed a napkin, which she'd already stained with her extra maple syrup and drippings of egg yolk. While wiping the outer rim of her lips hard and picking shards of ham out of her teeth with her tongue, she jabbed her fist at me. 'Son of a damn bitch, Liu. I knew that shit-stinking farmer knew more. Didn't I say that? Didn't I tell you that?'

She had not said this to me. She'd only complained of the smell of Boyd's barn. Although, truth be told, I, too, thought Boyd knew more. I wish I could tell you I was surprised he called. But I'd been through this so many times before. People get nervous when they sit with the FBI in their kitchen. They worry about how they appear, how they sound, whether they are targets themselves. They think about past indiscretions of their own and wonder if my inquiry is a cover for some other investigation, closer to home. It is not until we are long gone a few days – sometimes months – when a buried memory or a subconscious observation surfaces. And then these benevolent witnesses resurrect my card or Lola's and they call. Usually their revelations are meaningless, worthless, or things we'd already uncovered. 'Her car, it was definitely green, I remember clear as day now, Mr Liu,' they might say, to which I'd think, *Yup. A 1979, emerald, two-door Ford. We found it, with the bodies in the trunk, at the bottom of Lake Winnipesaukee last week. Thanks for the call.*

So when I heard Boyd's voice, I didn't expect much. Boy, oh Boyd, was I wrong.

But before we get into Boyd's ruby of an investigative gem, I should explain why Lola and I found ourselves at a diner in Chicago. As you'll recall, we had the fortune of falling into some lucrative videotapes at a gas station outside of South Bend, Indiana. We knew the day to watch and generally the time period: afternoon of the day Boyd sold his van, which happened to be his brother's birthday and the reason Boyd left the same day to go to 'Lou-C-ana' for an extended visit.

There were three tapes for this day: one at the pumps, one above the cash register, and one over the bathrooms with exterior doors. We found our suspect, full face and frowning – but wide-smiling in one frame – on all three tapes. *Jackpot.* We tracked him as soon as we captured sight of the van at the pumps, where he stayed for two-and-a-half minutes, and followed him to the counter at the cash register, after losing him for about three minutes, during which time he acquired a pint of chocolate milk and a package of Ding-Dongs. At the register, he asked for a 'pack of Marlboros,' which was easy to discern by way of his slow manner of speech and our trained eyes for lip-reading. Then he asked for 'the key to the bathroom,' and our lovely gas station owner obliged. Another four minutes passed, he returned the key, and we caught him one last time back out at the pumps, checking the gas cap, entering the driver's door, and driving away.

All of these images were sent to Virginia for serious dissection, along with the lifted fingerprints from Boyd's bathroom. At the end of the analysis, here's what we wound up with: a man in his early 40s, brown hair, tightly cut in the fashion of Caesar, small, round rat eyes, pupils so brown they appeared black, thin lips, almost no lips, and a fat nose with extra large nostrils. His lower eyelids sagged, revealing the inner flesh of his eye sockets. The medical experts said this might be a sign of lupus. The profilers and anthropologists pegged him as Sicilian, but American-bred. Smoker, obviously, and overweight, which showed only in his rounded belly and not anywhere else. He had no priors and no military record, so the fingerprints revealed nothing. We measured him at 5'9" and between 180–185 pounds.

Our man was wearing a Lou Mitchell's T-shirt. The analysts discovered that the color and style could have only been printed in the last year or two. I might not have been excited over the T-shirt if all I had to go on was the T-shirt; I'd probably have assumed he was just another tourist. But when he opened his wallet at the register, he made the mistake of laying it flat on the counter, and those sharp-eyed video-jockeys back at headquarters zeroed in on the one frame that said it all: 126:05:001 showed the very top of a frayed check on which several letters were visible above the inseam: L CHELL'S. Despite zooming in so far we could pinpoint individual molecules in the wallet's leather, we couldn't find the man's name, what with the apparent absence of a license and credit cards, so we began to call our rat-eyed suspect, Ding-Dong.

We seized upon the visible letters on Ding-Dong's check. The human behaviorists theorized that Ding-Dong's body shape, gait, burn-marked fingers, and habit of wiping his hands on his pants at the pump, meant he was a short-order cook. Everyone surmised he'd been one at Lou Mitchell's, given the T-shirt and by filling in the obscured letters on the check in his wallet to form the only possible solution. The medical experts also diagnosed him with a mild form of emphysema, just by video alone.

Lola and I hightailed to Chicago in search of anyone who might identify our short-breathed, short-order cook.

We were waiting at Lou Mitchell's on a man named Stan, the head chef, to finish the breakfast rush. We promised the new manager we wouldn't make any inquiries of the waitresses during their shifts and while they were out on the floor. So we sat and ordered the aforementioned breakfast. The manager had explained after we showed him a picture of Ding-Dong, 'I started here last year and I don't remember this guy. Your best bet is to talk to Stan. If someone worked here, Stan'd know.'

Our waitress, a hard-knuckle woman in her later 50s, came to collect our empty plates. Standing sideways to us with her face tilted to the side and down, and with a tone of familiar boredom, she said, 'The big man is ready for ya'. Go through the counta'. Left at the "frig". Can't miss him.'

Lola and I did as directed. As soon as we turned left at the 'frig', we saw him, a literal wall of man, standing before an eight-foot-long griddle. He was so wide, they had married two aprons together so as to stretch across his midsection.

'Stan?' I said.

Nothing.

'Stan?' I repeated.

'I heard you the first time, lawman. Come over here. Sit on these boxes of oil.'

95

I sat where directed. Lola, on the other hand, took her usual position as faithful sentry behind me.

From the side, Stan's head was the size and shape of a medicine ball: big and round. He had a well-maintained pork-chop beard and a mane of wild curls, which were slicked to mid-skull. The remaining locks broke out from the grease suppression into a clown's wig behind. Stan turned to face me. I have never seen a nose so big in my life. If giants ever existed on this planet, Stan was surely a descendent.

'What you want to ask me, lawman?' A splatter of batter plopped from his spatula to the floor, which I followed; he did not.

'Wondering if you know this man?' I held out the picture of our suspect.

Stan glazed the picture with his brown cow eyes, snorted, swiveled back to his grill, flipped three pancakes in quick succession, and grunted.

'Guess that means you know him,' I said.

'Man's a first-class idiot. He ain't been here in about two years. I kicked him out on his third day. Comes to me, says he worked a truck stop diner outside a' Detroit for five years. Says he's been short-order, sous chef, pastry chef, head chef, you name it. Lost everything on account a' some fight with the owner, he says. Says he's all down on his luck, wants to start over, can't he be something in my kitchen. So I give him the bacon station. First day, I knew right away, this man ain't never been in no kitchen. Burnt every strip he was supposed to fry up. Next day, I give him dishes. Screws that up too. Sending plates out with eggs and shit still stuck on 'em. I figured I better give him the Ol' Stan Lecture on Perfection and give him one more day. So I did. But, well dammit, he fucks up the third day too. And, well, shit, here it is, lawman, we Lou Damn Friggin' Mitchell's. We don't put up with no bullshit. We got the best damn friggin' breakfast in the city. Mayor Daley loves us. Zagat says God makes our omelets. Calls us "world-class".' Stan turned his attention to Lola, 'You know,' he said, pointing his spatula at her, 'Yeah, you know, lawwoman, I saw you Hoover my pancakes.'

Lola's highest emotion was to nod at Stan, which actually was a sign of respect. He understood, for he winked at her, but returned to providing me with a personal sermon.

'Lawman, anyway, we Lou Damn Friggin' Mitchell's, and I ain't got to take no bullshit from no one. Okay?' he said, as if I was questioning him on this obviously objective fact. I nodded an assurance that he was right.

Stan continued. 'Anyway, fourth day, I'm waiting for the idiot at the back entrance. I got a check in my hand, tell him he ain't to come back. Damn jerk says I got to pay him in cash. He can't cash no check. I should-a' known, right? I should-a' known he was the under-the-table kind. Well, we ain't no under-the-table kind of place, lawman.'

Stan turned to flip more pancakes as he waved a 'whatever' at me with a free hand behind his back.

'I suppose you need his name and whatever other information we have on him. Problem is, I sorta went around the regular procedure and hired him on the spot. So I don't have no application or nothing on him. Linda, she works the front, made him fill out a W-2 so she could cut him checks. Ask her to dig out the one for the jerk who called himself "Ron Smith" and worked here three days back in March of '91. But listen here, lawman, jerk's name was not no Ron Smith, we all know that, right?'

'I'm sure you're absolutely correct, Stan. Is there anything else you can tell us about him? Any tattoos? Did he say anything at all about where he was from, where he went to school, anything to help us?'

'For starters, he was a prick. Second, dumb as that box of oil you're sitting on. Couldn't fry up no bacon. Third, big fat liar. He didn't talk to me, didn't talk to no one. Unsociable motherfucker. I couldn't squeeze one fact out for you. 'Cept maybe he was a punctual psycho. He'd show up literally at 5:00 a.m. and leave at 3:00 p.m., punched on the exact click of the clock. I recall this in calculating his hours for Linda. Punch clock had it dead on, opening shift and closing shift, each of the three days. He said one thing that stands out. When he showed up at the back door, he says, "I have a thing about timing. I'll show up every day for you on time. But I must punch out exactly at the end of my shift. Call it OCD. Call it what you will. I am always on time. I have to be." That's what he says to me. Friggin' weirdo.'

'Stan, that's real helpful. You think he's ex-military or a vet?'

'Ain't no way idiot-man was in no army, Marines, no air force, no navy. No way. I served my time in the army and plenty'a boys come in here to work after their tours, and not one of 'em like this guy. Plus, he didn't care about his body none. And while I got no room to talk, most-a' the military men I know, care some, at least a little. His arms ain't never seen no day of lifting no weights. You can tell this in a man. He's just some crazy cock who has to be on time or he'll wig out or something.'

'Stan...' I started to say, but Stan swiveled his torso toward me, pointing his spatula in my face. I leaned back, away from his thrust; Lola, however, leaned in. Stan ignored her, for it was clear she was but a fly in his kitchen. They'd probably make a good pair, the two of them; Stan might have been Lola's match, if she were in to such things.

'Oh hell, lawman, he was a crazy son-of-a-bitch. I remember something. He had a nervous tick. Would blink his eyes a lot if you confronted him. Real annoying like. So this plus the gotta be on time thing, I think he really did have OCD.' Stan paused, blinking his eyes furious at me as a demonstration. 'Yup, all's I remember. That's it.'

Lola leaned back on this new intel. I reeled around in my mind where this tidbit might lead us. I'm sure Lola questioned what we could do with this information. I'm sure she doubted it would help at all. I felt the density of doubt, for Lola was usually right.

After rummaging through ten different boxes in the basement with Linda, we found the correct W-2 form for a 'Ron Smith.' We faxed it to headquarters, and as expected, the records experts soon confirmed it was a fake name with a fake social security number. So fake, they didn't even run it through the database. 'Liu, you should know by now that social security numbers don't start with a 99, unless this man is from the fictitious town of Talamazoo, Idaho.' And they snorted away in their special brand of dorkish, dark corner, fluorescent light, office laughter.

Back outside, Lola and I walked from Lou Mitchell's into the heart of Chicago's loop. We crossed the Chicago River, taking the pedestrian's path over an ornate, orange, arched iron bridge. The water below glowed Caribbean green, and ferries and water taxis glided in a harmonious chaos. Sightseers, lawyers, tourists, children, late-night jazz clubbers stumbling home, and stock market runners in piss-yellow jackets teemed about, the whole lot of them bumping into each other on their way to wherever, as though silver balls in a pinball machine. Lola and I kept a steady, slow pace amongst the bustle. We walked along to stand before the Sears Tower, both of us reflecting and silent, thinking separately about the morning's developments.

We'd been together five years at this point, and you might as well call us equals, even though our pay grades were different. I knew when she needed quiet, and she knew when I did. Although it kills me to say this, Lola and I worked in a synchronized tandem more refined than me and my own wife. Even our steps that morning clicked in synch, our stride the same, our gait, our breaths, our pauses and head shakes, our very beings choreographed as though a long-running tap-dance team on Broadway. This may have been the walk in which I admitted to my inner nagging that I was a terrible husband. I was never home. But would Sandra be disappointed in me if I quit? Would I be able to walk away from this personal hell, this obligation I'd imposed upon myself, partially as punishment and partially to rectify a past and grave error?

Down into the belly of the loop we sauntered. Tall buildings on each side of Madison Street made parts of our stretch as dark as twilight. When we came to the jewelry merchants on Lower Wacker, the raised train roared over our heads. In this part of town, the pigeons outnumber the office workers, who populate the area two streets back. We continued on, passing over Michigan Avenue to enter Grant Park. It was here that Lola and I sat upon a green bench. I crossed my legs in contemplation. She spread her own, jabbing her elbows on her thighs and hanging her head between her knees.

My phone rang. It was Boyd again. I was expecting him. I stood and walked in circles, listening to him out of Lola's straining ear.

I returned to the bench and mimicked Lola, our heads hanging between slumped shoulders. After a solitary minute, I exhaled loudly to call our two-person team to attention. I had something to report.

In my line of work, I've heard many crazy, insane fact patterns, combinations of reality that while real in individual parts seem incredulous when smashed together. Take for example the case in which a Romanian-run circus abandoned its old dancing bear in a densely wooded forest in Pennsylvania, the same place we thought a kidnapper had taken a ten-year-old girl the month before.

Tracking human scents, for this is how the declawed bear associated food, for three miles of concentric loops, she literally fell upon our kidnapper, suffocating him with a mama-bear paw on his windpipe. The ten-year-old girl, too horrified, tired, and beaten to respond, simply rolled to the bear's feet, sobbing. She later told us that in her delirium, the bear appeared to her to be Mary the Mother of God, with sunrays shining off her divine face and all around her pink cape. The bear lowered her head and with her snout nudged the girl to climb aboard. A motorist found the girl half-conscious on the bear's back, the bear whine-growling down the center of an old logging road. The girl wore a pink leotard; the dancing bear wore a pink tutu.

Thinking on Boyd's fresh story while I sat on that Chicago park bench, I heaved a sigh of disbelief, as though filtering all the air in the city through my lungs could compress his words to a truth I could believe.

In our slouched state, Lola twisted to me, and I did the same to her. 'You ready to tell me what Boyd said,' she asked.

'Get the car. We're going back to Indiana. We need to leave an hour ago.'

'Damn, Liu, I knew that shit-stinking farmer knew more.'

'You have no idea. You're never going to believe this one. Get the car.'

'Pink bear?'

'Pink bear.'

CHAPTER EIGHT

Day 25 in Captivity

There are days in your life that are horribly eerie but in hindsight are fabulously comic. Darkly comic, but comic nonetheless. There are people in your life who seem wildly strange, and they too in hindsight are actually darkly comic – they also remind you of your advantages, because they set the bar so low, breathing in your atmosphere, as if entitled to do so.

On Day 25, I had a visitor who I, even as I write these words, snicker in the memory of – this man. Maybe God and his black butterfly felt I needed a break from misery, so they sent me a good laugh, in hindsight. In hindsight. During the ordeal, I spent my energy fighting back fear, constantly flipping a stubborn switch in my brain to off.

There I was late afternoon, the dusk beginning to unfold over the house. My dinner delivery would be coming any minute. As I did every day, I gathered my tools of practice, even the ones I conjured out of air, and placed the physical and invisible implements in their rightful places. I sat on the bed, a palm to each knee, back straight, my belly soaring out like a plump, stuffed teddy bear.

Creak.

Creak, crack, closer.

Creak, crack, loud now.

Metal inserted, turning, seal broken, door opened.

No food.

'Stand.'

I stood.

'Come here.'

I went to my jailer. He put a paper grocery store bag over my head.

'Keep a hand on my shoulder, one on the railing. I didn't tie the bag so you can watch your feet down the stairs. Now come on. And don't ask any stupid, fucking questions.'

What the hell? You make me walk down stairs with my vision mostly obscured? What am I going to see at this point that would matter? Rephrase, what do you think I would see at this point that would matter? I know I would find an incalculable number of assets, perhaps a path to escape, but you don't know I know that. Ape.

'Yes, sir.'

So, as it was, I garnered no information about the world below the landing outside my jail cell, except that the stairs were wood with a faded middle from a missing runner. The floors on the lowest level were thin oak planks, and certainly scuffed, the varnish all but scraped off, from years of what looked like heavy use. We turned a few corners and entered a bright room. The light surged through the bag. He removed the bag.

'Here she is,' said my captor to my captor.

What is going on? What the hell? Am I losing my mind? There's two of them. What?

'Well, brother, she looks perfectly healthy to me. She'll fetch us a pretty penny,' said the duplicate of my captor to my captor.

Identical twins. This is a family business. Well, dip me in molten metal and bronze me in this spot, my mouth agape.

'Come, sit here, pleasant panther,' my twin captor said to me, gesturing with a femininely extended hand to a chair at an ornate dining room table. His nails were longer than a man's nails should be. I noted his purple paisley scarf.

An odd sound eked through when the tinkling piano of Tchaikovsky met my ear, coming from a warbling record player on a lace-doily-covered service hutch capping the end of the table. Mauve and green floral wallpaper busied the space into an outdated Victorian, the décor antiqued further with a dark and shiny dining set. This room's veneer, almost black and densely waxed, with creepy roses on the wall. Twelve high-backed chairs with pink-flowered cushions surrounded the table. Casserole dishes steamed in the middle. The heat was cranked to hell.

'Pretty panther, pretty, pretty panther, come here, sit next to me. My name is Brad,' said the twin. There was a nasal, high pitch to his sing-song voice. His long, tasseled scarf fluttered with his exaggerated movement.

So, this is Brad. Why is he calling me a panther? Brad must be the source of the scarf I gathered when I had the ultrasound.

Brad and my captor were an exact match: same face, same hair, nose, eyes, mouth, same height, even same potbelly. The only difference: Brad was clean and crisp; my captor, soft and mangled.

I sat in the chair next to Brad. He placed his featherweight hand lightly on my elbow; it felt clammy even through the cloth. *I'm sure Brad limp wrists a loose handshake. Mother would hate him. 'Never trust anyone who doesn't have a firm grip on your hand,' she'd say. 'And people who finger your fingers as a greeting have no spine, no substance, and no soul. You may, you must, dismiss them.'* He laid a large cell phone on the table, out of my reach.

'Brother, you didn't say our precious panther was such a cool diva,' Brad said, as he placed a dinner roll on my plate, another in the toile. *I will obliterate these plates someday.*

'Brad, let's just eat and get the girl back upstairs. I don't understand why you insist on eating with these things. They're as good as dead anyway,' says my so very uncouth captor.

'Tsk. Tsk. Brother, so gruff all the time,' Brad said and then looked at me. 'So sorry, growling panther, he has no manners. Don't mind him, he's just a brute. Let's enjoy our dinner. I'm so tired. I flew in from Thailand yesterday. Been at the dentist all day. Old Grumpy makes me stay at a flea-trap hotel in this Godforsaken town. So, so tired, panther. So tired. Leaving on a flight tomorrow to ... Oh panther, tsk tsk to me, going on about my fool self. I bet you just want to eat. Tee-hee-hee.'

What movie did I watch with Lenny, my boyfriend? Ah yes, Three On A Meathook. *The son and mother and father, all killers. A family of psychopaths.* Tchaikovsky morphed into the screeching soundtrack of a stabbing knife through a shower curtain.

Brad uncovered a pile of sliced meat on a platter and placed two pieces on my plate. I hoped the meat was veal, for the slab looked and smelled as such, although I could no longer trust my senses in this den of insanity. Brad also served a pyramid of glistening green beans, a dollop of mashed potatoes, and a delicate trail of glazed carrots. He cut the meat into tiny bites, leaning in to my side as though he were my doting new mother.

'Panther lady, my brother and I, perhaps just I, are, am, wondering,' and here his high voice switched to a forced, low grumbling, like he was talking funny-serious to a toddler, 'why you glare at him with such mean eyes?' He continued in a quick return to a higher voice, 'What? You don't like the food he gives you? Tee-hee-hee. Don't worry, we don't let him cook. He couldn't even hold a job flipping bacon at a diner! Remember, brother? Remember when you tried to get away from your Brad-y-poo? How'd that work out for you?'

Brad blinked at my captor.

'Ol' fatty has to work with me. He's too dumb to do anything else. Anyway, anyway, I prattle on. You probably give him mean eyes because he's such a fat slob.' Brad nudged my shoulder to laugh along with him. I exerted a short, 'Ha,' only to catch my captor's stare, a cold, dead stare, which was scattered with incessant blinking. This was the first time I noted him blinking, blinking, blinking.

'Shut the fuck up, Brad. Let's get this over with.' Blink. Blink.

'Now, brother, relax. The girl should enjoy a nice widdle dinny-poo. Right, panther?'

'Yes, sir.'

'Yes, sir?!' Brad howled. 'Yes, sir?! Oh brother, oh brother, she's a little baby, cute baby panther.'

Brad turned to his plate. My hands were on my lap. He took a bite, his eyes darting to my clenched fists. He scowled, losing his tittering lightness in a flash of squinting eyes.

'Pick your fucking fork up and eat the veal I made you. Now!' Brad shouted in a deep, loathing voice. 'Tee-hee-hee,' he added with a returned high tone.

I picked up my fork. I ate the baby calf.

'Now, brother, why is panther here calling me "sir"? Is this what you make her call you?'

My captor slumped, shoving mashed potatoes into his open, chewing mouth.

'Brother, brother. You're never going to get over daddy-poo, are you?' Brad twisted to me. 'Pretty panther, my brother here is very scarred. Our daddy, our sweet, sweet daddy, made us call him "sir". Even when we had the flu and were throwing up in our pressed pajamas, it was, "sir, I am so sorry for puking, sir." Oh, panther cat, guess what my sweet daddy did to my dumb brother once?'

'Brad, if you don't shut your shit-spewing mouth right now . . . ' Blink. Blink. Blink, blink, blink.

Brad interrupted with a deafening two-palm slam on the table. The glass teardrop chandelier shook as he stood to lean into a scream.

'Oh, brother, you will shut up,' Brad said, wielding a pointing knife across the table while audibly sucking a shard of meat from his teeth with his tongue.

My captor shut up. Brad sat down and scrunched his nose in a kitten smile to me.

Hmm, strange dynamic. The feminine twin has power over the fat slob twin. I leaned a fraction closer to Brad, perhaps wanting to forge an unconscious partnership in his mind.

'Brother, brother, brother, so touchy. Tsk, Tsk.' Brad said 'touchy' in a higher octave. 'Panther cat, listen to this, my sweet baby brother, he had trouble keeping our daddy's curfew. Oh Daddy, he kept his time on a military watch – one he had since he'd been corporal – and well, I was real good about being punctual. I was Daddy's favorite. Naturally.'

Brad said 'naturally' while inspecting his nails, pleased with himself.

'Anyway, dipshit here, well, he'd miss deadlines by a minute here, thirty seconds there, come in all huffin' and a' puffin' out of breath. One night when we were both eighteen – we're twins, you know. One night when we were eighteen, the day after high school graduation, in fact, Daddy sent him to get us some milk and Sanka from the corner store. Daddy says, "Son, I'm timing you. This is your test. You be back here at 0700 hours and not a second after. You hear?" And my dear brother goes, "Yes, sir," which was the right answer. So boy goes running out the door. Me and Daddy watch him tear down the street, and Daddy gnarls under his breath, "He's worthless. Slouch. Running like a moron." Something musta happen down at the store though. What was it, brother? What made you a whole two minutes late?'

Pause.

Brothers staring each other into death. Sweat pouring down my captor's jowels.

Blink. Blink. Blink.

Hatred between two men, twins.

Blink. Blink. Blink.

I caged my belly with my arms.

Blink. Blink. Blink.

'Doesn't matter anyway. My dear, dumb brother walks in the door, and Daddy taps his watch and says, "Boy, it is exactly 0702. You're two minutes late. You're spending a year in the brig."'

My captor dropped his fork. This time, however, he glared, no blinking, forcing all of his hatred on me, as though I was the one who sentenced him to the brig. It might have been because I had stopped eating, stalled enthralled, staring at Brad to feed me more of this story. I fought back asking, *what brig?*

'Panthy panther, you know what the brig was? Oh, of course you don't. Although my brother wailed and begged, Daddy dragged him down the basement stairs, flung open a false wall, pushed him inside a jail cell we'd built the summer before, and locked the door. Was my job to bring ol' dumb nuts his meals. I really put a lot of care into his food, panther. So, so important to stay healthy when you're confined. Daddy's lesson. I hope brother here is feeding you fine. Is he now? Giving you your meals?'

'Yes, sir.' I didn't look to my captor. I didn't care to collect his approval.

'If he doesn't, I'll step in and take over. So tell me, panther, for real, he's giving you your meals, yes?'

I don't want you to step in. I don't want to start my calculations over. Can't start over with a new routine. Too late. I'm so close to execution day. No, I will not have you step in.

'Yes, sir.'

'Sweety, sweetypie, just a'runnin' a well-oiled ship,' Brad said and clapped like a wind-up monkey with cymbals.

'Anyway, back to my story. Cranky-pants didn't leave his cell for one full year. Released at exactly 0702, one year later on the nose.' Brad touched his nose. 'Every day, Daddy made him write, "The devil keeps my time. He has me under his heel when I'm late". He filled up 365 notebooks, one a day, with that phrase. When my brother here was set "free at last, free at last", boy turns to Daddy and says, "Thank you, sir," which was the right answer.'

My jailer had not released his stare-down on me. His menacing meditation had switched to some deeper level of evil, now that I knew the source of his darkness. Blink. Blink. Blink. His look said he would show no mercy because he didn't want my pity – pity would mean he was weakened and his daddy was wrong. Blink. Blink. Blink. Pity said he wasn't good enough, a lower creature. His blinking burrowed a bit of fear in me, something that took a solid ten seconds to bite back and switch off. And switch off again. Blink. Blink.

Someone pushed my plate.

'Eat your vegetables, pantheon, we need you healthy,' Brad said.

'Eat your food because I'm about ready to carve that baby out of you,' my captor said.

Brad did not rebuke him. Instead, he nodded his head in agreement.

I took a sip of the milk Brad had poured me, wishing I could grab the steak knife under his upturned pinky and jam the blade into his scarf-enshrined neck. The red would blend nicely with the purple silk, I thought.

When dinner was done and cleared, Brad pranced out and back in with a slice of apple pie, just for me. 'Panthy pantherton, take this pie on up to your room. And thanks for having this little dinny-poo with me. I like to meet our productkeepers, here and there.' He flopped his free hand to and fro on the 'here' and the 'there.'

Product-keeper? You mean, a girl-with-child? You mean, a mother? You're so sick, I can't even get mad. Sick. So sick it's hilarious.

When Brad lifted his hand to rub my earlobe between his

thumb and index finger, I contemplated knocking him off his balance and using his forward motion by pulling and twisting his arm so he flipped on his back – all from his very own physics; then I would crush his windpipe with my heel, my physics. Just like my daddy-poo taught me. Once that maneuver was complete, I'd swiftly grab the fire poker at my left flank to impale my captor who would be standing stunned. But again, my condition dampened any chances of this obvious and easy solution, so I took hold of the apple pie as it was offered.

I marched half-blinded, bagged again, carrying my Americana dessert up to my cell, my captor at my back.

Normally he would have shoved me inside. This time he stopped, taking me in from his standing state. 'You look at me like I'm beneath you, bitch. Since Day One, you don't blink. Let me tell you something, I will gut you. You will not win. Don't go grinning over that little story my brother told you.'

He left me on this pleasant bedtime wish. Tucked me in with his twinkling, gnashing grin.

I better behave so he sticks with his established patterns.

CHAPTER NINE

DAY 30 IN CAPTIVITY

As expected, at 7:30 a.m., the smell of baking bread knocked me into my fourth Kitchen People cooking day. Along came the rattle of the shaking floor – the moving ceiling fan below – and the whirs and the churns of their spinning mixer. In my mind's eye, the apple-green appliance whipped up a batch of brownies. A cloud of baking chocolate filled the room and lingered high in the rafters, making way for the scent of melting cheese and a buttery crust. My nose twitched, my mouth watered, my stomach grumbled. Oh, but to have been afforded a lick of the bowl and a quick nibble of the pie as it came out of the oven. I cowered in a curved position on my jail bed, not wanting to make one single noise. My captor coughed in the hall, his back against the door, which banged with his every wheeze. He'd shown me his gun again earlier in the morning when he threw me and the bucket on the bed. 'Stay the fuck put, not one fucking sound, or baby gets a bullet today,' he had said.

The barrel of the gun was on my navel, likely on my baby's head. Asshole very well could have pulled the trigger for the freezing chill I felt even after he'd left. I didn't even twitch, shuddering mentally at the thought of metal gouging through my child, a horrid hallucination that would not retreat, like the incessant buzzing of a mosquito.

Sitting here seventeen years later, I have this quote I wrote to myself and taped above my desk: 'Whatever you're waiting for, be ready.' What I mean by this is, if you're waiting for something, don't really wait for it, take the steps to put it in place. One stone, one layer of mortar, another stone, one step at a time toward your goal's pyramid. Emotion by emotion. Brick by brick. The quote is a constant reminder to myself to live as though whatever I am waiting for is absolutely coming true, regardless of doubt, laws of physics, or worst of all, time.

Time, ticking time, like relentless water over a sharp rock, it dulls resolve. In the dip of the middle, when the seconds pound out their slow-witted mockery, one must think of any knot untied, any map not yet triple-checked, any shadow not yet measured, any task, any task, any, any God-loving task will do, so long as it is toward that one goal – whatever you're waiting for.

Many an afternoon of mine were almost comatic in the dip of the drip, drip trickle of time. I couldn't think of any more tasks and I'd turn catatonic, staring at my rough-hewn, barn-board jail cell wall. The beams became tree limbs, the ceiling a white-cloud sky. Then a trumpet call crack of the floor and him moving beyond would rouse me to rummage my mind for a task. With none found, I'd turn to the only routine to give me solace: practice. Whatever I was waiting for required practice, then practice again, then practice ten more times, and to start over a thousand more times.

I love Olympians. Especially solo Olympians who fight not for a team, but their very own souls. The swimmers, the track stars. And I'm a sucker for the back-stories detailing their grueling 4:00 a.m. workouts lasting to midnight. Like a Jack-in-the-Box, these athletes pop up and deflate, pop up, deflate, up, down, up, down, up, down, never lifting their feet firmly implanted in the box. At long last the bell blows, the gun fires, and off they go – muscles beating water, pumping over hurdles, splash they're gone, flash they're gone. Darting like a stingray past soggy competitors. Bolting beyond the speed of light. Whenever the expected champion wins, I literally scream my approval. They worked for it. They deserve it. Cream rises to the top, especially the self-stirring cream. Driven, determined, dedicated, death-defying, competition-obsessed – the game, they play, to win. I love every one of them.

On Day 30, I lay on my bed, waiting on the Kitchen People to leave so I could resume my practicing and stop the circular daymare of bullets in babies.

Around eleven, there was the familiar kissing-of-the-ass between my bakers and my jailer. As acid rose in my throat, I dry-heaved my displeasure onto my coverlet. But instead of melting somewhere else into the house like he normally did, as soon as the door shut, he pounded back up the stairs toward my room. This was not part of the routine. I hated any shift in my daily plan. A warm sweat rose on the back of my neck. Acid burned my throat. My heart returned to the beat of a hummingbird once again.

In he burst with his customary agitation.

'Get up,' he said.

I got up.

'Put these on.' He threw an old pair of Nikes at my feet. They were two sizes too big. I put them on and tied tight. *Asset #32, a pair of running shoes. Wait, where are my shoes? Have I been without them this whole time? How did I not notice?*

'Move,' he said, the gun at my back. We resumed the same gunman's shuffle we had had the first night of our arrival, me in front, him behind, me not having a clue as to where we were going. The only difference was, I was not bagged or blindfolded this time.

Oh God, please help me. Where are we going? Butterfly, you did not warn me. Why? Maybe you did. I was looking at the wall all morning. Why didn't I watch the window? Where is he taking me?

We went down the three flights of stairs but did not turn left, which would have brought us through the kitchen. We forged straight ahead to a back door that opened to a dirt patch, the grass having been worn away by people who must have once occupied a weathered picnic table outside the door. Cigarette butts carpeted the area. *A break spot for employees?* I yearned to turn around to see what the building looked like, but he heel-kicked me forward, and I was not afforded even a glance.

The dirt patch was about fifteen feet in circumference, then began a long stretch of unmowed grass parallel to the building we'd just exited; the grass strip was about four feet wide before tumbling over a ridge. He gun-prodded me to the ridge. Over the edge was a steep hill leading to a forest behind. One narrow path, about a foot wide, led down the hill and through the woods. We took the path. It was the middle of the day.

Where is he taking me? Is this the end? I'm eight months pregnant. If they had the equipment, the baby is viable. But would they risk Caesarean birth after all of this trouble? Where is he taking us? I rubbed my stomach with the fury of a cast-away rubbing sticks to start a fire. This was when I realized something about myself: whenever there was a direct threat to my child, the fear switch in me turned itself on. I'd never had this trouble before pregnancy. Having realized this glitch, going forward, I was more self-aware – better at tempering, or tamping, the unwelcome, woefully useless emotion of fear. Interesting though, psychologically, medically, and perhaps even philosophically, at least to me. Sometimes I wonder if my baby's emotions – his fetal fear – transferred to me in those moments. I was giving him life, but was he giving me life?

It had rained earlier in the morning, and the cold spring wetness clung to the ground and to every leaf. The buds on the trees stalled in the moisture. Not one sign of life stretched to unfurl in such weather. The sun slept, unwilling to fight the chill in the air. Thick clouds were a wet blanket overhead. I shivered without a coat.

'You're worthless. Cheap. A whore. Look at you. Slutting up yourself. Banging in heat and pregnant with sin. You're scum, you mean nothing, you mean nothing to this world,' he said. He kept the gun on my back and slithered his face around my neck, keeping his lips close to my cheek. After exhaling two hot breaths, he spit in my face and added, 'Worthless bitch.'

If I've taken responsibility, if I intend to work hard to make this work, is this not my journey? Yes, I am lucky to have resources, help, love, but do these benefits not make it my journey, still? A flawed and unique journey, but mine? Why is it up for universal discussion? Brought up by who, him? This criminal? Wait. Wait. This is not about me. Focus. This is about him justifying his depravity. Focus. Please. Focus. Breathe.

I was not sure what I had done to deserve his sanctimony, except be a woman and get myself pregnant – and so young. But arguing about the morality of it all, apologizing to him, to the world? To God? The woods, the trees, the morphing molecules of right and wrong in the air? None of that would temper him. I had followed his every command so far; all he wished to do was harm me. I lowered my head, steadying for more of his sermon of judgment, which he seemed so primed to give. His saliva slid slowly down my skin.

'Yeah, you heard me, you're fucking worthless. All these other girls, they cry and they beg me to help them. What are you? Some fucking crazy bitch? You just sit there, like nothing. You don't even want this baby, do you? You don't give a shit.'

Wrong. I wanted my baby more than I wanted to be rescued. Much more. Many a time I fantasized about the butterfly giving me a choice: would I choose to remain in the house of horrors and keep the baby or be rescued and lose the baby? Always I imagined this choice and immediately planned where I would place my born child on the bed while we slept in our eternal jail cell. My hand would cup his puffed belly, and I would kiss his sweet peach cheek.

'I bet you'll talk when we get to the quarry. Won't be so brave then.'

Why is he taking me to the quarry?

'Yeah, I bet you'll scream, bitch. What? What's that? What?'

I didn't know how to respond. Here I was, walking in front of him on a thin, twisted path, which took all my faculties to maneuver without tripping, and he's behind me asking *What?* Was this a rhetorical question? Sarcasm? How did he expect me to respond? Was he talking to himself?

I stopped, my head bent, my body still forward, my right foot hugging a fist-size stone at the arch, my left flat upon a root. He slowly crept up and became flush with my body, angling his arm with the gun around my midsection as though he were my lover hugging me from behind. He seethed in my ear like a mad, hissing snake, 'You answer my questions when I ask them, bitch. What, what do you think we're doing today?'

'I have no idea, sir.'

'Ah. Okay. Well, let me tell you something. You're going to climb this hill up there, a few more steps, yeah. And then you're going to see where I throw all you bitches. I am sick to shit of you lounging like you own the place. I want you to know what's coming to you and then maybe you won't sit so smug up in that room of yours. Looking like you might kill me any minute. You're such a dumb bitch.'

His breath still smelled like shit.

The warm sweat that had beaded up on my neck when we started this journey had cooled to freezing, but with his menacing breath now on it, the sweat warmed and flowed once more. A fever rose in me. I vomited. Bile spilled upon my right foot and the rock beneath.

He backed away. 'Move it,' was the only tenderness he gave to me being sick. He jabbed the gun at my back.

I climbed the hill he had mentioned, and the path became no more. We came upon a series of huge granite slabs, natural rock mountains. Green moss and lichen-covered spots, puberty fuzz on a teenage boy. I walked, stooped at an incline, an angle made more dramatic given my top-heavy state and unsure footing in my too-big shoes.

I slid backwards and into him once, but caught myself by planting my palms on the prickly lichen, which embedded and scraped my skin.

'Get up. Get up. Move,' he said. He didn't lend one hand to help me stand.

At the crest of the crop of rocks, we arrived.

We stood upon the top of a doughnut ring; carved in the middle was a hole filled with black water. Dynamited ridges cut vertical from the top of the rock wall into the water. *So they mined this once. A quarry. The quarry.*

The quarry was about the size of eight aboveground pools.

'They say it's forty feet deep in some spots. You want to dive on down there and find out, bitch?'

'No, sir.'

'No, sir? No, sir! Is that all you got? You fucking little bitch. Come down here. You'll cry once and for all.'

So he has unraveled. He's gone mad. All this sitting around, guarding me, being my food slave, has gotten to him more than me. He's sick. He's a sick man. Sick men are unpredictable. I can't calculate events on this. Listen. Listen. Do as he says.

I followed him before he could grab me by the neck and pull me.

We walked the rim of the quarry and down a gradual decline to a puddle spilling off the lower edge. While keeping one arm extended with the gun in my direction, he bent to retrieve a coiled, wet rope.

'Put your hands behind your back.'

Once I did as told, he placed the gun on the ground and, like a practiced sailor securing a boat to a bollard, wrapped the rope around my wrists and took the long end to a tree at the edge of the quarry, securing me in place as though I were his junkyard dog.

'Stand there and watch this,' he said.

He reached from the puddle into the darkness of the quarry, searching with his hands the side of the rock wall. He seemed to unhook something. Another rope, a slack rope. He pushed past me and found a boulder behind which he sat, placing his feet against the boulder so as to form a cantilever out of himself. He pulled the rope, straining his biceps, his legs, his jaw, in an effort to extract what seemed to be a rather heavy object tied to the end of the rope.

Panting, he took one break mid-pull and said, 'I strapped this one to an expensive, competition-grade wakeboard, the kind for oceans, yeah.' His chest heaved as he breathed, yet he smiled, pleased with himself in providing these insane details. 'On the bottom of the wakeboard, I tied a huge cement block. I pushed the whole thing, her on the wakeboard and the block, off the edge up there.' He arched his head to indicate the top of the quarry and paused to pant in his heavy breath before resuming his crazy speech and his pulling on the rope. 'At first, the board tilted headfirst, with her on it, under water, but then righted itself as the cement yanked it down and down. Oh, but she floats just below the surface all right. You'll see soon enough. Just as soon as I get this block off the bottom. Yeah, bitch, kept this one tied on in case I needed to convince one of you bitches of something. And wasn't that smart of me?'

'Yes, sir.'

Um, so ... Um? You? And then you? What?

Part of me, the unemotional side, was, admittedly, a bit intrigued by the details, the bizarre steps he'd taken to retrieve one of his victims. It was as though he'd built himself an elaborate underwater trophy. Frankly, I'm not quite sure of the physics of his contraption. Standing there, listening to him, I figured this trophy of his must not be too old. The tension of the pull between wakeboard, which would want to rise, and the cement block, which would want to stay put in the bottom muck of the quarry, would constantly pull on her continually decaying flesh. Thus, eventually, the very rope holding her tethered underwater would tear through her muscles, her organs, and her skeleton and her corpse would be torn apart. Pieces of her would either float to the surface or sink to the bottom.

Must have just thrown her in?

'Moved this bitch to the basement when I brought you here. She was on her way out. Yeah, bitch. Cut her baby out a few days ago, right up there on top of that rock, all while you sat on your ass, staring at your wall.'

I cannot even begin to explain my emotions in that moment. I don't normally allow many emotions at all, but when he actually showed me the spot where he took a baby, when he pulled to give me proof, I experienced the only pro-longed time in my life of involuntary fear, a five-minute period, give or take three minutes, when the fear switch turned itself on. I must have been in a state of shock, unable to flip any off switch in any lobe of my brain, for the horror of watching him pull an unknown girl out of the murky black knocked me into a void of pure oblivion. I do recall fixing on just one thing, a red cardinal, high on the highest limb of an oak at the top of the quarry. I kept waiting for him to swoop down and pick me up. I believe it was my only thought.

My captor resumed his effort, his body a heaving machine. A gurgling of the surface of water began, bubbles flooded the middle, as though a cauldron from hell boiled over. The cardinal flew away.

With a quick plunk, a rotting head of long hair broke the surface. Soon followed her whole bloated, decomposing corpse. The rope tied in a harness around her chest was, as he said, tied to a wakeboard, purple with black lettering. I assumed the cinder block was beneath her torso, waiting to plummet into the water grave just as soon as he let go the rope. He held her suspended as though he were a magician who had raised a straight-laying lady above a long steel table. Nausea overcame me in a hot wave from my belly, through my lungs and heart, riveting my shoulders, my neck, and swallowed my face.

Floating right before my eyes was the corpse of a girl with her abdomen sliced open, hip to hip. The gash, having festered in the water, appeared burnt at the edges, like paper burned in a fire. But these weren't burn marks, they were the stigmata of rotting flesh, the bacteria of the still water eating away at her open wound.

'Cut that baby out. Baby was dead. The doctor was too drunk to get his ass over here. So I did it. Yeah. Threw the bitch in here. Baby too. He's tied to a rock himself, way down there at the bottom with the others. She was still crying, bleeding all over my tarp. I'll have to buy a new one just for you, bitch. You're almost ready now.' He pointed to the top of the rock wall. 'Did it all out here so she wouldn't spill her trail of blood all over the house. Learned the hard way the first time. Doctor wants you to deliver naturally. Thinks we don't have to cut the babies out. But, we'll see about that. I'm so sick to shit of you. Not sure I want to wait much longer. So don't go giving me your evil fucking eye anymore.' He let go the rope. She sank.

And since I allowed the emotion in, I wobbled. I fainted.

* * *

There is a sweet grayness that comes upon waking from deep unconsciousness. It's like a blank slate, with nothing coming before and nothing expected. There is a weightless feeling in this space, the mind not clinging to any past of any sort and not planning either, not sure if it should sink back into a black or allow the white to wake it whole. There are no colors, only a gray fading to white, and with the white comes the beginnings of sounds, fading in and fading out, with an undulation back to gray, then the littlest of sounds again with a return of white.

A stick snaps at your resting head.

A cough.

Some words.

A quick slip into black, then gray again, then stark white when a push is felt at your back.

'Wake . . . p,' you hear.

'Wake up,' you hear more clearly.

Definite shapes begin behind your closed lids. Some colors come into play.

A push is felt, this time on your shoulders.

'Wake up, you damn bitch,' is definitely heard.

You open your eyes, the nausea returns. You are lying in moss at the edge of a quarry. Your arms are tied behind your back.

'Stand the fuck up. Now we'll see if you look at me like you do anymore.'

We walked back along the skinny, winding trail to my jailhouse, this time with him holding the end of rope tied around my wrists as though he were walking me, his dog. I did not focus on one single solitary thing. If you've never been in shock, you should understand that your senses are not talking to your conscious self. You do not see anything. You do not hear anything. You do not smell anything. So I did not register the color, the shape, the siding, the height, not even one window about the building we returned to. After, I still did not know what the exterior looked like, so I continued to imagine it a white farmhouse. The only fact I clung to in those horrifying moments was the fact that we were returning. *We're returning. I am not dead. He did not throw me in. He did not take my baby. He did not cut me. We're returning.* This was the only time in my life I welcomed the cell.

CHAPTER TEN

Day 32 in Captivity

These blank days, of nothing and empty skies
Behold, closer, beyond the void
A comfort comes
When everything goes mercifully white

S. Kirk

Two days post Kitchen People. Two days post quarry. And all I wanted was a bath. A nice lavender-salt bath, the kind where the water encases me in a hot quicksand. The kind I'd take in Mother's custom jet, extra-deep tub, with a view of the television she had mounted in her female-only, white marble bathroom. The kind where when my skin got too wrinkly and my core too heated, I'd slosh onto her fluffy, white bathmat, cocoon into her

132

thick white robe from the Ritz, and enter her adjoining walk-in closet to parade naked on a fictitious runway in her Jimmy Choos, her Manolos, and her strappy Valentinos, the pair with the crystals. Wishing for this white comfort, I looked around my dusty, brown jail cell and at my grimy skin and wished for the end. Plus, I was pretty exhausted from the double acting load I'd taken on since Day 30. I had started to perform amazing monologues of wailing fits, adding a chorus of incoherent pleas for my weak-ego'd captor to free me – and my baby.

He needed to feel powerful.

I gave him what he needed so he'd stick safely to our practiced routine.

And although I craved a bath like a lawyer craves coffee, I wasn't about to deviate from practice and interrupt our choreographed days with any new requests. I could have used the comforter as a cloth, dipping a corner into my cups of water so as to sponge bathe some critical body parts, but I'd wrestle a viper before I'd waste a single drop of liquid. I'd never squander an asset.

After a lunch of shepherd's pie on Day 32, I waited for him to collect my tray. I stood and shook, repulsed with my own body, the film on my legs, the grease in my hair. My efforts to cloth wash myself with a dirty, dirty washcloth in the bathroom each day, really were not good enough – frankly, given how used that cloth was, I think I made matters worse.

Day 32 blossomed warm under the brightness of the sun against the cloudless sky. My room, with the pine-lined walls, became a sauna, even hotter than the days when the Kitchen People came and their scents and oven steam rose like fire smoke into my cell.

Here came the rattle of the floor, announcing psycho on his way to snatch my empty tray. I sat on the bed, counting the number of pine boards from my feet to the door and from there, crawled my eyes up the white plaster wall and counted the cracks that veined out from the doorway. I already knew the answers, but I counted anyway, as I always did, as a way to memorize every pattern everywhere in every one of those days: 12 boards of varying width; 14 cracks, including the small tributaries.

Keys clanged against the metal outside my door, and I toggled my head in boredom at this whole routine. Sniffing the thick vapor of unmasked sweat from my armpits, I fought back exhaling in disgust. I sat up straighter when at last he opened the door and stepped to his regular spot on Floorboard #3.

'Give me your tray. Bathroom?'

'Yes, please.'

'Hurry up then. I haven't got all day.'

You haven't got all day? What the hell do you do all day? Oh yeah, nothing. You do nothing all day. You're worthless.

But I didn't shoot any smart looks, no evil eye, like I might have before. I lowered my gaze, handed forth the tray gingerly, and squirmed, nervously, to the bathroom, as he moved to block the stairwell down, as he always did.

Inside the bathroom, leaning against the door, I stopped to marvel at how big I'd become. Baby moved within, but slow, like an unhurried whale breaching the ocean with his hump. At full size then, my child folded onto himself in his cramped quarters. Although, I don't know how he could have been cramped: my torso was as large as a Weber barbecue.

I patted the baby and scanned the room. I haven't described the bathroom yet, have I? It must have been a former closet, since the square footage matched, well, a large closet: a wedge of space, crammed within an eave. The ceiling slanted over a claw-foot tub that took up nearly the entire floor space. You had to shimmy sideways past the tub and sit perfectly straight to use the white toilet. Sitting so, you might pontificate life by resting your bent elbow on the white pedestal sink beside the toilet. A cheap square of mirror hung slightly crooked, literally glued to the wall above. Crammed between toilet and sink was a one-foot-high, white trashcan, in which were two white plastic bags: the active one for trash, and one under the one in use. I had left both bags in place, for I hadn't come up with a use for them. They were those flimsy, annoying things they give you at the grocery store. The variety in which the bagboy inexplicably places one item per bag: ketchup bottle in one, milk in another, bread in another, and so on. You end up with fifty million bags. I hate these bags. I really, really hate these bags.

But, I digress.

The bathroom floor was made out of the same pine boards as in my bedroom. I'd scanned this white room so many times for assets, but everything visible was either bolted or glued in place or not terribly useful. I might carry the trashcan, but what was I going to do with a tiny wastebasket? The dirty washcloth on the sink was just a 6″ x 6″ piece of filth. Beyond these items, the bathroom had been cleared of any regular items that might have been assets. No evident cleaning chemicals, no nail clippers, no tweezers, hell, even floss would have been a great weapon.

Despite my acceptance that the bathroom was void of any useful items, after clicking the door shut, I scoured the small space once again and again found nothing. I shimmied sideways to the toilet – and, if you really must know, emptied my bladder. My baby belly touched the rounded rim of the bathtub, and my left elbow rested upon the sink. When complete with my afternoon relief, I stood and bent to place my face under the sink faucet to swallow as much water as my dry mouth could take. With the skanked washcloth I'd used for weeks, I quickly wiped my pits and elsewhere.

I twirled on my feet as I worked, ogling the tub with an

animalistic desire. Oh, but to twist the 'hot' knob and slip in, soak in heated liquid, and burn the stench from my body. I placed my left foot on the toilet seat, balancing on my right, and stretched to scratch my hairy leg, struggling with my girth in the packed quarters to reach the area above my ankle.

In this struggle, when my head was cocked downwards and sideways just so, I noticed something that had been waiting for me all along. So hidden, so coy. But very much, very literally, under my nose the whole time.

A bottle of bleach.

Right there. A one-gallon bottle. The label was missing, and because it was tucked so tight in the inward groove of the back of the toilet, the bottle was quite camouflaged. And don't you know, Hallelujah, Hallelujah, when I squatted to extract my new find, sure enough, I found that glorious albino chameleon ¾ full. *Sodium Hypochlorite, welcome to the party. Asset #36.*

My plan did not *require* this bonus Asset. Yet, even in these final hours, I thought of a perfect use for Clorox: an extra flourish of pain, something I hadn't realized I *needed* until I set eyes on that magnificent white vessel. I allowed a frivolous and unhinged moment of psychosis in thinking I might fall in love with bleach. Perhaps I did dabble in a couple of seconds of insanity when I hugged the plastic body to my engorged breasts and kissed the blue lid.

At the bottom of the trashcan was the extra plastic bag. I grabbed it and placed it in my pants: *Plastic Bag, Asset #37.*

I replaced the bottle. I wouldn't be able to extricate the bleach on this trip, but with the whole hot afternoon ahead, I thought I'd map out a plan.

'Get the fuck out,' he yelled, while predictably banging his fat fist on the door. The wood bounced. Every time he did this, I feared the antique paneling would crack and cave.

'Yes, sir. Here I come. Sorry, not feeling well.' Which wasn't true, but, in the quick interim of returning the bottle and watching the door bend to his pounding, I figured out how to safely extract the bottle. I didn't really need the afternoon to think on a plan.

'So sorry, I'm hurrying, just feeling queasy.'

'I don't give a shit. Get the fuck out.'

I opened the door, rounded my shoulders in the posture of the inferior and submissive, and scampered quick to my cell.

He locked me in with his stupid ring of keys.

What are the other keys for? Who cares.

For the next hour, I conjured sick and disgusting visions. I spun myself dizzy, and then quickly stopped to drop on all fours, dipping my head to balance a quick second on the crown of my skull, repeating and repeating. The sickest and most grotesque thought was, of course, the real memory of the girl's torso in the quarry. So I thought of that. Over and over.

Then, I invented a mini-movie of myself licking my captor's twin's back. Sure, Brad, his back had to be hairy and pimply, so I imagined dragging my tongue through his wiry back hair while popping his back pimples, all while he'd be licking a plate of blood-oozing veal. With this awful imagery firmly in my mind, I spun again, kept licking, kept popping, the veal bloodier each time, the pus thicker, embedding in the hair I licked, and twirling, and twirling, and when so dizzy and so disturbed, I jammed my finger down my throat and finally, finally, vomited. It's harder than you think to make yourself throw up. And it's not something I've done since, nor do I recommend self-purging as an appropriate act for practice. Sometimes, however, these vile acts must be done on a one-time basis for the greater good.

The blob splashed well away from the doorway, exactly where I aimed, and nowhere near where he'd step. I didn't want him to ever have any hesitations in entering my room and stepping in the exact same footpath he always followed.

Should I sit until dinner with this acidic odor, steaming in this heat? Or, should I call out to him, like I sometimes did when a bathroom emergency seized my physical self. I had no clue where he went between his visits to my cell. Perhaps he sat in some room below, perhaps he left to do errands, somewhere where I could not hear him. Eight out of the twelve times I had banged on the door and requested a special bathroom trip, in-between the regular mealtime bathroom visits, he had barged up the stairs, playing the annoyed prison guard. Thus, his stats on responding were high, eight out of twelve times. And I figured that was because he didn't want a mess to clean up. So, with the likelihood he'd respond again, and because eight out of twelve times made it safely part of the routine, I chose to call him to my room.

Plus, the awful odor of decay, which seemed accelerated in my fire-pit room, invaded my nose and pierced my brain, and reinforced my decision.

Oh hell no, I'm not smelling this all afternoon.

Rubbing my hands together, I waltzed to the door. I pictured myself a master healer, heating holistic hands to massage broken muscles for an absolute cure. With hot palms, I banged upon the door.

'Excuse me, sir. Excuse me. I got sick,' I yelled.

Sure enough, movement began in some pocket of the building below me. Then a pause, which I presume came because he questioned whether he heard anything.

'Excuse me,' I continued to bang and yell. 'Sir, I'm sick. I'm so sorry,' I said.

'Mother of all fuck, son of a damn bitch,' he shouted, as he stomped up the stairs.

I backed away from the door, and in he came.

'Holy What,' he said, pinching his nose, while finding the source on the floor.

'I'll clean it, sir. I'm so sorry. Please, please. I saw some bleach in the bathroom. Can I use it? Should I use it?' I fell to his feet, begging him, 'I'm so sorry.'

Still squirming in the smell, he backed up, took his position at the top of the stairs to indicate I should enter the bathroom, and said, 'Well, go on. Clean this shit up. And hurry the fuck up.'

Still on hands and knees, I crawled to the bathroom, grabbed the trashcan, the washcloth, the bleach, and crawled back. Quickly, I scooped the mess into the trash and poured two caps of cleaning chemical on the washcloth to rub the boards. Setting the bottle aside after scrubbing the spot, I took up the trash and cloth, returned to the bathroom, dumped everything in the toilet, rinsed the trashcan in the tub, wrung the cloth under running water, and returned to my room.

'Thank you, sir. I'm so sorry.'

'Don't fucking puke again. I'm watching Matlock,' he said, while once again locking my door.

So that's what you do all day. How predictable.

I guess we're back to a safe routine. All snug and comfy, aren't we now?

Bleach, Asset #36. Right on time. Tomorrow we go.

CHAPTER ELEVEN

Special Agent Roger Liu

You might choose to believe this, you might choose not to. For sure, this part is too fanciful, perhaps too magical, for any FBI field report.

Sometimes, and it used to be more frequent, I like to disappear. Say a meeting ended earlier than expected, and I wasn't required to be anywhere at the moment. I could call, say the office, say my wife, Sandra, or my hard-knuckle partner, Lola. But perhaps, I might figure, I could take this gift of stolen time and slip away down a cobblestone alley and into a little Italian restaurant I know has been there forever. If, for example, this early-ending meeting were in Boston, that restaurant might be called Marliaves, set on a hill on the edge of Downtown Crossing. I think it's been there since they invented bricks.

Perhaps I might coil tight in a black booth, my cell phone at my hip on the seat, untouched. The waitress would bring me a menu, but I wouldn't need it, for who would need to scour such a pedestrian item in stolen time. I am free here, untethered, and my divinity in this moment gives me a clarity as to a simple desire. 'I'll have the gnocchi *al dente* and a Coke, please.' The waitress soft shoes away to summon from some suspended place, my hot plate.

I love this feeling, no one in the whole world who might want to find me knows where I am in this very second. I am powerful. I command the world. No one can say I can't be here, for even I had not intended it. This gift, this free time. I might fall into a void between the universe's theoretical strings and remain forever in a gravity-defying pit.

I'd learned the power of hiding at age thirteen, but when I have these stolen moments of hidden peace, I surely don't allow my mind to wander to those wretched memories, nor the wretched day that shaped my whole life, my career. So, we won't go there even now – now when I tell you of my blessed stolen moments.

Sure, I'd love Sandra to be with me in these times of hiding, but that would be impossible. They're never planned, and she's busy on some tour, I'm sure. And no one is missing me anyway. I suppose I could have taken on more cases, jumped ahead with other work, called my mother, a friend, finished some nagging errand. Or, maybe all of those things would never get done anyway had I been struck by a bus after the meeting; but since I wasn't struck by a bus, I must be on borrowed time, gravy time, extra-frosting time. So I won't call and I won't work. I'll just sit here with my pasta and my soda and I'll stare into the restaurant's shadows or linger, listening to the couple in love in the next booth.

At the end of my life, I'd like to splice together all of these moments into one reel. I'm sure if I did, the splicing would reveal that one stolen moment was no different from the last or the next and so on, because I swear every time this happens, it's the same place mentally, just me, myself, sitting here smiling at the freedom of living in this exact moment and not one soul changing that perspective. Could be Marliaves, could be the reservoir in Manchester, New Hampshire, my hotel bed in Atlanta, the streets of Soho, or the park in Kentucky with a view of one brown horse and one tan horse. Always the same place for me: internal peace.

Of course, I can acquire this feeling of peace because I'm not on the run. I don't need to hide from anyone, except myself, except dire memories. If I were on the run, well, that would be a different story. Or, if I had something truly awful to hide, then in that case, I'm sure I wouldn't be sitting all sedate in some restaurant, ordering up anything, let alone *al dente*.

In my line of work, I've found there is a spectrum of

criminals. In one extreme, there is the mastermind megalo-maniac who leaves nothing to chance, no fingerprint stains, no tire treads, no strand of hair, no footprints. No witnesses. No accomplices. No nothing leading to nothing. In the other extreme, there are the bungling fools who might as well broadcast their crime in real time. In between, you have your garden-variety knuckleheads, who get a lot right, but get some critical pieces wrong, and on these, we pounce.

In the Dorothy M. Salucci case, what with the information Boyd called with, we had a bonafide extremist on our hands, of the bungling kind. And so, this is the part I bring you to, the part you might choose to believe, or choose to dismiss. Keep in mind, reality is often stranger than fiction, and so while you might be inclined to think the following impossible, it might serve to remind that some investigations are indeed solved. Whether the result is positive or negative is irrelevant to the fact of solving – also, the impression of positive or negative is, of course, subjective.

'Mr Liu, you ain't gonna believe what I got to tell you,' Boyd said.

There I was standing outside Lou Mitchell's in Chicago's loop, having left Lola to do her bidding on my breakfast plate.

'Yeah, what's up, Boyd?'

'You ain't never gonna believe this, Mr Liu. Hardly believe it myself. Ah shit . . . '

Silence.

'I got to call you back,' he said and hung up.

As you already know, I went back into Lou Mitchell's and found Lola eating my toast. After the whole ordeal with Big Stan, and Lola and I had walked to the park, Boyd called again.

'Mr Liu, I'm so sorry. So sorry to have hung up. You ain't gonna believe this.'

'Go on, Boyd, I got all day.'

I didn't really have all day, but I could probably listen to the sweet whistle in that chicken-farmer's voice for hours. Sort of reminded me of my grandpa, before everything went to hell.

'Mr Liu, I'm standing in my cousin Bobby's kitchen outside Warsaw, Indiana. I suggest you get on down here.'

Boyd proceeded to tell me he had driven about an hour from his home to Warsaw, Indiana, to pick up some specialty feed for his chickens. 'I tell you, had the hood a' my car not blown up cuz the latch broke, I mighta never been able to give you this information. God, He bless me when He broke the hood of my car.

'Mr Liu, I know the only thing, other than a new latch, that was gonna help me get my feed home before the rain hit – I got it piled up in the back bed and have no tarps on me – was to go on inta' a hardware store and get me a good roll a' Gorilla tape to hold the lid on my engine. That stuff'll hold a moose to a tree. So there I am, minding my own damn business like any

146

good Christian son at the town hardware, and holo, I couldn't believe my eyes. Here he was, Mr Liu, there was my van buyer, standing in line.'

'Did he see you?'

'No, Mr Liu, no sir, not a wink. I was behind him, and he was too bugged out to notice no one. In fact, the clerk had to say, "scuce me" about three times before he moved ahead in line. Man was far off to some other place in his mind. But wait, okay. Cuz there's more, uh-huh.'

'Go on, Boyd. Go on. But wait, when was this?'

'Just 'bout hour-ana-half ago. Right after he paid and left, I threw a twenty on tha' counta', told 'em to keep tha' change, hurried out, taped my lid up quick, watched him drive away in *my van*, and drove myself to a drug store I know down the road. It has a pay phone. That's when I called you first. I walk around with your card now, and I'm so glad I do. Anyway, listen, I had ta hang up cuz, guess what, here comes your man, again. He'd parked on the otha' side of the building and he was going in-ta the pharmacy. It's one a those old-school pharmacies, Mr Liu. They just sell the prescriptions. No food section. No big Pampers section. Can't you track him now by his doctor? Maybe don't need to though, cuz listen.'

'Wait, wait. Did he see you at the payphone?'

'Ain't no way. He didn't see me there and he didn't see

me at the hardware store neither. I stayed a good distance behind because I knew you'd want me to, Mr Liu. Wouldn'ta done you no good he saw me see him. He mighta flee, right? At the hardware store, I know he ain't seen me 'cuz I stood low and stayed behind a big ol' boy in a red-and-black hunter's jacket. So your man there, he was buying duct tape and also a shovel, and a roll a' tarp too. That's concerning ain't it, Mr Liu?'

'A bit, Boyd. And you say he didn't see you at the pharmacy either? Did you see him come out of the pharmacy?'

'No sir, I took off. Drove around, looking for another pay phone. I surely didn't want him seeing me. I shoulda followed him, you think, don't you? I'm so sorry. I jus' didn't want him to see me. But wait, wait, there's more.'

'Go on,' I said and starting thinking, *pink bear*.

'So I'm driving around looking for another pay phone and damn I tell you, pay phones are harder ta' find than you think, Mr Liu. Anyway, I suddenly rememba my cousin Bobby. I mentioned him to ya, yeah, his boy play for Indiana University, right, you rememba? You asked about the Hoosier plates?'

'Yes, Boyd, I remember. Go on, please.'

'So, I rememba Cousin Bobby, he live 'bout half-an-hour from the downtown in another town, takes so long cuza the dirt road and all and he got a big ol' cow farm. I was thinkin' I'd drive on into Cousin Bobby's to use his phone, plus he'd let me park in his tractor barn to cover up my feed 'fore tha' rain hit.

'So there I finally get, right on into Cousin Bobby's, and out he come, smiling his fat face farmer smile, and he says the strangest thing.'

'What's that?'

'He goes, "Damn Boyd, I was just about ta' call ya. I just got back from checking the outfield, past the ridge, and saw your van parked on the outskirts of the old school's field, under a willow tree. Why'd you leave it there?"'

'I didn't believe him until he took me up there. And damn, Mr Liu, there's my maroon van, Hoosier plates still on her front and her back. I told Bobby we had to creep back real slow, backwards and all, to make sure ain't no one saw us. And that's exactly what we did. Two grown men walking backwards through the pasture. We sittin' in Bobby's kitchen right now. We shakin', Mr Liu. We damn shakin' in our bones. Bobby's got a couple-a rifles, and we can go take care a' this for ya, if ya want. We ain't called the local boys yet, we want to do whatever you need, Mr Liu.'

'Just sit tight. Give me your address. I'll handle this. We'll be right there. Do not move from Bobby's kitchen.'

The damn suspect was out doing his errands all peaceful, as if free, as if on stolen time. Now we'd know whatever he bought at the hardware store and the pharmacy and we'd have all of the video evidence in those places and likely in between. Now we had his van, and I was pretty damn sure he was hiding out in the old school house Boyd so casually mentioned. We had him dead-to-rights. Well, I thought we had him dead-to-rights.

CHAPTER TWELVE

DAY OF

I read once or heard once that a human can drown in just two inches of water. I had water, Asset #33, which I used on Day 33. And hence, the full name of my plot, '15/33.'

I woke as usual at 7:22 a.m. Asset #14, the television, told me this, as did Asset #16, the radio. I made the bed as I always did and waited, sitting on the white coverlet until 8:00 a.m. for breakfast. At exactly 7:59, just on time, the floorboards rattled, and thus approached my punctual jailer. He unlocked the door and handed me the tray with the chipped toile china plate – chipped because I purposefully dropped the thing one day before – for fun. *Blueberry muffins from the Kitchen People. And, of course, the milk, and the cup of water. I hate blueberries, but the butter-sugar top looks good.*

'Thank you.'

Whole extra water routine.

He left.

The bored conductor yawns as he waves his wand through rote motions. Awake! This orchestra will soon play the rock version of a practiced hymn; a solo crowd will be shocked. Ratchet up the pace, maestro.

After the field trip to the quarry, which at the time I consciously blanked from my memory, and up to this day, Day 33, I had peppered my regular routine with screaming and crying fits, all for the sole benefit of my captor's weak ego. In addition to these well-planned spells of emotional acting, I truthfully increased my internal resolve. I also sped up the timeline. I had planned on waiting two more weeks, two more rounds of Kitchen People, so I'd be beyond question in my calculations and practice. So I'd have plenty of water. But what with the trek to the pit of horror, I chose to cut to the finish. I allowed three days to pass so as to ease him back into a safe routine and reduce his agitation, trick him into a sedate trust, by giving him what his demented state needed: wailing, crying, a subject who treated him like an Alpha, moon-eyed him from beneath his knees as a person of power, a mighty man rising from the earth, a pillar, a ruler, a Pharaoh, the only king of my world. *Fucking inbred.*

Tricking someone into thinking he has power is the ultimate power play.

The execution of my plan would have to wait for the delivery of lunch on Day 33 because 7:22 a.m. - 8:00 a.m. did not afford enough time for the set-up. I ate the muffin quickly and waited until 8:30 for his return. Sitting on the edge of the mattress after my meal, I flossed my teeth with thread I'd pulled from the hem of the comforter. Mashed muffin crumbs beaded in a saliva chain on the make-do floss, as I forced the string in and out of the tight joints of my teeth. Moving from molars to incisors, I did find it curious to be so fixed on the blood my rough dental care produced.

I'll need to see the dentist when I'm out of here.

I found it humiliating to have to perform such private work in a bedroom – how uncivilized to treat my sleeping space as a bathroom.

I'm better than this.

I checked my nails, displeased with jagged cuticles. Waiting. Preening and waiting.

Fortunately, he fell into my trap and came on cue.

Strike the rumbling kettledrum.

He opened the door. I handed him the tray.

Whole wash my face, body, teeth, and drink from faucet routine – this time by just splashing water. I wasn't about to use the nasty washcloth anymore.

The orchestra shifts closer to the edge of their seats, gripping strings and filling lungs. A violin joins the drum to heighten the passion. Anticipation crawls up the spine of the stiff-backed pianist.

I waddled back to the room. I considered this phase of 15/33, successfully completed, *check.*

The minutiae of this day is so ingrained in my mind movie. Microseconds of actions and observations are burned so deeply I practically see them play out now: seventeen years of replay. When he thrust me back into my confines after the morning bathroom trip, the iciness of his grip on my forearm was so cold I thought he might stick to my skin, like lips on an icy glass. Slowly I craned my neck to see a stain on his chin, stuck within the stubble he'd failed to shave. The yellowy blotch looked to be egg yolk, which I presumed he'd horked down after giving me my muffin and before picking up my tray.

He gets protein in a hot breakfast but gives me empty calories in a cold pastry.

I wanted him to have the decency to wipe his face before being in my presence. I wanted him to have the grace to apologize for breathing his hot stench around me, for clouding my air with his BO and halitosis, for thinking he could enjoy a meal while I was in the same house as him, for having no warmth in his touch, for not seeing the plan unfold around him, for his blindness, his stupidity, his existence, and his past, a past that made me a victim – trickle-down torture. I wanted that yellow stain to not exist. I wished I'd never seen the gooey mass on his blackhead-filled, dry-skin, lazy face, but it was there, and I was there, and hard work had to be done that day.

He's out of my hair for a good three-and-a-half hours. Get to work. Phase II.

I really didn't need three-and-a-half hours. I needed perhaps an hour for the set-up. With the extra time, I practiced. *I must stand here.* I stood there. *I must drop this then.* I pretended to drop a cord. *I must pick this up and push, right away.* I practiced with the floorboard. *I must unhook this as I leave the room.* I didn't practice this last part for fear of squandering my *coup de grace*, my grand finale, my triple insurance for death.

The hour approached. If I were a ballerina, I'd be on point, my toes, my legs, my whole body in a stiff cement posture. The child growing inside me turned; his foot moved across my belly. Five toes and a heel were visible from him pressing within. *I love you, baby. Hold on. Game time.*

A fast wind rustled through the treetop outside the triangular window and in its wake, the sky darkened, and a sudden shower fried in a flash.

The team of flutes sounds like swarming bees, the violins are in a fury, kicking up a cyclone, the grand piano is on fire, the ivory practically pounds to dust.

Minutes later, the sky remained gray and dripping, not fully giving up on rain, but not raining outright either. If the air had been warm, the day would have been steamy, like summers in

Savannah at Nana's house. But since the air was cool and we were on a non-exotic, flat farm, the wetness was the kind to chill bones, crack marrow.

My son will not be born here. He will not enter the world, cold and damp. My child will not be taken.

My condition, this condition, propelled me to action. Because I was a full eight months then, I could not afford to physically attack my captor, even though he'd given ample opportunities. I could have jabbed a dagger of broken china or the sharpened end of a TV antenna into his neck. I could have dismantled the baseboard and beat him with a bedpost. Trust me, I thought of all of these options. They were ruled out though because they would require agility and lunging and jumping, abilities I lacked in my late condition. Besides, I might miss. I could not do the necessary deed entirely physically, and I did not want to stress the baby with a foolish attempt. Instead, I used as many assets as I could, the power of physics, basic biology, systems of levers and pulleys, and unbridled vengeance.

My father is a physicist and a black belt in jiu-jitsu, trained by the navy. With these two industries, he taught the benefit of using an aggressor's weight and movement against him in battle. I knew from my mother, a hardened cynic, 'You should never underestimate a person's stupidity or laziness.' Any opponent will eventually slip up, and thus, to her teachings,

'Never waste an opponent's moment of weakness. Do not hesitate in slicing an exposed jugular.' She meant it figuratively, but I tried in vain to apply it literally.

My captor displayed numerous moments of weakness, of stupidity, of laziness. I'll sum them up: the van, the Kitchen People, the pencil sharpener, the setting and following of patterns, the inability to fight his own weakened ego, the decision to put the barrel of a gun on my unborn baby, the offers for more water, the TV, the radio, and finally, the act of leaving his ring of keys in the door whenever he unlocked it to enter.

By Day 33, I was secure concluding the Kitchen People would be absent until Day 37. The Doctor and The Obvious Couple would not visit, for I had shown no signs of labor – nor would I have shared them with my captor anyway. Brad, I presumed, had been successful in flying the coup.

It will be him and me alone, just as 15/33 requires.

The dangling radio said it was 11:51, nine minutes to showtime. I stood in my designated spot and tried to fix upon the time, suspended in the air on the radio which spun on the rope to which it was tied. The minutes were so slow then, and so was my heartbeat. I believe the only anxiety I felt was the anxiety of getting this gig over with. The practice I'd had to this point was as though I'd memorized a passionate love speech, one that at first writing might have elicited trembles of heartbeats and perhaps even tears, but after ten thousand recitations had

become a mass of words, disconnected to human feeling –
much the way a President might read from a teleprompter or
a bad actor might deliver lines when reading straight from a
script. 'I love you' is said as three robotic words, no dip of voice
or shoulders, no hand extended on the 'love', no pupils dilated,
no crease of the forehead to emphasize the point. 'I. Love. You.'
is simply said while the speaker simultaneously checks the time
on his watch. *There is no love with such a declaration if he checks
his watch; but love is felt, indeed the room pulses, when he says as
much and fights his knees from sinking to the ground or fails to
blink from the blinding light invading his widened eyes.*

And so, much like the tin man declaring love, my practiced
hand itched to complete the task. I probably could have killed
him blindfolded and asleep at this point, the actions I planned
had been repeated so often.

At 11:55, I signaled my star, a bag of bleach, to take its place
in the spotlight. Bleach is corrosive. I once read an article in
which Scott Curriden of Scripps Research Environmental
Health and Safety was quoted as saying, 'Bleach can drill a hole
through stainless steel.' So I waited as long as I could to pour
my ¾ gallon of bleach into the flimsy plastic bag and pinch
the bag by loosely tying the top with some of the red yarn I'd
unraveled. Next, standing by the door, I pulled the other end
of the yarn, which was thrown over the beam closest to the
door, along with another cord holding another item – wait

for it – so the pouch of bleach rested beneath this other heavy item. Both objects dangled directly over Floorboard #3.

Bleach is corrosive, as I've mentioned, which we know from scientists. And bleach burns like a Mother You-Know-Whater when it's splashed in your eyes or your mouth or your face, which we know from common sense.

The clock ticked to 11:59 and the sun simultaneously flared, sending a beam to cut through the dust particles in the air. The smell of my own sweat fogged me in the tight space I quarantined myself to, firm against the wall by the door. I'm sure my odor hadn't increased due to any nervousness, but rather was abundantly apparent as I prepared to say goodbye to all the details of that horrible den.

An ever-so-slight tremble began. The floorboards rattled. *Lunch.* I plastered my back to the wall, solid in the designated spot by the door. Outside, he placed the tray on the floor. The click clack of plastic against wood signaled me to stand rigid and ready.

Keys jingled and metal scraped within the keyhole.

The door opened.

He opened it wide, just what I needed, just as always, just as expected, as planned.

After collecting the food from the floor, he bent without looking up and stepped to the exact spot he always did, just as I had marked and measured three times a day since Day 5.

Floorboard #3. He looked straight ahead at the bed, which was now a contraption of death. What did he think, expecting me to be sitting there waiting for lunch but seeing ... the mattress tipped, wedged between the bed frame and the wall, and the box spring on the floor, cut open and hallowed, lined with that plastic, and filled with water, and thus, transfigured into a literal pool. A quarry with cotton sides *in* the house, only steps from the door. In the second of insight I allowed him, I hoped he saw a ready canvas, waiting only for its main subject, him, and thus would be my completed masterpiece. I hoped he would chastise himself for giving me plastic on that box spring, chastise himself for being too lazy to remove it and properly place the bed on slats. His vision would be of that box spring now expertly layered in the plastic, half-filled with water, and the standing mattress against the wall, like an opened lid to this well, waiting to close once he entered. The wood frame of the bed, he should have noted, had several skinny rungs missing. Did he wonder where those had gone? And hanging and twirling and singing in the sky above was the radio on a rope made out of a red knit blanket. The radio's plug was in the socket at the foot of the bed.

Did he connect water with electricity? Did he feel the rising zap in the room, coming from the socket, my plan, my head? Did he sense the tension so high in the blaring opera above the bed, so high I thought bolts of lighting flashed around the room?

I'm sure if I had allowed another second to pass, he'd have cranked his head to see me standing to his left and by the opened door. He'd have asked a bewildered and grunted *How?* I never gave him the opportunity, of course, but I have a chance now for a quick explanation.

On that working night from Day 4 to Day 5, I used the razor from the pencil sharpener, which had been summarily dismantled by the sharp end of the bucket handle, and cut the plastic covering and the fabric on the inside of the box spring. The cutting is what took so long. I had only the razor to work with and it was small. Even a microscopic tear might foil the plan, so I worked methodically, like an art restorer to a damaged Rembrandt, precious square inch by precious square inch, ensuring each cut was surgeon-worthy straight. I kept the plastic on the sides and bottom of the box spring and secured it in place with the flat tacks, collectively Asset #24. I'll explain about the tacks in a minute. I lined the box spring between its now exposed support boards with the cut plastic and secured the inner well – now an empty pool – with more of the flat tacks. I reinforced certain spots with a patchwork of pieces of my black raincoat, which I had torn apart. He never noticed it missing.

'Your opponent will often be blind to your design, being consumed with his own. Do not subconsciously seek accolades of your ingenuity and thus call attention – be sated by your own approval. Be confident you will win,' so said the quote, scrawled on a napkin and framed in my mother's home office. My father was the author, having written the inspiration before jumping from a plane in his Navy wetsuit to extract some kidnapped figurehead from an island prison. Such were the subjects of our family dinner conversations, even after mother's trial wins became the norm and even after my father retired to a full life of science.

On Day 33, he likely could not believe the spectacle of this box spring well, filled with the lukewarm water he offered me at every meal – by the way, when I guzzled water from the bathroom faucet, this is how I got the hydration needed for my condition. Above the bed-pool hung the radio, plugged in to the outlet on the wall by the headboard. A symphony of unparalleled voracity blared.

Wild notes. Oh wild melody. Rage on.

Just before my captor arrived on Day 33 to deliver my lunch, I marveled at this scene myself. *When I said, 'Thank you', each time you offered me more water, I meant, 'Thank you. Thank you for letting me drown you, electrocute you'.*

The band is beyond divinity at this point, so furious I can no longer hear a single note. What music, what rapture. I am overcome.

One second after he entered the room and stepped in the place I had studied for weeks, I let go the pouch of bleach

(Asset #36), and also the ultrasound machine's extension cord (Asset #22), which held the TV suspended above his head. The pouch hit first and burst, only to be squished further a millisecond later by the crash of the television. Both missiles hit squarely on what was once the soft spot of his newborn skull.

The bleach must have reached his eyeballs because instead of cradling his crushed head, his weak arms, weak because he was passing out, went to his eyes as he gave out a high-pitched moan. I hold freeze-frames of his actions from this point on. Frame-by-frame, he rocked his left eye with the back of his left hand, while his right arm did the same with his right eye. Even in memory, I do not hear, as I did not hear in those microseconds, what must have been spitting swears and screaming coming from his wide-open mouth. I heard that radio offering praise from an opera. I heard a violin scream a high note of approval. And I heard the crackle of urgent electricity, seeping from the socket and anxious to play its part. Water in the box spring rippled from the sudden thud of the TV when it crashed to the wood floor, after falling from his head to his right shoulder and bouncing off his back. A metal corner gouged somewhere along his neckline, releasing blood to run down his spine – like a ribbon on a balloon.

Before his complete collapse, I moved on to my next weapon, which I picked up in the same motion as when I released the bleach and TV. The loose floorboard in my hands became a battering ram. I laid it flat against his back from his left side where I stood. Using his falling motion, I pushed the requisite force – based on his weight and height – to drop him to his knees, propel him forward, and insure he'd fall headfirst in the water – which he was primed to do anyway. He splashed into my quarry, and I slipped out behind his now fallen feet to the hall, looking in. Simultaneously, I unhooked more of the red yarn, which I'd braided to form a rope, from a nail by the door. I fashioned the rope out of the yarn from the red knit blanket, Asset #5, which I began unraveling, as you know, on Day 20. He never noticed the uncoiling because I folded the blanket on its own disembowelment every single morning at dawn. The once dangling radio hit the water where his bleached and crushed head and torso lay, submerged. The crack and the sizzle of electrocution filled the room. Me outside, him within.

All of this took less than ten seconds, about the time he took to nab me from my street.

Now that, my friends, is justice. Cold, hard, burning, skull-splitting, electrified justice.

15/33 consisted of a three-part escape plan: TV, with unnecessary but added bonus of bleach pouch, electrocution, and drowning, each of which could have caused his death. If the TV missed, I still would have picked up the floorboard and pushed, expecting him to likely trip. If necessary, I would have mustered physical force and whaled him with the floorboard until he collapsed, then I'd turn to my failsafe and shoot him in the eyes and neck and groin with the bow and four arrows in the holster strapped to my back.

Arrows and holster? I had so many assets. The bow was constructed of the elastic from the attic and my trusty now unbent bucket handle. The arrows were sharpened rungs I had removed from the bed frame and whittled with the ends of the TV antennas – the rungs and antennas being falsely re-secured each morning into their intended, decorative/sort-of-functional spots. The holster was the sleeve of my raincoat, pinch-tied at the bottom with more of the yarn, the strap made out of wiring I ripped from the guts of the ultrasound machine. Thankfully, the arrows were superfluous, then, which is why I didn't fret over the inability to use them in practice. Praise God and his black angel butterfly, for I had the positional advantage, the element of surprise, and from my relentless study, I knew his movements, patterns, gait, steps, height, and weight so precisely, I very well could have metamorphized into the man.

What about those tacks? You'll remember, on the first night in the van, I slept less than he did. It's funny what sweat will do to duct tape and that van was hot and I had extra pounds. I felt the magic of my heat on the tape all of Day 1, and slowly but surely, my thin wrists loosened within my confinement. Finally, while he snored, I tested how far I might pull an arm free. Sure enough, fifty minutes into his slumber, my right arm slid out. Unsure of how long I had, and since the olive oven barred the side sliding door and a chain barred the back doors, I was likely out of time to free my left arm and legs – although I continued to fiddle. I bent to the backpack, retrieved the tacks – a commercial-sized pack of one thousand so stuffed the tacks didn't rattle – and pocketed them in my lined, black raincoat. He stirred. I sat up straight. I put my hand back through the duct tape, slouched, and pretended to sleep. He yawned and turned in his chair. I felt him look at me.

'Stupid fucking whore,' he'd said.

Idiot. I will kill you with these tacks, I had thought.

Thirty-three days later, I froze outside my jail cell as his sizzling and muscle-jumping body rounded out. When he fell, his body was limp, his legs collapsed and sprawled on the floor in pigeon-toe, but his torso lifted to slump over the low bed frame and into the water in the box spring. The oddest part of everything was how his hips kept rising with every zap of electricity and banging the side of the bed – as if he were dream-humping the long board while sleeping submerged in the water. The water appeared blue with yellow streaks, swirling and spilling around him and to the floor. Sparks poured from the wall socket, threatening to catch and burn the whole joint, but didn't, given that they burned to black dots on the floorboards. Pops accompanied the sparks, as did bubbles of his breath when his body settled into death and the angered electricity calmed. I waited until all popping stopped, like when you microwave popcorn, those last, slow seconds of one, two-three, silence, a fourth and final kernel pops. 'Ding!' the microwave blares, 'All done.'

A drone of dying lights sent a warping over the house: the electrocution had shorted the electricity. Although midday, the musty hall fell dark and a quiet dropped a cloth of eerie silence. I reached for an arrow on my back, standing as still as a stone statue in the park, mid-step, sword unsheathed. No noises came from his chamber of death. No footsteps fell behind me, above me, below me, or anywhere. I was outside my room. I shut the door and locked him within. I took the keys.

Silence.

My heart beat loud in my ears.

A swallow fluttered by the window in the stairwell, a herald tweeting, 'The coast is clear.'

I hope you enjoyed your swim in my little pool, motherfucker. I spit on the door.

I went downstairs and entered the kitchen. I had imagined it so often with the floral print fabric, wood worktables, white sink, and apple-green mixer, I felt deceived to find something wholly different. The truth in the vision winded me. Instead of a country kitchen, before me were two long stainless steel tables – commercial-kitchen style. The stove was big and black, the mixer, boring egg-white. There were no colors in this room. There were no aprons with pink piping. No fat cat lounging on a rug. And, there was another surprise for me too.

Upon the steel table closest to me, I found a second china plate of food. This was surely not mine; mine was shattered upstairs, under the electrified remains of my perpetrator's feet. This plate was wrapped in plastic with a Post-it on top. Beside it was an identical mug of milk and cup of water. I stepped closer. The note said, 'D.' I looked in the trash. On top, plain as day, was another piece of saran wrap with a Post-it, but this one said, 'L,' my first initial. *How did I not see this before?* We were not alone in the building. *Another girl. And her name begins with D.*

Still, this diversion was not a part of my plan. *Stay focused, finish 15/33, and then re-plan.* I found some envelopes with the address and a phone, dialed 911, and demanded the chief of police. I got him.

'Listen to me carefully, write this down. I will talk slow. I am Lisa Yyland. I am the pregnant girl who was kidnapped a month ago from Barnstead, New Hampshire. I am at 77 Meadowview Road. Do not come in a cop car. Do not put this on the radio. Do not make a scene. You will jeopardize me and another girl they've taken. Come in one regular car. Come quick. Do not put this on the radio. Do not make a scene. Are you following this?'

'Yes.'

I hung up.

Now I could attend to this other victim. I stepped outside. Finally, the full architecture. For once I was right, it was white. As I had noted previously, the footprint housed four different wings, three floors to each with a common attic adding a fourth level. A faded sign on the side said, 'Appletree Boarding School.' The kitchen was so new though; the peeled paint of the exterior seemed misplaced. I thought of the scene in *Romancing the Stone* when Kathleen Turner and Michael Douglas visit Juan to get a ride in his 'Little Pepe', a truck. Juan's house was a run-down shack on the outside, but a virtual palace on the inside.

The girl, D, might be anywhere, and I was not about to go climbing all sorts of stairs looking for her. I wasn't going to yell either. Fortunately, something caught my eye. In the far left wing was a matching triangular window, at the same height as mine. I walked around the whole structure. There were no other windows like them. Instead, all of the other windows were large, some taking up the whole wall of a room. I concluded that had she been in any of those rooms, there would be curtains. I looked up again at the triangular window and I swear the black butterfly fluttered in the pane, as if pointing the way.

I opened the doorway of this far-left wing and climbed three flights of stairs. The stairwell matched mine exactly. The third floor housed the same bathroom, in the same spot.

I rattled the floorboards outside a locked room.

'D?' I said.

Nothing.

'D, what's your name? I just escaped from the other wing. Is someone there?'

A loud crash, something fell.

'Hello, hello! Please, let me out!' She screamed this phrase repeatedly, frantic she became, as I clawed through the ring of keys, which I had collected from my own locked door, and found the right one. Interestingly, her lock was antiquated, a simple turnkey lock so unlike my titanium upgrade. *Why was she so trusted? Underestimated?* I would have picked this lock on the first night. As her door opened, a blond girl struggled to sit on her bed. A pile of books was strewn along the floor, so I presumed they were the source of the crash. D wore a purple dress and one black Converse All Stars sneaker; her other foot was bare. I wondered again where my shoes were, as I scrunched my toes in the gifted, too-large Nikes. *Why was she allowed to keep her shoe?* This D was very pregnant, just as I.

'The cops are coming. They're coming right now.'

As I said this, the sound of tires and an engine rumbled outside.

Why didn't I hear cars pull up in my wing? She must have

heard whenever the Kitchen People arrived, The Doctor, The Obvious Couple, the Girl Scouts and their mother, Brad. Did she scream for help each time? They must not have heard her.

'My name is Dorothy Salucci. I need a doctor.'

A car door slammed. *That can't be the cops yet. I called 3.5 minutes ago. Must be the cops. Someone is walking around outside. Where are they going?*

Beads of sweat dotted her pale face. Her eyes drooped in sickness, not lethargy. One of her legs was swollen and red; her right shin appeared as though it would burst. Her hair was matted with grease, the bangs pulled aside by one bobby pin.

Where are they?

Dorothy's dungeon mirrored mine in many respects: wood bed without mattress on the bottom slats, just resting in the frame, plastic covered her box spring, the beams were the same, the window, the wood floor. But she had no TV. She had no radio. No pencil case, no ruler, no pencils, no paper, and no pencil sharpener. And I guessed, no tacks. She did have two assets, however, that I did not: knitting needles and several books.

Screaming began in another part of the building. My wing.

I tried to lift Dorothy, get her to move.

A door slammed. Again, my wing.

'Come, Dorothy, come now.'

She froze.

'Dorothy, Dorothy, we need to leave, now!'
Running feet outside the building below us.
And up the stairs.
Dorothy pasted herself to the wall behind her bed.
I pulled her arm.
A floorboard rattled behind us in the hall.
That's when I accepted my colossal miscalculation.

CHAPTER THIRTEEN

SPECIAL AGENT ROGER LIU

As soon as I hung up with Boyd, Lola and I found our way to the Skyway, the one road to Indiana that afforded a quickened, lights-and-siren-blaring path. I called the local Indiana police station and warned of our imminent arrival, instructing the chief to not move a muscle or make one solitary call on the open wire. He said, 'No problem,' and promised to bring his troops off the street by way of an innocuous code.

When we hit Gary, Indiana, we abandoned the lights and sirens, opting to blend into Indiana's straw-and-wheat air like other unmarked motorists on this cold spring day. The sky was a steel blanket of gray with just a faint hint of fighting blue. The sun, a distant memory behind the murky froth.

Lola's instincts were up on a high wire, for her sweat of Old

Spice pervaded every last inch of the interior. I opened the passenger window as she drove.

'Shut the damn window, Liu, I'm dying over here with that pumping sound in my ears.'

The fast-moving air annoyed me too, and I suppose it annoyed even more a woman with a hound's senses. I pushed the button to shut the window.

We beat our way into the police station, which had been turned into a makeshift command central of two men. The one-floor box of a structure had gray desks facing a waist-high wood partition, which itself faced the door. The wall of patrolmen in local blues I had expected to meet us was absent. An older officer extended his hand to mine.

'Agent Liu, Chief Marshall. This is my deputy, Hank. Sorry, I know you were expecting more of us. But soon as I hung up with ya, I realized, out of all the damn days, all my boys are attendin' a funeral for the wife of their old chief. They're all two-and-a-half hours away. But listen here, listen here.'

The chief stepped closer, peering into my eyes to accentuate his announcement.

'Listen here. You won't believe this. Your kidnapped girl just called. I can't believe the timing.'

'Dorothy called here?' I asked, incredulous.

'Dorothy? Who's Dorothy? No, the girl said her name was Lisa Yyland.'

'Pink bear,' Lola whispered.

'Come again?' Chief Marshall asked.

'Never mind, never mind. Did you say Lisa Yyland?' I said.

'Yeah, you can hear it on our recording. She called three minutes ago. I've been trying your phone number. She said to go on up to the old boarding school. She's waiting. Said not to use sirens or we'd jeopardize her and another girl.'

Another girl. Another girl. I bet that girl is Dorothy.

'Who is Lisa Yyland? If you're looking for a Dorothy, do you know?'

'Yes, we know. A team went to inspect Lisa's home when she vanished from New Hampshire about a month ago. A week after the girl, Dorothy, we've been trailing. Lisa had packed a big backpack the morning she went missing, clothes, a box of her mother's hair dye, lots of food, and other items. They thought the contents all stacked up to one conclusion: a suspicious runaway. Her case landed with another team, based solely on these facts. Fucking metrics. Damned computer models. I knew she was part of the cases we're tracking.' I wiped my forehead with a fist and clenched my teeth, fighting a prehistoric growl.

'Roger, come on. Let's get over there, now,' Lola beckoned, pulling on my crooked elbow.

Lola had enough tact to call me Roger instead of Liu in front of other people, which was not lost on me. Also, she never called me Roger unless she needed me to snap out of it.

'Chief, you can take us to this place?'

'Sure as hell can. We'll use Sammy's Volvo. Sammy's our operator. No one will suspect that rusty beast.' The chief pointed to a fat man eating a donut, slumped in a chair, barely awake, in front of a switchboard in what seemed to be a back closet. Fat Sammy nodded, kept chewing, and handed the chief his keys without any words. The powdered sugar on his lips and chin, along with his uniform shirt missing two buttons, reminded me we were in a small, small town.

We climbed into Sammy's orange Volvo, Chief Marshall, his deputy, Lola, and me. Gas station coffee cups and dog food from an open Purina bag rolled at my and Lola's feet in the back. Our guns were loaded, cocked in the holsters, and ready for a bloodbath. Lola hung her nose out the window, following the scent of something along the way. Her muscles twitched in anticipation, her fingers straightened to a rigor mortis upon her clenched thighs. My emotions matched her physical message.

CHAPTER FOURTEEN

I turned from facing Dorothy to see my twin captor, and in so doing, became immediately cognizant of my duty to protect four people: me, my unborn child, hysterical Dorothy, and Dorothy's unborn child. I evaluated the tears bubbling like lava from his bloodshot eyes. A sludge of wetness sagged the top layer of his face in a mudslide of sorts, as though his skin were melting. Concerned I was delusional and witnessing the decay of a wax figure, I inspected closer and realized his crying was cutting lines, like the receding tide to soft sand, and smudging his thick foundation. *Makeup? Yes, makeup. Wow.* Soon enough, his underlying giant pores revealed him as the true and exact twin of the man I'd just killed. His deep breathing was of the variety summoned from only unfathomable grief. Like a hungry, bee-stung bull, he practically ground his feet in the floorboards, preparing to charge and impale.

Four quick conclusions surfaced for me:

Brad found the remains of his brother;

Brad had his own set of keys to our dungeons – they dangled from his loose grip. Fortunately, I had plunked my set into my back holster once I entered Dorothy's room;

Brad had, in fact, not flown away;

Brad intends to harm us in a very bad way – worse than even before.

'My brother!' he screeched, pacing Dorothy's room and lunging in my face.

'My brother, my brother, my brother,' he kept saying, turning and pacing and flinging arms here and there.

Around his third lunge of growling, I caught glimpse of a dent in one of the four gold buttons on the right sleeve of his rather flamboyant, navy-blue, velvet blazer. *He seems so impeccable, despite his tirade. But the dent . . .*

When he back armed my left temple like I was the tennis ball and his forearm the racket, I figured that perhaps the dent was merely a future vision, for I'm sure my skull is what caused the dent. Perhaps in my constant evaluation and planning of each miniscule step, I had primed my brain to anticipate near-future actions. Of course, I can't prove this theory, but I'd like to study the phenomenon with neuroscientists someday.

With the blow, every emotional switch I might have allowed on, although none were truly on, were securely turned off. A satisfaction of nothingness washed over me as I crashed to the floor. I became no more than a vessel. A robot. An automaton. A murder-seeking android.

With wincing eye, I followed one of my bedpost arrows roll free of my holster. I clutched it in the same motion as grabbing the bow from my now prone back. Laying on my side on Dorothy's floor, I positioned the arrow in the sling and waited for my new pacing jailer to again turn to face me – all of which occurred in the three seconds from his arm hitting my head. Practice. Practice. Practice will make you like this – detaches your physical actions from a horror of reality. Ask any soldier in any war.

Dorothy was up standing on her mattress, screaming all hellfire as though lead soprano in an opera about horrific agony, written entirely in C7. Perhaps even air shattered upon her deafening pitch. How I longed to replace her voice with my yard-sale radio and the pianissimo assai of the keys. I did not turn to calm her; I did not have the time. There I lay before her, she stripping vocal chords on the bed behind, me aiming an arrow at our mutual foe. My eye closest to where he hit me swelled. A trickle of blood blinded that side of my vision. My top eye, however, was clear of bruise, clear of blood, and sharp and free of pain.

He spun to me. My quarry trapped only four feet away, I lifted the blade of the arrow toward his eyes. And, not giving him any chance to retreat or even freeze to collect his thoughts, I let go the arrow with a simple plunk of the bowstring.

Go arrow. Nail him.

The arrow wobbled mid-air, but like a heat-seeking missile, adjusted itself upward and straight, all while keeping speed. Landing bull's eye in the sensitive chasm between his nose cartilage and the bone part of his left cheek, about an inch below his lower lid, the determined wood blade bore deep enough to stab itself in place. *If only I had had the chance the practice on a hay-bale, I could have impaled his eye and possibly his brain.*

Beastly screaming ensued. He lifted his arm and pulled the arrow from his face, which I considered the stupidest reaction. *Leave the knife in place if you're stabbed. Get to a doctor. The blade will sear the blood,* my father once taught, while explaining the military wound on his right flank. *I walked ten miles with the insurgent's kitchen knife in my obliques. Had I removed it, neither you nor I would be here today.*

An eruption of blood burst from Brad's cheek and drained down his velvet jacket to plop on the floorboards. A large drop moving too fast splashed to spray my hands. Dorothy, God love her, quit her screaming and jumped to my side to begin hurling books at Brad's bleeding head. *Catcher in the Rye, Breakfast of Champions, One Hundred Years of Solitude,*

Something Wicked This Way Comes, several other classics typical of school learning – J.D. Salinger, Vonnegut, Marquez, Bradbury – all became weapons in our war. *Collective Asset #39: Literature.*

Brad, reduced to a whimpering weakling, skuttle-waddled to the hall, and, with one hand pressed firmly on the blood hole in his face, slammed through the motions of locking the door in a fitful, keys-dropping manner. I was less concerned with being a prisoner again and more concerned with having a wounded animal to contend with. Wounded animals, those grief-stricken and vulnerable, have nothing to lose and no one to coax them to their senses.

So I had a rabid hyena on my hands outside the room. Inside, a hysterical teen: Dorothy had returned to the bed with a harrowing writhing of sound. My black butterfly, although I stood drop-shouldered on a weathered floorboard, one that seemed a place for pacing, and I searched and pleaded the triangular window for him to flutter up, failed to show.

How could you miss Brad's possible presence? How on Earth did you miscalculate by so much? I chastised myself.

Admittedly, my self-expectations have always been unrealistically high. I do expect Me to be omniscient, although I know very well I am not. It is a wish, I guess, a wish that I could harness all of the knowledge in the universe and make good use of a collective intelligence. Solve all of the theories out there on space and time and matter vs. dark matter. The creation of life. The meaning of everything.

Humbled, always when reminded of my human handicap, I merely expect more of myself, never relenting to reality.

I circled the perimeter my new jail, reminding myself I'd called the cops. *This is soon over, relax, relax, breathe. They should be here any minute now. They better get here before he comes back up. I better map out a plan in case something's wrong. What if whoever answered the phone is in on it?*

Dorothy lay on her bed in the curled position of a dying fawn. Her moaning interrupted my plan making. I wasn't used to including anyone in my personal strategies, whether in my lab at home or whether in incarceration. I was also not used to holding, let alone beginning, a conversation with a girl my own age. Back home, I had no girlfriends. My only friend was Lenny, my friend since age four, my boyfriend since age fourteen. Lenny was a poet, who had a surplus of emotion, and we found that when mixed with me, we evened each other out. Lenny had an uncanny grip on the English language; he saw patterns so quickly in a list of seemingly unrelated words, our teachers struggled to challenge him. In fifth grade, they placed Lenny in a special class of one, and a specialist from the State of New Hampshire Council on Higher Education came once a week to deliver Lenny a packet of challenges. People with PhDs and MDs and XYZs bandied the word 'savant' around as casually as though labeling him with ADD. But I think Nana, known simply as Nana, presented the best diagnosis of all.

Nana had flown in to New Hampshire from her estate in Savannah just about eight months before Day 33. My parents had gone to Boston for a 'Broadway in Boston' play, so Nana, Lenny, and I played Scrabble on our butcher-block counter, all of us snug on the bar stools with cushioned backs. Of course, Lenny was winning by some will-crushing seventy points, and I had deciphered there was no point in continuing the game.

'Nana, let's just make fudge because there is no point in continuing,' I said. 'I've done the math, and we can't possibly win, so we might as well call the game now. Or, how about chess? Lenny is terrible at war strategy, and we can destroy him.'

'You mean you can destroy both of us,' Nana said.

'Well, okay, if you see it that way,' I said. I had flicked on my Affection switch, so I allowed Nana an eyes-wide and simple grin, which she returned with a fuzzy-eyebrowed Nana-wink. I liked the way her wrinkled skin looked so soft and white, so very white to match her white, curled hair. She seemed like a luminous ghost to me – a happy specter in my life. Her red blouse with lime flowers, her long, red corduroy skirt with a pink silk ribbon as a belt, her red, leather clogs with purple straps – so white of hair and face, and yet so colorful – like a rainbow wrapped her soul.

Nana was a published author of a regionally popular crime series. Her target demographic consisted of ladies her age who, unlike her, spent time in rocking chairs on retirement lakes or in brick nursing homes. Unlike her audience, Nana never relented to age: she wrote and sewed, sewed and wrote, and made fudge when she visited me.

On this particular night eight months prior to Day 33, Lenny and I had just begun our junior year. It was a Friday in mid-October. The air was unseasonably warm, and a breeze whooshed in through the open kitchen windows, fluttering the arched drapes above the soapstone sink. Nana slid off her stool to quiet the tea kettle when it began to whistle.

'You know,' she said. 'Lenny here is just like us. The difference, my dear, is he is the lucky host of whatever literary parasite Charles Dickens suffered, or Bob Dylan suffers. Some glorious strain mere mortals find impossible to bottle. How I wish I were so afflicted.'

As she wrapped the kettle handle with a quilted potholder, I passed Lenny a vacant stare – the kind he says that freaks him out.

'Lisa, don't start,' he said, while snapping his fingers to break the spell. But I was already mentally gone, lost to a solitary, invisible hiding place, well within study mode.

When Nana reduced Lenny's literary gift to a microbiological ailment, something clicked in me, some question of science made me hungry for evaluation. Perhaps her friendly comment should have been taken lightly as intended, a humorous lilt to our weekend song. Perhaps I shouldn't have elevated her theory to proven biology – but, mixed with the warped mentality of a teenager, I found myself in a hormonal fit of science and desire. Yes, perhaps I wished to catch Lenny's disease of words. Perhaps I caused our amorous protections to fail: our child was conceived that night, in Lenny's car, after we'd filled ourselves on a batch of Nana's fudge. I was 100 percent thinking of microbial inoculation and zero percent about ovulation. Science Fiction vs. Established Medicine. The one slip I allowed – a slip made possible given my brief stumble in the battle with hormones. I really hated being a teenager.

As soon as my next period came and went without need of Tampax, I resolved to never again allow pedestrian physical desire to cloud my regular precision thinking. I pleaded with Lenny for forgiveness and promised to not derail his life, promised to take on the sole responsibility. We sat once more on the cushioned stools in my kitchen when I delivered him the news and my apology. My parents were at work and Nana back in Savannah. When I mentioned I'd endure the responsibility alone, emotional Lenny teared up.

'Never,' he said.

'Lenny, no. This is my fault.'

'No, it's my fault. I wanted this.'

'You wanted this?'

'Marry me, Lisa.'

Quickly, I calculated our ages and the ensuing events of our teens and twenties. The whistling kettle once again announced a profound shift in our lives, so as I slid sideways from the counter to remove it from the hot element, I responded with my truthful and calculated answer.

'Yes. But in precisely fourteen years, when we are thirty, after we've earned our degrees and I've established myself in science and you in writing.'

'Fine,' he said, wiping his eyes with his sleeve and reaching for a pen to document his inner turmoil in a chicken-scratch poem on a Chinette napkin.

To me, this was the height of romance. To Lenny, I have no idea. He spent the weekend at the library researching poets who had written about their children and came to school on Monday, bright-eyed and practically skipping to class.

How Nana would cringe to know her whimsical analogy prompted me so – I'd never tell her any of this. Even seventeen years later, I wince at writing this account, fearing her eighty-eight-year-old eyes might discover the truth about her great-grandson.

Somehow, back then in Dorothy's jail cell, I was thinking on Nana and the night of her fateful words eight months prior. I swept up to Dorothy's bed, her body curved toward me like a misshapen croissant, bulging with dough in the middle. I had no clue how to comfort her, and telling her how I'd killed our other kidnapper in my own jail cell would likely alienate her. She probably didn't have the same taste in justice as I did.

Brad was downstairs pacing and throwing objects, completely unglued by the sounds of his manic screaming. A chair or a coffee table must have been smashed against a wall by the thud that ricocheted three floors up to us.

This will stop soon. Where are the cops? The cops will come. They will save us. Where the hell are they? They should be here soon. Should they be here by now?

I knew I could pick Dorothy's country lock in a second flat; I'd already assessed this asset when I entered: old lock, easy to crack, Asset #38. But there was no point in doing anything until the cops came or, if they didn't, until Brad left the building. Fortunately, sounds outside and below were easier to hear in Dorothy's wing. I was pretty sure if we kept quiet, we'd find a window of time to pick the lock and haul on out. So, instead of pacing and evaluating further, my only mission was to quiet Dorothy. We'd have to listen, listen, wait, and, if the cops failed to show, use patience – Asset #11 – for Brad to leave. And then, then we'd have to hustle.

Dorothy lay convulsing, and it was then I noted her wrinkled and unlined purple dress, something Mother would never have allowed me to wear – what with its assembly-line construction and poor quality. I contemplated, for the first time in captivity, my own attire. My black maternity pants, hand stitched in France, still surprisingly held their shape and with few wrinkles. Mother had purchased me two pairs the day after she discovered my pregnancy. 'We are not to be uncivilized in this ordeal, Lisa. You will dress appropriately. No more of this baggy nonsense. Your appearance counts for many things, said and unsaid, personal and impersonal,' she said, while flicking an invisible crumb from her starched shirt and straightening diamond cufflinks, which rested below her embroidered initials. 'It has squash to do with wealth. I could have purchased you ten cheap maternity dresses for the price of these two pairs of pants, as most pregnant women would do. But quality bespeaks quality. And it is financially stupid to trump quality with quantity. A colossal waste of money.' She brushed the air with her fingers as though setting financial ruin to a dusty corner, out of her exalted view. I did wonder at the time why my style would trouble her more than my state, but I understand now it was simply her way of coping.

The quality of my pants held little answer on how to calm Dorothy – no resolution appeared in the tight seams of a French cotton blend. She began to dry-heave from sobbing so hard, and then came her incoherent tirades and fist pounding on the mattress. My head bounced upon her every punch.

Surely unwound, poor Dorothy fell off whatever mental hold she had previously had. I guessed that had her eyes set on mine, I'd witness her pupils roll about, like those black-and-white googly eyes you buy at craft stores.

Where the hell are the cops? It's definitely been too long now. I've thought of Nana. I've thought of Mother. I'm sitting here on the floor, bleeding from my face. Something's off. Something's wrong. I need to fix this. Get us out.

Some heavy object crashed into some other heavy object downstairs, followed by a brain-splitting howl that went something like this: 'Yeeee-anannaa – My brotherrr!'

Forget someone saving us. Plan for no one. Plan only on yourself. Focus on Dorothy. Keep her quiet. He'll have to leave. Get some tool or something. He'll leave, and then we need to be ready. Get Dorothy calm.

The only peace I could offer Dorothy was to sit cross-legged and place a hand flat by her pillow. My other hand stayed raised to stem the blood from my still-bleeding face. I thought having my hand so close to her would allow her to grab hold of me as her tether, should she find the ability to focus on the things surrounding her in reality. But this act of mine was just the mimic of something I saw Nana do for my father the day his sister, her daughter, died. Nana was crying too, but was so drained herself, she was able to offer only this minor silent gesture to my dad. He was very close to Aunt Lindy. They were nine months apart in age, and her cancer was fast and merciless.

Mother and I gave Nana and my father comfort in our own way. We spent the crying time building a highly detailed itinerary for a month-long excursion through all of Italy for the four of us: me, Mother, Dad, and Nana. I'm not sure Mother and I ever exchanged any words to directly acknowledge Aunt Lindy's death. I took her cue on the proper emotion to display by remaining quiet in the house and focused on minute-by-minute planning of museums, churches, and restaurants. I did miss Aunt Lindy, but grieving her would not be productive to healing my father, nor toward studying Lindy's blood samples, which I'd been able to extract when the nurses turned their backs. Aunt Lindy palmed me one of their vials and whispered in my ear, 'With that mind, find a cure or fight injustice someday, girl. Don't let your brain go to waste.' She swallowed hard, fighting through her incurably dry mouth to continue, 'And screw those doctors who prod you about your emotions. Love is the only one that matters, and I think you've got that lassoed and reined.'

Was it love I should allow for this girl on the bed? This wretched young woman in the throes of something beyond me? Someone like me in her state, but experiencing some emotion I had no ability to comprehend in the moment. With a tepid hand on her pilled cotton sheet, I felt the warmth of

Dorothy's cheek. I studied her scrawny arms and wondered if she'd eaten a thing in her confinement. Surely she hadn't had her lunch yet – I'd killed her delivery man.

The sun at this point was a futile smear of grainy white behind blackened clouds – a failure of a day. The shadows in Dorothy's chill room made me think night was upon us, although the hour could not have been long past noon.

The sounds were different in this part of the building. Nature clamored outside: the mooing of cows and occasional bells somewhere long off in the distance. Also, because a rock or something had been thrown to cause a hole in her high triangular window, the nipping breeze creaked in, carrying the scent of grass and manure. Further adding to this sensory overload was the flinging of things and spitting swearing of our agitated captor downstairs. A caged beast – the bars: his own insanity.

Cops aren't coming. Execute a new exit.

Yet despite all of this incessant noise, Dorothy somehow stepped down her emotions when I set my hand beside her head. She clutched my fingers so tight, I thought I might be the cliff and she the fallen climber, her nails clawing a ledge of rock over the edge of the world. But I dared not move an inch, for with her widening and deeper breaths, she inexplicably slipped slowly into an eyes-batting nap. In her last blink before sleep, her big and wet blue eyes caught mine. Our faces were a mere foot apart. In that moment, Dorothy M. Salucci became my best friend ever in my life. I turned Love on – specifically for her – in the hope such an emotion would motivate me to replan and save us both, us four.

Love is the easiest emotion to switch off, but the hardest to turn on. In contrast, the easiest emotions to switch on, but hardest to turn off are: hate, remorse, guilt, and easiest of all, fear. 'Falling in Love' is an entirely different beast. In fact, 'Falling in Love' should not be classified as an emotion at all. Falling in Love is an involuntary state caused by a measurable chemical reaction, which leads to an addictive cycle your physical self seeks constantly to maintain. So far, I have only ever fallen in love once, the day a miniscule life fluttered within my body. What a day for me – to be so jolted with such awareness, a feeling masquerading itself as an emotion, tricking its way into my heart and burying there. I'd do anything to protect and prolong this addiction to Higher Love, one that barged into my life and offered no switches.

Garden-Variety Love, on the other hand, is most definitely an emotion, one with a stubborn, although productive when on, switch. And thus, it was this switch I jammed open in watching Dorothy rest, her wet cheek upon my now bloodless fingers.

CHAPTER FIFTEEN

Special Agent Roger Liu

Sometimes when I think about that day, I want to strangle whoever is closest and throw a brick through the nearest window. How frustrating to be so close and so cobbled.

Middle Indiana is like upstate New York, only flatter. So, flatter than flat. Running straight, as in literally straight, through the town of our destination was an infuriating four-lane 'route' with one billion stoplights, the number of which must have been installed to rile passers-through, but none of the townies, who seem just fine mosey peddling along, jamming to full-stops at yellows. The tar of this main road was a worn, faded gray, a color made possible by a million beat-down days of country sun – the kind of days when armies of invisible beetles hiss in unison. But the day of which I speak could only wish for some hot hell; no, the day of which I speak was a cold spring day, and though the insufferable gray tar was still faded, spots were blotched a darker hue by the intermittent drops of rain that escaped from the black clouds above.

We drove like quiet phantoms through town, past the gas stations and the emptied parking lots of mom-and-pop hardware stores and five-and-dimes. A couple of women rolled shopping carts along the edge of the road, way beyond any supermarket in sight. Silently we crept, cognizant inside the vehicle of our inner wish to not alarm any perpetrators complicit in the scheme we aimed to unravel. The orange Volvo in which we rode, however, was a siren itself, the missing muffler a foghorn of our presence.

We passed an abandoned building with the telltale watchtower of a KFC. The boarded windows were spray-painted 'ELEC' in blue with an arrow pointed down to some presumed underground cabling. I wondered why ELEC was not in orange, an indulgent thought given the task at hand.

Over the roar of Sammy's busted-up Volvo, the chief tried to speak to me and Lola in the back. I folded forward, resting a hand on the corner of his bucket seat.

'What?' I yelled.

I unbuckled my seatbelt to scooch closer, but even with the proximity, I still could not hear the chief. The tumble of the engine rattled my eardrums as though I sat on stage at a Led Zepplin concert.

The chief turned his head from the road, twisting for a view of me and Lola. I slid back, but did not rebuckle. I looked to Lola, whose grip on her thighs had only tightened further. Her fingertips must have been blue.

'You been trailing this case for long, Agents?' the chief asked.

'Um, Chief...' Lola said, pointing ahead.

I turned myself, for I, too, had not been watching the road.

I'm not sure if I shouted about the advancing truck, or if Lola shouted about the truck's shocking velocity, barreling in our direction. I recall the chief facing front once again and his quick spin of the wheel to avoid the collision. I strangely recall freeze-frames of actions thereafter, such as my arm springing sideways to brace Lola, who was buckled, as her arm did the same to me, and the chief's deputy holding the rim of his hat, as though he feared an oncoming windstorm up there in the front seat. I also recall wondering why the deputy didn't shout about the out-of-control truck, but then the other freeze-frame I recall was of him lifting his head from the map he read on his lap.

Some people say a crash is experienced in slow motion and that the sounds play as single notes, crinkling out one by one, an accordion slowly unfolding. I, on the other hand, experienced a lightning bolt of pain in my ears from the sonic boom that erupted as the engine of Sammy's Volvo crashed headfirst into a lamppost, which guarded the entrance to a strip mall. An instant of black overcame me the moment my head slammed against the roof. The next thing I knew, Lola hooked her arms under my arms to heroically pull me from the wreckage. Hollywood would have declared, 'It's a wrap,' for as the heels of my shoes hit the pavement, the steel post fell to demolish more of poor Sammy's car.

There we lay, panting for breath, cradling our bloodied heads, me and Lola, while the chief and his deputy, also pulled free by Lola, slumped unconscious. I strained up to sit, using my shaking arms for a brace, and searched the battlefield. The chief lay on the driver's side, prone on the pavement, his shoulders distorted and both arms obviously dislocated, what with their rag-doll angles. The deputy was on the passenger side, also prone on the pavement. He had a bleeding gash from his forehead, across his closed right eye, down his cheek, and ending somewhere under his chin. *What a hideous scar that will make*, I thought. The hat he fussed with teetered topside down five feet from his left ankle, which flopped cockeyed in the wrong direction. The humming static from the chief's walkie-talkie told me Sammy-the-donut-eating-dispatcher was off to God Knows Where. We were alone.

With the chief and his deputy badly hurt, his dispatcher uselessly unavailable, the remainder of the puny police force two-and-a-half hours away at a funeral, and my back-up, who

I'd called when we left the station house and had the address of Appletree Boarding School, likewise two to three hours off, I had only one call to make.

'Lola, my phone, where's my phone?' I said, sitting up straighter and closing my eyes as I talked. The blood racing to my skull throbbed loudly, demanding I stop talking.

'Lola, my phone, my phone, get my phone.'

Through my squinting eyes, I saw her crawl across the lot, her hands pressed firmly in the loose gravel of the top layer of tar. She entered again the clunking and smashed car, the doors still ajar from her extractions. I thought she might back out on all fours with my phone antenna in her teeth, like a hunting dog retrieving a dead duck.

Images of others vaguely came to appear in my periphery. Knocking began within the car, which forced me to inspect it more closely. Flames flattened out, escaping the steaming hood, the engine aflame. Urgent, orange flames spread and contracted, spread and contracted, blazing fingers desperately searching to touch skin and scar. A trail of gas snaked beneath the trunk, creeping closer to my foot.

'Lola, get out of the car, now! Fire!'

I don't think she heard me, because I don't think I was really yelling. I felt trapped in one of those dreams, trying to scream my lungs out, but unable to muster even a gurgle.

I tried again.

'Lola! Fire.' I scrambled to wobbling legs, and just as I did, she backed out, standing tall, threw the phone in my face, and burst in the direction of the chief and the deputy who remained unconscious and too close to the engine.

I allowed the phone to plummet to the ground and likewise wobbled toward the chief and deputy. Taking my share of the work, I pulled the deputy opposite the direction Lola pulled the chief, just far enough and fast enough to miss the flaming paint that began to rain down upon the scene as the car burst up and out.

Once settled, I reclined to the ground and watched the inferno in a mesmerized hypnosis. The fire raged madly, seemingly furious upon being set free, as if it had been bottled for centuries under the hood of Sammy's Volvo.

And I am always this way with a fire, remembering the time my father set our barn ablaze when I was five. On the day of the barn fire, just one week into owning the chickens and with my mother and baby brother shopping, my father asked me to run inside and fetch us both a cold Pepsi. However fast I was, however long it took me to scramble my five-year-old feet inside, fling open the refrigerator, fist the two bottles, and run back on out to find my father, well, that was how long it took for the dead grass my dad had raked up for a bonfire to catch a gust of Great Lakes wind and stick within the crevices of the dried barn boards. There I stood, useless, clenching Pepsis, as though I were choking two geese. A wall of wicked fire, running upwards from ground to sky, no sideways flames, no doubt of direction, flames streaming up and up and pushing me, plastered back to the house.

'Get inside,' my father must have screamed, his arms gesturing wildly. 'Get inside,' he must have repeated loudly, but all I heard was the roaring hiss of the red-orange flames, which insisted I do nothing but stare. Many years later in middle Indiana, doing the same as I watched, unblinking, the Volvo burn, a shadow formed overhead. One of the women with a shopping cart who we'd passed only moments before attempted to umbrella me from the irregular drops of rain.

'You hurt? You hear me?' She mouthed. I couldn't hear her words.

'My phone,' I said to her, pointing to where I'd dropped it, ten feet away.

'The who?'

'My phone. My phone. Please, there, my phone.'

The woman, about mid-fifties, with a dirty blond matted perm, housecoat, and road-stained slippers, shuffled to where I pointed, bent like an elderly grandma, and shuffled back, handing me my phone with her mouth in slackjaw.

Shouting from the strip mall began – but only as a collective mass of moving sound, which I tuned out either because my eardrums had burst or because I needed to focus on the one call I had to make. Lola sat gasping for breath with the chief's wrist in her hands, counting his pulse by keeping time on her Sanyo watch. By the look of her enlarged nostrils and squished nose, I could tell she was concerned with the silence between his heartbeats.

I'm pretty sure my judgment was clouded when I made the call. I'm pretty sure I deliberately broke all sorts of department codes. But in that moment, I felt I had no choice.

'Boyd,' I said when he answered. 'I'm going to need your help after all.'

CHAPTER SIXTEEN

Dorothy, this vision I hold of her, like an old precious Polaroid in my purse, the photo changed only by the warping of color over time, but still and forever the same in terms of heart-caving nostalgia. Dorothy, sweetly sleeping, courtesy shock, courtesy sickness, her blond curls rising and falling with every inhale, every exhale. I wanted to keep my own breath in time with hers so that I might be a sleeping beauty just like her. To have someone stand watch over me, protect me from wolves, from dragons – yet, only lovely Dorothy, my new friend, my only friend, the closest one to my desire to mother a child, only she was worthy of such administrations. Only Dorothy deserved pause before the storm. I, I was a mere weapon.

How was she able to sleep? I understand, I truly understand.

In the moment I gave her my hand on her pillow, she likely allowed herself to succumb to whatever battle of insomnia and fever she'd been beating back. I was to save her. She handed me her fate.

And I had work to do. And though I'd turned Love on for Dorothy, no other switch was on. Not even one for annoyance. I had abandoned all hope on cops showing up, so I put the possibility of them showing up, out of my mind.

Hole-in-his-Face-Brad-y-Poo's moaning began to carry outside, moving in the direction of my wing and the kitchen and his dead, burnt brother. I figured he would not be long in returning. And I guessed he'd likely recover from his brother's corpse some tool or apparatus or artifact of demented sentiment, whatever, and then he'd reenter the kitchen. There, he'd soon figure I had used the phone, seeing as I left the envelope with the address under the dangling cord. With hand heel to forehead like a dunce saying 'duh,' he'd finally realize I'd called the cops. I wasn't going to underestimate the smarter of the dumb twins. Sleeping Dorothy and I had all of four minutes to escape and get to the van.

I collected and stashed Asset #40 – Dorothy's knitting needles – in my back holster, while kicking Dorothy to wake up. I removed Asset #41, the bobby pin in her hair, and slid to the locked door. Only two months prior, I had maneuvered a mini-needle through Jackson Brown's shaved skin to finely stitch her paw, which she'd slashed on a jagged roof edge while chasing a cooing dove. So since I was really a surgeon inside, picking the country lock on Dorothy's cell door was as easy as popping a canister of Pillsbury cinnamon rolls with the flat end of a fork. Pop.

With the door open, waking Dorothy became a liability and a duty. I slid back to her bed and as soon as I arrived, I bent to her lifting head. Cupping a hand, the one with the blood from my eye, I held firm to her dry, cracked lips, staring into her now startled eyes.

'Dorothy, keep your mouth shut. And I mean shut tight if you want to live. Follow me, now. Get up, now.'

I didn't let go because I wasn't sure she understood.

'Do you understand me? If you make one noise, we're toast. You have to shut up and follow me. Understand?' My holster banged into my up-bent shoulder, rattling the knitting needles, bedpost arrows, and keys inside.

Dorothy nodded her head to indicate she understood.

Slowly I released hold on her mouth; she wiped my blood from her lips.

Are we blood sisters now? Is this what it means to have a best friend?

Stop.

Stop these ridiculous thoughts. Get to the van.

Honestly, you'd think I'd kidnapped the girl. I had to push

her from behind, prodding with my index and middle fingers on her spine as though a gun. Her one skinny leg and her one swelled leg wobbled from fatigue and emotional retching, and she continually turned to face me with a puppy-dog, quizzical gaze. 'Turn and walk. Be quiet,' I kept saying.

Step by step we crossed the threshold. She seemed so hesitant to take the flight down, checking me constantly with an expression of 'You sure? You sure?' I pushed harder with my finger gun. Her back felt knobby and knotted, not fleshy as it should have been in her late state.

Given the wetness outside, the stairwell's thick air of must and dank hit our noses in a swift uppercut, so much heavier than in times of sunlight. Like a smelling salt, the mold must have slapped Dorothy to a sharper alertness, for she jumped and froze. I pushed again.

I wasn't mad at Dorothy. I had scant emotion. I just needed her to focus and quicken her feeble pace. Dorothy herself was most definitely not an asset. But she was my instant friend and now my ward, and we'd formed an unspoken bond no one else could ever really understand, even myself. So although I growled directives at her, I did take two pauses to pat her back to say, 'Come on now, be strong. You can do this,' which is what Mother said to my father on the day he had to throw the first shovel of dirt on Aunt Lindy's grave.

We were about midway down the stairs, close to the top of

the last flight. I fisted Dorothy's greasy hair to halt her descent and hold her still. Fearing his return, I strained to hear any shuffle along the tar and gravel outside. Dorothy's shallow breathing filled the stairwell with a rumbling static, like an old lady with pneumonia, that crickety wheeze of breath encumbered by phlegm. With her wrist in my hand, her heartbeat tapped too quick; with my bloody palm to her forehead, her temperature nearly burned me. Again she locked eyes with me, and in this second moment of tightening our bond, without her saying the words, I answered, 'I know.'

By my estimation, we had about a minute and a half to reach the bottom floor, exit the building, cross the small parking lot, and enter the forest path before Brad emerged from my wing. I had visualized the outside world and the path back to the van since the first day in this hellhole, even though I had been blindfolded and bagged when I'd arrived. I counted the steps, recorded the give of the ground, touched the air for climate, and had replayed those details into a visual memory of terrain, topography, and temperature. In my mind, I'd made the trek from van to building and building to van a hundred thousand times. And you know what? Apart from the building being a white building – a former boarding school – instead of a white farmhouse, I was dead-on exact on every detail. Goes to show what your senses and your memory, your prior learnings and your confidence, will give you if you're able to strip out the nonproductive distractions of fear and anticipation. Listen. Smell. Taste. See. Live. Evaluate. In real time.

Most people perceive only 1 percent of the colors in the vast spectrum of hues. The rare humans who visualize more than 1 percent report either a disappointment with everyone else's dull perception of life or claim to have visited Heaven in their dreams. They have a type of super-sense, these lucky souls.

A recent article in *Scientific American* reminded me of the super-sense I experienced during my time in the Appletree prison. Summarizing research published in the *Journal of Neuroscience* on the cross-modal neuroplasticity of the deaf and blind, the article proclaimed, 'This research ... is a reminder that our brains have some hidden superpowers.' If you're not aware of cross-modal neuroplasticity, basically it is the ability of the brain to reorganize itself in the areas where a person may be sense-deprived. For example, how 'deaf individuals perceive sensory stimuli, making them susceptible to a perceptual illusion that hearing people do not experience.' I really liked the introductory paragraph of the actual Journal article, which stated rather succinctly, I thought: 'Experience shapes brain development throughout life, but neuroplasticity is variable from one brain system to another.'

So I, a deaf person, a blind person, a person deprived of varying senses, one who with practice, built models of reality, a separate dimension of senses that overlaid with the world in a very true way. Perhaps emotions are merely another set of senses, and the absence of them makes for precision hearing, touching, smelling, seeing, imagining.

Perhaps.

Who knows.

Detecting no scrubble of his footfall, we scrambled to the bottom of the stairs and shuffled our way outside. Looking left, looking right, I found no sign of Brad, so I pushed Dorothy diagonally across the tarred area to the opening of the path to the van. Our bodies were practically merged we were so close. We cut a shadow of two mountains stuck together with those bellies, which I studied with awe when we reached the mouth of the trail.

Are we one girl? The same girl? Are we all the same at sixteen? So ready for life, and yet so young. I have to save us both. Us four.

I leaned from behind to speak in Dorothy's ear as I collected the keys from my holster. The heat emanating from her body made me think she might combust; my face grew flushed. I hadn't noticed the sprinkles of rain until they cooled me of her warmth.

'Dorothy, walk straight ahead exactly one minute. Running would be faster if you can. Trust me, I know it's scary in there, and it will be dark, but it opens onto a large field with cows and a big willow tree. Under the tree is a van. We'll take the van. I've got the key. Let's go.'

Dorothy nodded her head in a slow, nauseated way, and took one step into the forest. I followed, glued to her body. Our steps were in synch and so close together, as though we walked with tied legs, the sound of the door shutting behind us was slightly muffled by the thud of our double-footfall.

'Oh, hell no! You girls stop now!' Brad's voice was a high pitch of crazed depravity.

I shoved the ring of keys in Dorothy's hand.

'Go now! Do what I said. One minute. Run! Go, go, go. The van key is the one that says Chevy. Go. Go.'

These were the last words I ever spoke to Dorothy M. Salucci.

I ran straight toward Brad, a knitting needle in one hand and a bedpost arrow in the other.

CHAPTER SEVENTEEN

SPECIAL AGENT ROGER LIU

'Son. Of. A. Damn. Bitch. Lola. Sonofadamnbitch!' I said, after slamming the flip on my giant cell phone and cringing from the incessant ringing in my ears. Boyd had answered my call, and I think he agreed to check the schoolhouse and bring his gun, but I couldn't hear him. Then he'd called back, I think within five minutes – I knew only because I'd set the ringer to vibrate. Boyd's words melded together in a muffle to me, which must have registered on my face, for Lola crawled past the flaming car, grabbed the phone even though I hadn't said a word to her, and listened to whatever Boyd was yammering on about. She relayed Boyd's news – once again shocking and near unbelievable – by scrawling out a summary in the notebook she kept in the square pocket of her man pants.

Here's what her note said:

B find DSaluc at his van. ?? Woods? No Lisa. B say, 'Ain't no sign of no other girl. Ain't no one around here.' B used phone in school kitchen. B reports, 'Some kinda smell downright awful in here, coming from the upstairs. Smells like death.'

After this fairly appropriate, file-worthy note, she added her thoughts on a second page of paper, while saying the words slowly so I could read her lips:

'And how the hell's Boyd supposed to understand what an awful smell is? That shit-stinking chicken farmer.'

The Bureau required all of our notes and observations, especially those we wrote, to go into the official record. But you try and stop Lola from spouting off on her constant opinions. I ripped her second note, wishing she wouldn't editorialize so much.

'With all the burning cars and people – like your dumb ass – I got to save, spare me the pleas about my opinions, Liu,' she hissed when I tossed the pieces of her note to the now slick ground.

I knew what she said, mostly because I read her moving lips; the ringing, the ringing, how awful that ringing had risen. I was a mad deaf man, fighting to hear clearly again. I felt I was still dreaming, running so fast, beating my legs to pump harder and harder, my chest heaving in the stress to move forward, but moving nowhere, an inch an hour. Ring, ring, ring, the ringing drowned everything out, blurring the world.

I clawed my hands, cupped my ears, searched the falling sky for any other sense, any color, only to find the mottled gray of an unfurling curtain – and the shadows of black, how they, too, fell like ghosts. The clouds had merged into a coiled thunderhead, and yet, despite the ominous darkness, relinquished only bits of water as though to torture us all in that strip mall parking lot. And the fire didn't care; no liquid could quench its anger. Sammy's Volvo, stripped of much of her paint, became a warped box of burnt steel. Only blotches of orange remained in the parts untouched by flames.

One of those irritating raindrops, a fat one, plunked on the bridge of my nose, rolled on the crest before plunging left to ride the cavern of my cheek, and landed on the topmost rim of my lips. The friction of the water's movement itched me to an untenable annoyance, so I quickly rubbed my face hard with the sleeve of my moist, gray jacket. The ringing seemed to soften when I fixed on this other sense.

After reading Lola's disdainful opinion of Boyd's report on the smell of death, I shot her the 'Seriously' look while covering both my ears as though this would dampen further the bleating bells. She backed down.

An ambulance and a fire truck came onto my and Lola's accident scene, the ambulance practically skiing in on two tires. By this point, Lola and I were standing and separately guarding the chief and the deputy. Onlookers had formed a half circle behind us, all safely at bay given Lola's ferocious commands and spitting yells. While she kept our boundary intact, I scanned the crowd for anyone who might have an off-road truck.

A woman in a quilted Carhartt jacket stood taller and wider than her compatriots. She had long, thick, farm-girl hair, and under her jacket she wore a flannel shirt, buttoned to the top and untucked over a pair of white-washed jeans. Mud melted up over the toes of her boots, the kind with a thick rubber sole. I placed her at about mid-forties. Apart from the Viking stature, she was rather attractive.

'Ma'am,' I shouted, nodding to her.

'Me?' She mouthed, inaudible to me. At this point, I suffered a dulled ringing accompanied by an auditory windstorm.

'You got a truck?' I yelled.

'Ford F-150,' she said. I moved closer and faced my ear directly on her speaking mouth. She pointed to a shiny, black Ford F-150, sure as rain, right behind her. Slow raindrops cut lines down her fogged windows.

'All wheel?'

'Of course,' her lips said, the woman sniffing back a bit of indignation. A man with mutton chops crossed his arms and nodded my way while screwing his face toward her, and with a nose flick, said, 'This guy for real?' in his gesture.

'Ma'am, we're going to need your truck,' Lola intervened, having caught on to my struggle and to my intention.

I stepped closer and pulled the Viking woman out of earshot of everyone else. 'And if you could direct us to the old boarding school?'

She again sniffed, but added a disbelieving smile.

'Wow. Hmpph,' Lola later told me the woman said. 'I taught there twenty years, until the foreclosure. I've been wondering what the hell's been going on up at the Appletree. Yeah, I can give you directions, all right.'

I rolled my shoulders, scrunching in shoulder to shoulder, attempting to quell the screeching wind within my broken ears. Lola took over, although she too seemed distressed in the way she kept twitching her nose. The stench of burning metal and leather was probably unbearable to her superior olfactory sense.

CHAPTER EIGHTEEN

'Cool your heels, put that bandy down,' Brad said in his awkward manner of speech. He then, not awkwardly but very deliberately, aimed a nine-millimeter to my face.

I paused in the driveway, Dorothy's knitting needle and my arrow still poised. And there we stalled in an odd stand-off: me, pregnant and panting with MacGyver'd weapons, him, draped in a bloody jacket and with a cocked gun. Although our version of the classic stand-off was so far from a proper Western, in retrospect, I've always painted this memory with tumbleweed bouncing on its way to nowhere and crossing our toe-to-toe line.

Where are the damn cops?

But nothing. No one came.

Still, we froze in place.

Out beyond, toward the van, a cacophony of yelling erupted, which surely wasn't the sound I had expected, such as the clunking of the van's engine. The medley was of Dorothy's high-pitch scream and then the more distinct chorus of men shouting. I, mistakenly, pivoted to listen to the noise beyond the pines.

'Boyd! Boyd! Catch her, she's falling!' I heard one man shout.

Must be the cops.

Exposing a quick vulnerability, I unwittingly allowed Brad to make up the distance between us. He grabbed me by the side, causing me to spill my handheld assets, and dragged me in a standing top slant. My sneakered heels parted the film of dirt on the driveway into two paper-thin trenches.

What is it with these brothers dragging me backwards?

Brad held his breath in his unrelenting effort to haul me to his two-door VW Bug, an older model in pearl white. In he pushed me, the gun to my temple. And without removing the aim of the barrel on me, he crab-walked backwards and sideways to the Bug's engine. The rain had smeared the windshield with foggy dots, filtering Brad into a watercolor impression of himself as he rounded the car.

I considered opening the door and rolling down an embankment once our speed reached 25 mph, and I would have taken my shot at the physics of velocity and downward motion to safely jettison my body, but I had an eight-month-old baby in my carriage and I had vowed that not one fine fiber of his budding hair would be ruffled. In fact, my running lunge toward Brad only minutes before was really just a ploy to distract him from Dorothy's escape – I had planned to cut left and run down the dirt part of the long driveway, in the hopes the cops would soon intercept. But Brad, panther-quick Brad, called my bluff by pulling his gun, which I suspect is the weapon he recovered from his brother upstairs.

I should have taken his gun.

Off we drove down a dirt road in the woods, in the same direction as the quarry, and adjacent to the curvy, narrow path my captor had forced me down only days before.

The apathetic sky half-heartedly offered rain, but the canopy shielded the car of most of the drops. I stared straight ahead, counting the passing oaks, the passing pines, the lovely birch, and a couple of saplings of unknown vegetation. The forest, although dark from the black clouds, bloomed in uncurling new leaves, leaves of lime and emerald. Had the sun been in control that day, I'm sure brushstrokes of light would have accented the bright hues of green and made shadows dance in a kaleidoscope forest, transforming it to a magical place – for those with the vision to see such things.

Here I am going on about the beauty of a cold forest when I'm really telling of a drive of horror. But the truth is, I did consider how I might capture the scene in a painting and how I might reduce the play of shadows in shades of gray and deep green and offset those with highlights of lime and sunshine yellows. So if part of this retelling is trying to convey how one without emotion might think in this situation, I'm just recounting the mental and physical facts, as they were.

The tumble of tires over a dry stream caused me to look in his direction. Brad's nostrils were flared, his eyes glistened from sobbing, and the blood from his face hole dripped to his velvet jacket. When he sensed my eyes on him, he snarled.

'Bitch. I'm taking that baby today,' he said.

I looked forward, concentrating on the black rings of a white birch and how they complemented her budding yellow-green leaves. The tree reminded me of one in the grove behind my home, the one in which I'd hidden Jackson Brown. Such a memory in that moment gave me the resolve to harden further, to generate even more strength. I pushed levers in my brain so roughly, I killed any lingering shred of fear. Yes, practice in my jail cell prepared me for this – the unfortunate inevitable reality. I may have miscalculated Brad's travel patterns, but I had not failed to prepare for the worst.

The birch allowed me to calibrate a steady self-command, a warrior mode. I sat straighter in the car, as though leaning against the tree's solid trunk.

Brad, apparently expecting me to beg his mercy, slammed on

the brakes, and I folded forward at the waist, bracing against a head slam with quick hands on the dashboard. I was drawn in, however, for I had buckled myself. The forest surrounded us, but for the dirt road behind. Ahead, the road went on about another fifty feet and abruptly stopped at a pile of deadwood that dammed the end-point. There was no other direction to drive except backwards. End of the line.

'Ronny told me you were a cold bitch. He called you a crazy bitch. A crazy fucking bitch. Oh, I'm taking your baby. And you will pay for what you did. No one knows where you are now. And no one is going to find my exit, little bitch panther bitch.'

How eloquent. What poem are you quoting, Walt Whitman?

What exit? There is no exit. You're full of shit. You got yourself trapped. You don't know what to do next. I can see the dancing in your nervous eyes. Idiot. You're so dumb, dumb as your brother. Couldn't even plan an escape contingency. How foolish. How juvenile.

'I know what you're thinking, panther bitch. You think I need the doctor to slice that baby out of you. Ha ha ha,' he chortled, and on his special, patented low voice, he added, 'Who do you think used to cut those girls up before he came? Huh? Me, bitch! Me! And my brother. I got all the tools I need in the trunk. I'll take your baby, throw you in the quarry, and hike on out of here unseen.'

Okay, he might be telling the truth now. Perhaps this is the plan.

I pursed my lips and flattened my face, involuntarily signaling I was slightly impressed with his strategy. I almost said, 'Touché.' Instead, I chose to raise his bet, launching our game of Crazy Poker into full swing.

'You know, Brad. That's a nice plan and all. But I don't think you have the stomach for any more blood today,' I said, winking slowly to match my sly smile. 'I mean, the hole in your face is getting real ugly, going to scar your pretty little face pretty bad, precious.' And then I blew him an air kiss.

I have to admit something here. Really, I do. I don't want you to get the wrong impression. I don't want you to think me brave, to say such a thing. Actually, I find it rather fun to be wicked. I do, okay. I admit this much here. Frankly, I do have a bit of evil in me, a notion I can't quite shut off all the way, a feeling of pleasure when someone else squirms in my presence. Please don't tell the doctors who have so far agreed to not label me a sociopath.

I must have shocked him – which is exactly what I intended to do – for as though I'd tagged him in freeze tag, he stared at me, unblinking. The water from his eyes stopped bubbling anew, but the older tears fell down his cheek and mixed with the blood, creating a pinkish sludge that pooled in the stubble on his chin.

Dear Brad, you look so terrible. Tee-hee-hee.

He stared on and on. The sporadic raindrops pinged the hood of the car, here and there, their light tapping nearly silenced by the engine's purr. All else was quiet, even frozen Brad zipped his lips. Ping. Purrr. Silence. Purrr. Silence. Ping.

Do you see him? A creepy, blood-faced man, shaken, uncoiled, bug-eyed on me. He wakes me from sound sleep, seventeen years later. I bolt up in bed, the world darkened still by him. I noted the time on the car's analog clock when we stopped: 1:14. At 1:34, Brad was still staring.

So I stared back.

I tried to scare him with my glare, but I'm sure had anyone stumbled upon us in the forest, and had Brad not been face-gored by a sharpened bedpost, they might have thought we were in the throes of falling in love, pupils dilated and us virtually holding roses in our teeth by the appearance of our eyes-locked gaze.

They say staring at a wild animal is a sign of aggression and a sure way to invite an attack. But doing the same to a cobra is a way to tame, which is something I'd witnessed only a week before they kidnapped me. On the night Mother discovered my pregnancy and thus the night before she had the doctor evaluate my pregnancy, I hid in her study, watching her watch a video from her law firm. She had no idea I was in the room at the time, nor that I was pregnant. This would be the night of my stark reveal.

Mother, my father, and I had just finished a celebratory dinner of fried pork chops and applesauce to commemorate Mother being home from her four-month trial in New York – which she won, of course. At our four-person kitchen table, it was hard to tell who sat at the head. Nevertheless, I chose the most unlit corner and bulked myself within my dad's faded Navy sweatshirt, which four months prior, before I started showing, used to be huge on me. Since I no longer had a chance of hiding in just the baggy clothes alone, I draped a pink-and-green quilt around my body, sniffing and fake coughing and claiming my muscles ached.

After dinner, I went to my room, finished some advanced calculus, and inspected my round form in a bedroom mirror. After removing my father's Navy sweatshirt, I tiptoed down the stairs and slid, silently, into Mother's darkened office, where she was working. The glow of her television cast electric blue on her sitting in one of her Dracula throne chairs. She sat in her bubble of TV light, and I stood beyond that bubble, well hidden in the shadows created by the mahogany bookshelves and matching paneled walls of her study.

In the past, I had wedged myself in the same shadowed corner to study Mother's inner thoughts and also to gather data on how to react – truly react – to certain social situations, for this was where she sometimes watched movies my father considered 'chick flicks.' Whenever Patrick Swayze collapsed into Demi Moore's all-encompassing kiss in *Ghost*, Mother would clutch her neck, stroke her own skin, and breathe in deep. I figured I should do this whenever Lenny kissed me, so I did. He seemed to appreciate the gesture, so I allowed moments of joy when my physical senses flared upon Lenny's tighter embrace.

On this particular occasion in which I spied on Mother, she was not watching a movie, but rather the raw footage of a wildlife television show – Mother's client being a mega-entertainment conglomeration, which owned the rights. The show, the station, the producer, hell, everyone, were being sued by the estate of a somewhat famous wilderness 'expert.' This man, the wrongful death complaint alleged, had been 'pressured, goaded, and threatened' into approaching a cobra during an ill-fated trip to the deep backwaters of India.

Mother sat in her study watching the footage of the incident. So sets out our wilderness man, perfect wilderness boots and pressed khakis and proper chest patch and all, all of which was filmed and in a raw, unedited state. Mother leaned forward in her chair, stalling her note taking, when the 'expert' lay on his belly in the India high grass to level his eyes with an arched and mesmerized cobra. Their faces were five feet apart. Mother checked her antique cuckoo clock, wrote down the time, and returned to study her client's on-screen star in the moments before his death. She raised her hand to her mouth, tapping a finger on her teeth as though anxious, and I know, I just know, the edges of her lips were curled in a slight grin, a simple excitement of anticipation. I thought in that moment Mother was resigned to the ultimate power of death. So I too, accepted death as base fact. But I didn't allow myself the pleasure she seemed to hold in witnessing the finality of life. I smoothed a palm gently over my belly, calming the child within.

The man in the video stared at the snake for a good long hour, which is a calculation I had to guesstimate given the fact that Mother grew bored with waiting and began to fast-forward. Play. Fast-forward. Skid. Rewind. Fast. Stop. Play. A quick twitch of the cobra caused the wilderness star to also twitch, but he did not avert the snake's gaze. The cobra backed down slow at first, lowering his head, but recoiled quickly, and oddly, in a strange and swift backwards hiss, disappearing beneath his rock. Just then, a tiger leapt from beyond the scope of the camera and into the frame, landing on our man's back and eating his neck.

Mother rocketed from her chair, her notes and pen tumbling to the floor. 'Holy shit!'

Watching her watch the mauling, I blinked a few times, as is usual to keep one's eyes moist when watching a television show. I checked the time, thinking I had another twenty minutes before I'd have to select my clothes for school and crawl into bed.

The tiger, taking his jowel-licking time, disemboweled our

man – such gory nature all being caught on video because the cameraman dropped the camera, still rolling, and had obviously fled the scene.

'What a damn beautiful beast,' Mother said, plunking into her leather seat.

I stepped out of the shadow.

'What, Mother?' I said.

She pushed into the chair, locking her elbows when she pressed her hands on the armrests to pin herself into a deeper safety.

'Lisa! Holy hell. What the hell?! You scared the shit out of me. Have you been standing there the whole time?'

'Yes.'

'Son of a bitch, Lisa. You can't be hiding on me. Son of a damn bitch. You gave me a heart attack.'

'Oh, um, well, I didn't mean to scare you. I was just wondering what you said.'

'I don't know ... what?'

Flustered, she scanned the floor and bent to gather her papers and pen, stopping after picking up each object to shake her head confused-bewildered-angry at me.

'Did you say "beautiful beast"?'

'Oh, Lisa, I guess so,' she said in an exasperated but stunned voice. She huffed back down to the edge of her seat, taking me in head to toe.

'What does it matter?' She asked, looking more closely at my body.

'Well, I wondered what or who is the beautiful beast in the video, is all. The man, the cobra, or the tiger?'

'The tig, the tig … er,' her voice wavered on drawn-out words. She squinted, zeroing in on my waist, which bulged in a tight white T-shirt. I stiffened my posture like a flat-foot ballerina awaiting the *Premier Maitre de ballet's* inspection. While pinching my shoulders for a more perfect stance, I lifted my chin as though pride would trump judgment.

'But the tiger killed the man. He is beautiful to you?'

'He did kill the man, but the man trespassed on his territory.'

Mother fixed on the rise of my torso and the descent to my pelvis. I moved closer and into the bubble of blue. A beam shot sideways as a spotlight, and realization ruled the room. Denial could live no more.

Hesitant and with an unsure voice, yet still continuing her precision answer – because Mother was loath to abandon her stream of thought, she continued, 'He is beautiful for his cunning strategy and ability to strike fear in the cobra.'

I straightened as she palmed my swelled belly.

I felt like a tiger as she fell to her knees.

Was she the cobra and the safe distance between us the mauled man?

Perhaps the analogy is too strained. Or too true. Nevertheless, I didn't mean to tame her, and I didn't mean to hurt her. I didn't mean any harm at all to my mother. I suppose the nature of me is just that though: her weakness, her blindspot, and thus, my own.

Not until I was trapped in the VW with staring Brad, did I realize how hurtful I'd been to Mother. Sure, she was distant – she too suffered a cold demeanor. We were similar, I believe. Although, as far as I know, Mother had never been evaluated as a psychological oddity like me, and she does cry and curl her fist in fits of anger. So I do not believe she is emotionally challenged/gifted in a medical sense, like me. All I know of her past is, she has some past, and we are never to talk about her parents. I have one Nana is all: Nana, my literary rainbow ghost.

Despite Mother's tall walls and her thick boundaries, she did try with respect to me.

I didn't.

In staring at Brad, I resolved to try harder with Mother. She was not the cause of our distance. I was. I should have told her sooner. I should have shared the pregnancy, not to reveal a vulnerability, but to connect.

As Mother allowed the feel of her hand on my pulsing bump to soak in the reality of her impending grandmotherhood, she likely concluded yelling would lead to nothing. She'd tried a couple of times when I was a toddler; each time I hadn't understood what a raised voice meant, so I had simply started laughing because that's what people did when things got loud on the television shows my father enjoyed. So the night of her discovery, Mother pointed to the door as an indication I should leave her be. When I woke the next morning, rested and hair mussed, I found her in her study with her clothes from the previous evening still on, one leg slung up over an armrest of her chair, and a stiletto dangling from her big toe. Two bottles of my parents' best vintage were scattered on her Persian rug. My father sat cross-legged on the floor opposite her, his head cradled in his muscular hands.

Staring at a cobra can tame him, if done right, so I kept staring at creepy Brad in the front seat of that damn VW, in the middle of the Indiana woods, stalled on our way to Brad's demented plan to butcher me and steal my child. On and on we stared, on and on clicked the clock, on and on the one-tap, two-tap, rain pinged the windshield, the roof.

And then Brad got even creepier.

'Panthertown.'

This again.

'Oh deary-o, you are a clawed and wild panther. You got me,' Brad chuckled, as he pressed a white handkerchief he'd extracted from his frumpled shirt pocket to the blood dripping off his chin. With his free hand, he picked lint from his jacket.

'Panzy, woops, I mean Panthy, look at my outfit. Such a mess,' he said in a debutante, sing-song voice, which lowered one hundred octaves when he swiftly leaned across to growl, 'You fucking cunt. My jacket is a fucking mess.' He leaned back on a tittering, 'Ahem.'

You will never enjoy another second of your life for calling me the C word.

CHAPTER NINETEEN

SPECIAL AGENT ROGER LIU

Lola hastened instructions to the paramedics about the chief and his deputy, flashed her badge, and pantomimed for me to do the same. My ears were still whooshing, whirring out everyone's voices. The woman in the housecoat and with the shopping cart who had fetched my phone, toddled to the other end of the strip mall and bent into a trashcan, oblivious to the sirens and the screaming and the fire and the smoke around her. How wonderful to not exist in this dimension, I thought.

Lola guided my missteps, like I was a drunk done with his last shot of the night, to the Viking woman's F-150. As she jammed the shift to first, second, third, and fourth, I watched how she poked her nose out the driver's window as if smelling her way. However odd, this vision of Lola prompted a vast nothingness, a near-complete absence of sound, which replaced the wind in my ears. I didn't panic. I allowed the relief, and in so doing, realized the sharpening of my vision once again – even sharper than before.

Did I mention how I trained to be a sharpshooter early in my career? Did I mention my better-than-20/20 vision? Lola and I combined made for a virtual Superhero of sight and smell. This is probably why the Bureau paired us together in the first place. So without the distraction of sound, I could have seen to Texas if hills and buildings weren't in the way.

Lola hunched her shoulders and scrunched her nose as though truly bothered to be alive. I tried to focus on anything other than the silence, reading the signs on whatever lonely stores and restaurants we passed along the straight way on the straight road. The rain was the annoying, cold kind, the kind that won't decide to stop or fall. A melancholic rain. Although mid-day, the sky was as dark as dusk.

A wide-mouth bass mailbox made me think of my childhood neighborhood, but then again, any of the cases I worked made me think of childhood. Given my possible hyperthymesia, which I usually controlled pretty well – unlike others with true hyperthymesia – my 'exceptional memory' took over, and I once again fell slave to scenes I hated to remember. The replay of one day in particular invaded my thinking, a cyclical spiral I'd entered so often in life. Here it is, cat's out of the bag, I guess I'll let you in on a little secret I've held back from you until now. I told you earlier that I decided to join the FBI to 'please my parents' or support my college girlfriend-cum-fiancée, but we didn't know each other well in the beginning of this dual memoir.

When I turned thirteen, my father got a job planning power plants for a big construction outfit in Chicago. We moved from the lap of luxury in Buffalo to a brick bungalow in a suburb about twenty minutes west of downtown Chicago, called Riverside. Riverside is filled with Frank Lloyd Wright masterpieces, peaceful birds and towering trees, quiet streets, and an addictive ice-cream shop, appropriately named Grumpies.

The same gentleman who designed Central Park, Frederick Law Olmstead, designed Riverside. Olmstead had this vision to create a town where each house had a view of a park. Thus, you will find that Riverside streets are circular, looping knots, interrupted by wedges of tiny plots of grass and full-blown parks, such as Turtle Park – which features a green-painted cement turtle.

Way back when I was a boy, because of Riverside's design, real estate agents claimed crime was low: the rat's nest of streets making easy getaways for robbers, well, not so easy. If you were a criminal in Riverside, you best know the lay of the land, the twist of the pretzel streets, and the misdirection of curving parks. You best be an insider.

Turtle Park was in the middle of everything, surrounded by layers of gnarly streets, as if the center of a grapevine wreath. It was here that something gravely significant revealed my seeing gift. When I say significant, I mean the kind of event so profound it slaps the direction of your life into a new direction, takes any emotions and settled fears, grabs and pushes them inside out, and creates a whole new set of fears you never thought possible; they exist thereafter as a constant undercurrent, the theme song to every waking minute.

This particular event also planted the bug my parents thereafter suffered: a desire that I go into law enforcement. Throughout my subsequent childhood, teenage period, and college, however, I fought back by burying that day in writing comedy, creating comic strips, and acting in dramatic plays.

Nevertheless, by my senior year in college, the St John's Jesuit priest I'd been playing chess with convinced me to face my fears. Taking his Godly advice to the extreme, I did the most drastic thing possible: I entered the very field that had for so long haunted me, kidnapping.

* * *

There we were: thirteen-year-old me, my mother, my father, and my eight-year-old brother, Reese, who we never called Reese. We called him Mozi. The day was a cloudless, high-blue July, windless and hot, so my parents walked us from our

232

bungalow to Grumpies for ice cream. About an eight-block walk. Midway back home, we stopped at Turtle Park.

Mozi and I had already biked and raced the whole town, twenty times over, sometimes with our day-babysitter. Having my pesky autobiographical memory, I'd conceptualized each square inch into 3-D models in my mind. I knew the Frank Lloyd mansion, the one that looked like a rectangular starship on the corner of Turtle Park, measured .5 miles from our bungalow. I knew the basketball-sized rock by its driveway had ten nicks on the top. I knew five Victorians, three stone mansions, two new construction mega-homes, a Cape, a gambrel, and a run-down ranch surrounded Turtle Park. The distance from house to house allowed for multi-legged foot races between me and Mozi, all of which I could have easily won, but throughout I'd scatter losses, so as to allow my four-eyes, thick-lensed, short-stature, younger brother, a modicum of self-respect. I loved Mozi. How light he was. A 'silly pants,' my mother called him. He made everyone laugh. Everyone pegged him to be a comedian someday.

I was never ever going to be like Mozi; and he was never ever going to be like me. But oh, how I tried to model his early years, to resurrect for all of us that long-ago lost boy of sweetness and laughter.

We'd gotten our ice creams, now dripping from cones and onto our wrists, and we sat like a family of quacking ducks around a lake, only the cement turtle in Turtle Park was our lake. Dunking his spent and mushy cone in the trash, Mozi said, 'Hide and Seek, you're it, Pop.' Then he ran, and I ran, and our mother struggled to get her balance from standing up to join in the fun. My father tossed his own cone in the trash and said, 'Game on,' hiding his eyes in his sleeves.

Between Turtle Park and another large field with a baseball diamond, a U-shaped road formed a division bordered with pines and oaks. Mozi ran like heavy rain across the U road and to the far end of the second park, while I stayed in Turtle Park, climbing a tree to perch myself within the lush canopy. I had full view of Mozi, who wedged himself in a bush about two hundred yards away.

On the edge of the second park snaked another road, sewn like a thin ribbon of black to the green of the grassy field. Mozi hid about two feet from this ribbon road, visible to drivers, but invisible to a father, who counted with closed eyes, and to a mother, who hid in a jungle gym beneath a slide and facing the wrong direction. And even if they were looking Mozi's way, I doubt their eyesight carried that far. But mine did. I didn't realize then that I was different. I thought I saw what everyone else saw.

A brown Datsun, parked ten yards from Mozi, slowly rolled along the edge of the park toward Mozi's hiding bush. The license plate, plainly visible to me, was immediately out of place but instantly familiar: Idaho, XXY56790. The eye doctor they called to trial to support my testimony said most people can read license plates 'three to four car lengths away.' And while the tree in which I perched was about 'forty car lengths away,' my 'visual acuity' was 'better than the best recorded and nearly immeasurable.' This was in rebuttal to the defense lawyers who claimed I could not possibly have pegged the license plate from so far away. 'He's obviously been coached,' they argued. They also objected to what I testified I saw the driver of the Datsun say.

As the car reached Mozi, the driver and passenger doors opened. Two men in tracksuits, one red, one black, exited. The driver stood by his opened door, scoping for onlookers, of which there were none, except for invisible me in the tree. The other, the one in the black suit, strolled over to Mozi, plucked him from the bush, and ran with him under his arm, his hand firmly over Mozi's mouth. He threw him into the back seat of the Datsun, got in next to him, and continued to bottle his screams. The driver said – I read his lips: 'Midnight.' And they sped off.

I jumped from the tree, landing square, my knees buckling beneath me. I trip-ran to a full-out sprint, yelling to my unaware parents behind me, 'Mozi. They took Mozi. They took Mozi. They took Mozi.'

Not waiting for them to catch up or understand, I kept

running and I kept screaming. 'They took Mozi. They took Mozi.' I didn't have time to stop and explain how I'd previously mapped the Datsun they took him in, how I could recite the number of windows and doors on the house where it usually parked so innocuously, before.

I'm pretty sure I didn't breathe the entire four blocks to our bungalow. I ripped open the side door, using the key my parents hid under the mat, flung my body down the basement stairs, grabbed my BB gun and a box of BBs, flew outside, and threw the gun and pellets and then myself over the fence to the schoolyard beside the house. I heard my parents about a block back yelling for me, but they hadn't had the chance to see me flee over the fence, and I didn't pause one second to let them catch up.

I snaked my way around the school, through the play yard, and down and around and around and around several windy, tree-lined streets and onto the outskirts of town, where split levels and small ranches took the place of the nicer bungalows, space-ship Lloyd Wrights, and Victorians further in. Our babysitter had walked us this way three times because her boyfriend lived in this particular quadrant.

I came upon a cul-de-sac of three split-level homes, set in a demilune around a crescent sliver of grass in the center, which cars circumnavigated and children Hot-Wheel'ed in a perfect circle. The babysitter's boyfriend's garage apartment was two roads over, and to get there, I'd be out of visual range of the house I needed to watch, given the twistiness of the streets and the merged canopy of the oaks and sycamores. Leading to the cul-de-sac was, strangely, nothing. No homes with a clean line of shot on the target, no houses on or at the end of the straightaway that led there either. An empty lot of abandoned construction further divided me from seeking help. The place to which I'd run was indeed a rare, secluded outpost, so different from the congestion of homes elsewhere in the village. The three homes in the cul-de-sac were architectural triplets, obviously built by the same developer. One house, a white split, seemed empty, given the newspapers piled up. Another, white bottom with brown top, screamed of a definite vacancy, given the no-curtain view of the empty living room and the uncut grass. The yellow caution tape around the missing stairs further confirmed the property's abandonment. The third, the one on the left, royal-blue peeling paint with white shutters, appeared unoccupied, but for the brown Datsun in the driveway. Exactly where I'd plotted it on one of our walks. Same plate: Idaho XXY56790. The screen door on the royal-blue split air-braked to a close, having seconds before been opened and crossed.

Statistically speaking, most kidnap victims are hidden or their bodies dumped within miles from where stolen.

A quandary. On the one hand, I couldn't barge on in for

fear the two grown men would tackle and take me too. Plus, I worried there were other men in there. On the other hand, I didn't dare take my sight off the house in case they decided to flee with my beloved Mozi. I held a pained hope the reference to 'midnight' meant they'd leave at midnight, at which point, I'd be ready to ambush them. I had one choice: I'd have to wait and hide in the sycamore across from the house, poise my gun at the side and front exits, and fire away as soon as midnight hit and they set out to leave.

It was only noon.

Lord only knows what torture Mozi endured inside.

That day in the tree. Oh, that day in the tree.

If you're reeling reading this, shouting at the page about another way out of this mess, an easier and obvious solution, good for you. I was thirteen, not as experienced as you in the ways of the world.

I quickly shimmied up the trunk, the BB gun hanging to my back, the pellets in my pocket. About ten feet up, a straight and perfect branch, one intended by God for a swing, allowed me to hoist one leg up higher, and then the other. There I sat on that blessed fat branch, pressing my side against the trunk, and holding another, smaller, crooked branch above me for balance. And I waited. And waited.

Every so often, I'd have to jostle my bottom, left cheek, right cheek, left, right, squeezing blood back into my tingling mass. Then my feet, my legs, arms, and hands, same drill. The biggest battle that day was keeping my muscles awake in such cramped quarters. As a newfound sniper but a quick learner, however, I figured out how to increase blood flow with the simplest of maneuvers, and I practiced aiming and shooting without having to steady myself. By about dusk, I graduated to Expert Shooter In A Tree. I also became an ornithologist, a studied observer of the comings and goings of a mother cardinal who fed her babies in a nest five feet from me on a leaf-domed branch. At some point I grew jealous of their safe little family, eating worms and chirping in a boastful way, clattering on about how untouched by evil they felt. Snug in their teeny, tiny twig home, they'd poke up their gumball heads and bobble about, seemingly to coax me to laugh along to their cooing. I may have pointed my gun in their direction, angry at their happiness. But I thought better of such a senseless act and focused my hatred on the man in the black suit and the man in the red suit.

Around dinnertime, I saw a flurry of activity over at my babysitter's boyfriend's apartment. My parents pulled in and to much commotion and hugging and crying, they met up with my babysitter and her boyfriend, all of them lighting candles and carrying flashlights. I couldn't hear anything they said, just doors shutting and opening. So I didn't yell over for help and I wasn't going to leave Mozi for any amount of time. Just in case. What if they drove off? *What if they leave and we never find him again?* I had to stay put, I figured.

Now with hindsight and better reason, there were a million things I could have done. Not a day goes by I don't berate myself for my poor problem solving that day.

Sometime after dinner, a metallic-green boat of a car waffled around the circle. The old man driver slowly turned his wheel, outright singing a song to himself and totally unaware of the boy above him in the tree. A squirrel came a little too close until I fly-swatted him to scat.

Here came the darker darkness, and the gaslamps lit. The cul-de-sac housed one lamp in the right pocket, which glowed as though an old London street, long ago, when candles ruled the world. The moon was a useless fingernail, barely casting enough light to tie your shoes. My legs were on their tenth round of sleep, and I began to shake them, carefully, holding tight to the branch above where I sat. I'd given up on feeling anything in my ass hours before.

Sometime around 10 p.m., quick flashes of Blacksuit and Redsuit were visible through the half-drawn curtains of the living room window I spied. Blacksuit would cross through to a hallway beyond the living room's wall, and Redsuit would follow, carrying a backpack. Back and forth the two of them went, back and forth with bags and papers and items. They were packing and preparing. I searched hard for Mozi, but did not see him. With the house's lights, all became visible within and around the place, as though a lone star in a black sky. The contrast made scoping targets simple.

Although I waited a good long twelve hours, holding vigil and focused on that awful blue house, I tensed in shock when the side door finally creaked open and out stepped Blacksuit, a backpack slung sloppily over his left shoulder and a duffel bag in his right hand. He searched the perimeter of the front lawn for any enemies hiding behind bushes. My G.I. Joe digital watch ticked to 12:02 a.m. And then I cupped my mouth to stifle a gasp in reaction to who came next.

Mozi, sloppy on his feet and far too compliant in the way he quietly marched behind Blacksuit, dragged himself out of the side door, Redsuit prodding him forward. Mozi's droopy shoulders told me he'd been heavily drugged. The three of them walked single file toward the Datsun, appearing to the world to be refugee brothers, a warped and weird family, setting out to run the border at night.

I leveled my gun, aimed at Blacksuit's right eye, and fired. Bull's eye. Snapped him dead on. He crouched to his knees in the driveway, screaming. Redsuit took hold of Mozi, as if to use him as a shield, but Mozi was so short, the driver's torso and head, although bent, were in full view. I fired again, this time at Redsuit's left eye. Bull's eye. Snapped him too, dead on.

'Mozi, Mozi, run, buddy! Run to me. Run Mozi,' I

screamed, while jumping from the tree. My second tree jump of the day. This time my sleeping legs failed me when I landed, and the gun flew from my arms. But adrenaline, now adrenaline, what a friend. Fighting every instinct I had to give in to the debilitating fire in my legs, I stood, wobbling, grabbed my gun and aimed again at the men, who were howling in the driveway.

'Mozi, Mozi, run, buddy!'

But Mozi appeared too drugged and scattered. He teetered forward, he sort of saw me, he teetered more. He was only one foot away from Blacksuit and Redsuit. I had to get closer.

Walking like a determined and murderous soldier approaching an unarmed enemy, I cocked my gun, kept it forward, and issued no warnings. I fired again, hitting an arm here, a leg there, any part made vulnerable to my shooting. Their bodies writhed in pain under my power. One of them turned an ear to me, so I aimed for the small hole and set a bead straight into his hearing canal. I'm pretty sure that shot hurt even more than the eye. Well, maybe not. But who gives a shit.

'Mozi, get over to me now,' I shouted.

Behind me, finally, someone noticed.

'What the hell is going on?' A woman behind me yelled.

'Call the cops!' I said. 'Call the cops!'

I later learned she'd been out walking her poodle and collie. The two men limped quick to their Datsun, and without even shutting the doors before backing up, peeled out of the driveway, out of the cul-de-sac, and out of town. Cops snatched the idiots in a failed shoot-out at a McDonald's in nearby Cicero.

Mozi fell on the grass, and I ran to meet and encapsulate him. He had no clue what was going on. That night. That night, Mozi slept mercifully oblivious, given the pills the doctors gave him.

Mozi has never talked about his day with those scumbags. Never said what went on in that house. But Mozi never put on his funny red cape again. Never sang a funny song. I'm sure I haven't seen him smile in all these years. After his second suicide attempt and his third failed marriage, Mozi moved into my parents' house, refusing to ever set foot in their basement or any basement, anywhere, ever again.

Once I took Mozi on a fly-fishing trip to Montana – my hope to extract from him the poison so flooding his veins. All he did was fish. And one night, he cried in his tent. I didn't want to embarrass him, so I stood helplessly outside, pacing around the bonfire, staring at the flames like I do, biting my thumbnails, and confused as to what step I should take. I prayed the zipper would come down, and he'd crawl out to find and talk to me. I wanted so badly to enter his tent and hold him. Squeeze all the bad memories away. But he never came out.

I'm still so heartbroken whenever Mozi waddles in his slippers into a room; a vastness follows him, sucking away whatever energy he might have carried with him. The blackness under his eyes, his drooping lids, these are the signs of his sleepness nights.

So I hunt. I hunt all those deplorable, worthless nobodies, those vacant suits of meat who deserve nothing, those demons who abscond with children and deserve less than we'd give a rabid rat.

My parents formed their newfound goal, a relentless hope that their babies would never be taken again, a responsibility they poured into me. They dragged me to the shooting range, insisted I take up archery. Whispered in my sleeping dreams how I should train for law enforcement. This was their vicarious wish, their way of coping with the horror. My seeing gift was out of the bag, and I became the regional record-holder on bull's eye arrow shots and telescoping those with a second arrow.

Oh, whatever.

Here's the point: I can take any shot. Any damn shot.

The Feds first tried to force the sharpshooter program on me. But I insisted on kidnappings. They either relented to my persistence or conspired to be voluntarily unaware of the psych tests that must have warned otherwise. Eventually, they assigned Lola as my partner or problem, depending on how viewed. I'd definitely say problem when we first met, but very soon thereafter, a partner in the highest sense.

* * *

So as Lola and I drove through the very middle of flat Indiana in a borrowed F-150, and as my vision sharpened and my hearing dulled, I set my sights on shooting someone that day. Everyone who took a child and taunted me, also took Mozi, scared Mozi, stole his humor, over and over again. And I felt every single one of them should suffer terrible pain and unbearable humiliation.

We turned where our truck owner told us to turn. The all-season tires scattered rocks along a dirt road, which had parts paved and parts unpaved. Unpruned apple trees, knotted and jagged with age, bordered the drive, and out beyond rolled the longest field full of cows I'd ever seen. How quaint I thought the fall arrival must have been for students when this country school was in its prime. Now it drooped in coldness and neglect, tortured by the lethargic rain, which barely cared to fall on this forgotten place. Everything was draped in a blackness above and an evil within.

CHAPTER TWENTY

I had the ultimate asset in Brad's VW: his gun, Asset #42, if only I could pry it from his bloody fingers. After he called me the C word, my eyes began to flutter and roll deep within their sockets. This happens to me once in a great while. It is this involuntary state my mind takes me to when my overactive cerebral cortex is in overdrive. Trance-like I become, and the sensation of lightness, busyness, zapping in my brain feels so great – like a perfect buzz with the best of wine, only you become sharper in thought, not blurred like you would with alcohol. The feeling is rather addictive, but you can't force it – you must simply wait and allow for the tingling to take over.

All I needed was a distraction to Brad's left. If he turned his head, his right arm – the one closest to me and which held the gun – would shift back. If I acted on this split second when his muscles would be in repose by pushing with one hand on his right shoulder, his elbow would jam into his seat and his forearm weaken. His grip would loosen. With my other hand, and with the element of surprise further lessening his hold, I could snag the gun. I'd have all of one second to make the move once a distraction hit.

But what distraction?

We were stalled in the middle of the woods. Trapped at the end of what must have been a mining road.

The rain fell, again, only here and there. The watery plopping was not even loud enough to call to mind the firing of my first-grade school shooting episode.

A squirrel might hop tree to tree. A bird might swoop limb to limb. These movements were not enough of a true distraction. I had no assets outside that car. Or none that I knew of, just then.

I could have said, 'Hey, look, over there, a polar bear.' And since he was a dumb-nuts psychopath, he may have craned his neck. But first he would question me, even if for only a nanosecond, and in so questioning, he'd tighten his grip. I needed a truly alarming jolt to make him twist, for this was what would push him physically and mentally into my plan. Shock and jelly muscles. These are what I needed.

Since I could find no distractions in scouring the forest outside the VW, my eyes continued to flutter, flipping through options, calculating and connecting dots, drawing lines, designing a new plan. The car was littered with assets. And as I logged them, my eyes rolling, he taunted me with wicked words.

'You crazy little bitch, you lunatic. Look at you,' he said, his face curled in disgust.

A screwdriver on the floor of the backseat, two feet from my left hand, down, left angle, Asset #43.

'Stop blinking your fucking eyes!'

Roll of duct tape around the stick shift, Asset #44.

A pen on the floor by my right foot, hitting the pinky toe side of my Nikes, Asset #45 . . .

The tie around his neck, Asset #46.

His phone in the cubby, Asset #47.

'Panther, you scare me. You try, oh ha ha.'

I fluttered on, even though the blinking was becoming less and less natural and more and more forced. I thought a charade of craziness might lull him to feel safe in his own. He seemed to be getting distracted. His grip lessened on the gun, which I could tell by the return of some wrinkles on his waxed knuckles.

And then . . .

Like a glorious gift, when I was about to consider very closely the screwdriver, to my great surprise, an outside distraction actually came. If I weren't so practiced and empty, I probably would have been stunned.

'Put your fucking hands up in the air,' a man yelled from outside the car.

I didn't even look up. Brad twisted toward the voice in the woods, just as I had only seconds before hoped he would, and I simultaneously shoved his right shoulder into the seat. His elbow pushed back, his grip opened, and I grabbed that damn gun.

I looked up to see a mixed-ethnic man, half-Asian, half-Caucasian, his legs A-framed, and his gun poised. His gray suit screamed federal agent.

Behind the car was a thick woman with a short haircut and a masculine nose. Her gray pants and white button shirt also screamed federal agent. She, too, had Brad in her gun's scope. Beside her was not an apparent agent, but a farmer-looking old man with a cocked and aimed rifle.

'Get out of the fucking car you piece of shit, asshole,' the woman demanded.

'Lola, take cover, I got this. Boyd, stay put. Yeah. Stay put, old boy,' the male agent said, a bit too calmly. He squinted to aim, and I believe he winked at me, as if thrilled to perform a murder on my behalf.

I could tell he meant to hurt Brad.

I liked him immediately.

I squirmed backwards, intending to exit the car, and realized too late that I was still buckled in. And then Brad took the wild option, one I had considered but ruled out because I thought it too insane, even for him. Before I could exit the car, he floored the gas, going faster than appropriate down the short stretch of remaining road. We barely missed the passing trees when he jerked the wheel swiftly left and off the road. Low-lying limbs scratched the sides of the car as we continued on and up the granite slant of the low end of the quarry.

Into the water we plunged.

The gun fell beyond my reach.

CHAPTER TWENTY-ONE

We arrived at Appletree, and just as soon as we did, Boyd came hauling out the door of one of the wings. Appletree Boarding School, so said the weathered sign on the side. Boyd slung his rifle up over his shoulder. He beckoned us to get out of the truck and run to him. My hearing was coming back in waves, a disconcerting undulation of dying and then replenished noise. A whoosh, a crackle, a series of disjointed words, up with volume and then a quick decline.

Boyd's words came to me in a flood. 'Come on now, y'all. Bobby's pretty sure they took the dirt road that goes to the quarry. They trapped in there, for sure. Prolly hidin' an all. Bobby just ran up here to tell me so and he's off to the hospital with the otha girl. Otha girl says there's anotha girl. Girl is Dorothy, the one Bobby's got. This seem right, Mr Liu?'

'Yes, Boyd. Where do we go?'

'Come on now, I'll show y'all.'

Procedure says I should have confiscated Boyd's gun and made him point the way, insisted he stick close to the schoolhouse and call any other authorities there might be in surrounding communities.

Fuck procedure. Lola and I needed back-up. And I didn't have any time to spare on others getting mobilized.

Boyd, turns out, is a champion hunter. Hunted his whole life. Back then, he held the Indiana State Title for largest buck taken with a single shot. So Boyd knew how to traipse lightly on fallen leaves. The sight of him, it was almost cute, tip toeing like a creeping Fred Astaire through the woods. Lola and I were trained on how to follow footprints and muffle our own approach, so we did just so. But frankly, I couldn't hear much of anything anyway, so I'm no judge on how quiet we really were. My hearing had gone back to a muffled wind. I'd catch only pieces of Lola's whispers.

'Liu ... there ... smell ... gas ... car ... engine running.'

I didn't smell any car. The aroma to me was just the forest, the wet leaves, the musty bark, the crispness of damp dirt. I think this is the exact same scent most everyone else on the planet would catch when walking in the woods. But since Lola was the connoisseur of odor, I followed her nose.

Boyd nodded his approval, for he was headed that way anyway.

Sure enough, we came upon the back end of a parked VW. Smog billowed out of the tailpipe, plainly visible on the cold air.

I crept slowly closer and to the driver's side. And as clear as if only one foot in front of me, I saw Lisa, seemingly in a trance, blinking her eyes wildly. She looked exactly like the school photo they had scanned in her file – the file they gave to the wrong team. Who I thought was Ding-Dong faced her, not me. He seemed to be shouting in her face. How odd they appeared, victim and perpetrator, sitting in a car in the middle of the woods, staring each other down.

I shouted for him to put his fucking hands up in the air.

Lola followed by demanding something. I heard only 'piece of shit.'

I watched as Lisa stopped blinking when the man turned to see me. Watched as she pushed his shoulder and grabbed his gun.

Did she really just do that? I was so thrown to see such an act by a child. But again, my vision. I was only ten yards away. I saw exactly what I saw as if I was in the car with her and watching her actions in a slow-mo replay. *The girl took his gun.*

Still, I held my aim.

I think something must have hatched in me. A calmness I had never known. I believe I felt nothing, actually, which was comforting. Maybe all I felt was relief that I would again scratch that ancient itch in me, be able to once again maim an awful human. I had so many accomplices to help: Lola, Boyd, and even the victim. I'd read her file, knew she was gifted, recalled her struggle with emotions. She appeared so calm in that car as she took his gun.

I even saw her slight smirk in holding the handle. A look of pride.

I knock and I knock and you answer.

The devil indeed is a she.

Why didn't I take the shot when I could have? Why didn't I burst his skull? Yes, I surely could have. It would have all been over so much sooner. But from where I stood, the only shot I could take would have been fatal. The man sunk so low in the low VW seat, and the door was so high, only his beedy head stuck up in the glass of the door. A head shot would surely be the end. I didn't mind killing him. That wasn't the problem. The problem was I truly wanted him to suffer for the rest of his life. I wanted him disfigured, hurting, and holed up in solitary confinement, or even better, embroiled in the general population of a state run prison. I may have been a federal agent on a federal mission, but I'd work behind the scenes to place his case on a silver platter for the state. A low-resource Indiana prison would be so much better for this bag of meat, especially if I could – and I would – send word to fellow inmates of his crimes against children. Oh yes I would, and Lola would too, but only after she'd taken her own turn with him. In private. For which I'd play the fool.

Why is Lola like she is? Look, that's her backstory, and damn, I dare you to try to crowbar the past out of her. All I know is the foster families took a toll on her, and that's all I've ever got, even after all these years. But hey, if you want to pry, go right ahead, Barbara Walters.

Now I know I could have taken the shot, and I would have clicked to reason and done so had I been given just two more seconds to contemplate what I was doing. Surely, in just two more seconds of thought, my lovely Sandra would have whispered in my ear, just by my memory of her. I was robbed of introspection, however, when in a flash he sped ahead. Lisa fell back in her seat, jostled off whatever game she was surely playing, and struggled to find her balance. And though I was relieved she was still alive, when they disappeared through the trees and over a ridge, I felt nothing but awful dread.

Boyd directed us left to a winding path through the woods. He said not one word to us, only led a compliant train under a canopy of cold trees. The sky was a darker gray with spots of black, a cancer mold in the pockets that were once a nice fighting blue.

At a clearing, a piling of granite slabs arched up in a circle. A quarry appeared, and suddenly my experience forced me to accept that whatever Boyd was about to show us would destroy any strain of relief at finding Lisa alive. Lola was motioning wildly, running like mad to the quarry's edge. Ahead of me, she turned and screamed by the looks of the veins popping from her neck. But a weird whistling blocked her words, and then a whoosh, and suddenly sound returned, and the bubbling of water met my ears. I raced to meet Lola and Boyd at the quarry's edge, only to see the Bug's taillights sink under the black surface. Ripples of water splashed the granite walls, but oddly, in a slow way and without much force, as if the water was as thick as syrup and thus difficult to displace.

Lola and I kicked off our shoes, scuttling to a low spot that would provide an easier entrance.

'Now don't, y'all. Don't just go flopping in there, now,' Boyd said, halting our quick progress.

'What the hell are you talking about, chicken man?' Lola shouted, her forehead crinkled in pain. She pointed her gun at Boyd. I did too. Neither Lola nor I trusted anyone, usually. We only needed the smallest of reasons.

Boyd placed his rifle on the ground and his hands in the air. I lowered my weapon, relieved my chicken farmer was still a good man and all my senses intact.

'Now, now, I just mean, now. Be real careful and all,' he rushed to say. 'This here's a mine they abandoned some forty years ago. Before this here place was a school an' all. My daddy and Bobby's daddy use-ta hunt this here property. They say old cars been thrown in there. Scrap metal. Junk. Y'all go jumpin' in, you're likely to get a leg tangled and drown yourself.'

Do you see how following a bureau procedure might have gotten me or Lola killed? Sometimes trusting the locals really can help. Yeah, well, tell the chiefs who run the Bureau about deviating from the game plan. About abandoning their damn metrics. Go ahead, tell them all about how instinct and heightened senses really should rule. See how far you get. And then come talk to me and Lola.

Sandra would probably stop me here with a gentle look of warning, a squint of her eye and a subtle tuck of her head. She'd place her rose-lotioned hand on my arm as her silent way of calming me. She'd say I've gotten a little heated and out of my regular character in remembering and retelling all of this. And she'd be right, as she typically is. Back then, before entering the quarry, I did try to find one humorous item about the scene around me. But then I thought, why would I even think it's appropriate to consider comedy now? Perhaps I was simply stretching hard for Sandra to save me, feeling bereft at being so separated from her, out there, cold, diving into dark, trying to save a drowning girl and her baby. A chain of safety is what I wanted: Lisa saving her child, me saving Lisa, Sandra saving me. But Sandra wasn't there. Sandra was never with me when I trudged into hell.

Cautiously, gingerly with testing feet, but as quick as I could, I stepped into the water. That's when I noticed the rope tied to the side of the well.

CHAPTER TWENTY-TWO

DAY 33 CONTINUES

I was buckled in. Brad was not. As we nosedived into the water, I calculated our fall at about a slight ten-degree angle. We were, thankfully, on the low end of the quarry. Across the way, the wall was about thirty feet high from surface to ledge; a fall from that end would have been much harder to take. Our fall was only about four feet. So really, it was more like we were driving down a boat ramp. Nevertheless, although short-lived, our descent was pretty fast, so we entered the water hard.

Only days before, my now dead but then alive captor informed that the quarry was forty feet deep in some spots, so I braced to keep falling and falling. But actually, we stopped short almost as soon as the car was submerged, hood first. All in, I'd say we were ten feet deep. No big deal, as far as I was concerned. Still, let's not minimize the situation. People have drowned in as little as two inches of water. Exhibit A, the man in my cell.

The back end of the VW began to sink and we settled flat. We'd landed on a cliff in the quarry, and I could tell it was a cliff, because although we'd kicked up a ton of sediment and the water was murky, out before us the water was lighter on top, and darker below, much darker below. This meant, just ahead, the water dropped steeply to a deeper hell.

Also, something floated on a rope in front of us, and the rope seemed to extend further down from where the car rested. I knew exactly what was on that rope, even though the grainy water needed to settle for clearer view.

Beside me, Brad slumped on the steering wheel, passed out from hitting his head or out of sheer shock over his dumb self, I have no idea. Either way, I was thankful I didn't have him thrashing about like a fool. Asset #48, Unconscious Brad.

Water began to rise in the car, creeping in the cracks in the doors and the up-rolled windows. My too-big Nikes were covered, next my shins. Rising, rising, rising to my hips. The water around us became clearer and clearer; I marveled at how fast this quarry recovered herself, as if all she had done was swallow yet another victim, another pile of metal, into her vast, dark stomach. *Ho-hum*, her liquid body seemed to groan.

The floor of the quarry was a junkyard: bent rebar, a child-size metal tractor flipped upside down, buckets, bricks, chains, and indeed, a chain link fence that crawled out of the depths in front of the car and onto the cliff, as though a long, curling tongue reaching out of a devil mouth.

The water kept washing in, like liquid being forced through closed teeth. Next, my hips were covered, my wide belly, my baby. I sat still.

Out before me, the picture was opaque, but she was visible, floating on the wakeboard, the rope harnessed around her cut torso. She shifted slightly in her underwater grave, tethered and buoyed in death, her hair slowly waving in the scant movement of the water. Together, her and her contraption appeared like a shriveled balloon, inexplicably flying high above a deserted car dealership, somewhere out West, somewhere where no one drives anymore, unless lost and out of gas. Waiting for vultures.

To my right, that man agent began crashing his flat hands on my passenger door window, pounding, pounding, pounding with his palms. Bam, bam, pounding, pounding, and so returned the school gunman, firing his gun. The pop, the screams, the banging, the ringing of his bullets through the classroom.

I fought my anger switch from turning on. I stayed the course; I sat still. I clutched my own fists, fist in fist. I turned to the agent, who remained furious at the window – his thuds dulled by the water – and yanking on the door – his strain slowed by aquatic gravity. Of course all of his flailing was useless.

I held up my hand to stop him, fanning my palm against the glass. Because my head was still in breathable air, but the water up to my neck, I said, 'The water has to equalize on both sides first. Then the pressure will be even and the door will open. Calm down!'

Doesn't anyone remember anything from high school physics?

The water covered the roots of my hair. I unbuckled. I reached for Brad's ring of keys, hanging from the ignition, and turned to the agent, who was foolishly still banging like a wild school shooter on my window.

Will this noise always haunt me? Will I forever be reminded of that day? Who can I hunt down to stop this infernal racket? Who can I torture with this sound?

I eyed the agent and raised my hands to gesture, 'Well, what are you waiting for?'

He tried the handle once again and opened the door.

I swam ten feet to the top.

CHAPTER TWENTY-THREE

SPECIAL AGENT ROGER LIU

I followed Lisa to ensure she got to the surface and into Lola's arms. Once secure, I swam back down, and although weighed with reluctance, I snatched the driver from what should have been his watery grave. I pushed him to the surface, and Big Boyd yanked him out at the armpits. Only Boyd had the wherewithal to give him mouth to mouth, which, as a farmer, he somehow knew. I don't know how. I really don't care. I wouldn't have put my lips on that cold fish.

The driver coughed into a fighting life, screaming and wailing and flopping on the granite rocks. Lola waltzed over and kicked him in a thigh. I was bent, laboring for my own breath, and standing close to Lisa.

'You're going to wish we left you down there, scumbag. Keep your mouth shut. Keep your damn mouth shut before I yank every single one of your teeth out.' Twisting her head to Boyd, she added, 'Chicken Man, hold his hands behind his back.'

'His name is Brad,' Lisa yelled over, calmly, but with definite distaste, as though 'Brad' were a laughably embarrassing name.

'You have the right to remain silent ...' I delivered the Miranda in a quick monotone, letting him understand how perturbed I was to have to read him rights he didn't deserve. I had to do the Miranda, because Lola never would have. She cuffed him roughly, and because he wouldn't stop wheezing for breath and whining about everything, she ripped a scarf from within her blouse and tied it tight around his mouth. Only a muffled groaning continued.

Boyd stepped back and raised his rifle at Brad.

'Ah, shit, Chicken Man, don't shoot him. I like the sentiment, but we can't shoot him now,' Lola said, thawing toward Boyd.

'Ma'am, I ain't gonna shoot the bastard 'less he try to run. And if he do, well, now, I need another trophy head for my wall,' Boyd said, never losing his gaze on Brad. 'Hey there, boy, you like these here kiddies. Well now, know this, I'm the state's record holder in single shot huntin'. Uh, huh. So's, I sorta want you to run an' all. Go ahead. Go ahead. Run like a rabbit.'

Lola smiled at Boyd. And I did too. He was now firmly part of our gang.

Lisa, standing with her arms crossed at the side of the quarry, leaning close to that rope I'd seen tied to the wall, lifted one side of her mouth, which I soon learned meant she smiled too. So, there we were, all four of us, a newfound band of vigilantes. At least we had the legitimacy of my and Lola's badges for cover. I considered the oddness of the coincidence that Boyd should sell our kidnapper his van and this kidnapper should park said van on Boyd's family property, miles away from where he'd purchased the vehicle. To others, it sure would sound suspicious on one end of the believability spectrum and impossible on the other. But I remembered too the words of the woman who witnessed the 'Hoosier State' on the license plate and how she and her husband watched 'Hoosiers' the night before. 'Divine coincidence,' she'd said. Divine coincidence, indeed. It was as if she'd provided a clue or a premonition, perhaps a subtext to the whole investigation.

I crept closer to Lisa, who was shivering from the cold. Stifling my own chill from the water, I lowered into my shoulders, like a turtle to his shell, and shook one leg, then the other. Water dripped off me like I was a squeezed sponge. My drenched gray suit buckled at the elbows. A thermos of hot coffee would have been nice right then, a daily comfort turned unrealistic luxury in that moment. I might as well have wished for a unicorn to swoop from a tree and carry us to Candyland for gumdrops and licorice.

Lisa hugged and rubbed her bulging belly, seemingly in

an effort to warm the baby within. She did not appear quite ready to flee the scene, as I expect any other victim would have been. She was also not hysterical, not crying, not shouting for her parents. She wasn't demanding the regular demands, not a doctor, not anything you'd think. Silently, she watched me approach her, seemingly considering my stride, possibly counting my steps. With Lola and Boyd pressing handcuffed Brad against a tree, I attempted to collect Lisa so we could leave the woods.

'I'm Lisa Yyland. Don't you fucking call an ambulance or put one damn thing on a radio. I want to catch the rest of the bastards who did this.'

Her soul-absent glare bored into my bones. Her disconnection to this scene, her determination, her power, everything about her overcame me. I fell into a stupor. A shock. I held my hand up behind me, a warning to the others, turned only my head, and as though possessed by her, repeated her exact words, 'Don't fucking call an ambulance or put one damn thing on the radio.'

'We're going to trap the rest of them today, and you're not to call my parents yet. No one is to know I've been found. And if you need any convincing, if you think maybe you need to call my parents first, perhaps alert a higher authority, let me show you something. Unhook that rope, sit behind that rock, and pull.'

The rope. I had avoided looking in its direction while under-water. I knew the rope had something awful on the other end. I did exactly as Lisa directed me: I unhooked the rope, sat behind a rock, and pulled.

Now I've seen many horrible, gruesome things in my career. I'll spare you. Suffice it to say, at that point in my life, I should have been numb to torsos without heads and heads without faces and bodies crushed, burned, battered, and broken beyond recognition. But something about the black quarry, the shivering trees turning their backs, the steel-colored sky, the vacant, vacuumed air, and the dead-lock sneer Lisa gave the bubbling water, made me gag upon sight of a young girl's broken gut when her corpse cut the surface of the water. I imagined Lola in the future at some meal we'd silently pick through after this horrible day, 'Liu, with what I got to see in basements and crawl spaces and abandoned quarries, spare me the pleas about "your food" or "your tobacco" or "your drinking" or "your belching",' or whatever it was she bathed in to soothe her barbed memories.

Lisa held a frigid hypnosis at the dead girl. She had one arm across her bulging stomach and another up to her chin, as though she were delivering a hearty philosophical college lecture. Her wet hair was plastered to her skull and face.

I dropped the rope when Lisa turned away from the water. The body and board plummeted back to the depths of the quarry. Lisa walked up along the top of the quarry, down the other side, and to Boyd and Lola and Brad. When Lisa winked at Brad in her passing and shot his face with an air gun, blowing invisible smoke from the top of her finger, I wished she were my daughter. She exited down the path Boyd had led us on, offering no invitation for us to follow, but of course we did, landing in her soggy footsteps and trying to catch up, gun prodding the whimpering Brad to move along.

Lola and I knew well enough to just follow. We motioned to Boyd with our fingers to our mouths for him to likewise stay silent. All the way back to the schoolhouse, across a small area for parking, down a wooded path, at the end of which was an empty space beneath a willow tree, we marched. Pregnant Lisa paced like an angry cat, and when Boyd went to say something, I shushed him.

Again we followed our teenage ruler back through the wooded path and to the school house. We stood waiting for directions, all looking at Lisa, in front of one of the wings. Lola had placed Brad, cuffed and legs tied to a hook, in the bed of the F-150.

'I don't know where The Doctor works. Where is Dorothy? She must have gotten away in the van.' Lisa said to me.

'What do you mean? Who is The Doctor?' I said.

'He's the one who delivers the babies,' Lisa said.

'The otha girl, she Dorothy? My cousin took her to the 'mergency room.'

Lisa nodded a confused approval.

I was about to ask more questions when out of the corner of my right eye, I saw Lola, sniffing her way through another door at another wing. She seemed entranced by something beyond the door, entering the building without motioning me or anyone else to follow.

'She probably smells the asshole I burned up in my jail cell. Tell her not to touch the water. It might still be electrified.'

Behind me, Boyd said, 'Ay-yup. That's the smell I told ya about. Door up there is locked.'

Lisa handed me the keys she held clutched in her hand.

I ran to Lola.

What we found on the third floor trumps any story of any circus bear dressed in pink.

* * *

After Lola and I saw what we saw in what I learned was Lisa's former room of incarceration, Lisa said nothing more to plead her case. All she said was, 'Agent, we'll set up a sting for this afternoon. I'll lure them in. You catch them.'

Lola was already convinced, nodding her head to Lisa, agreeing with whatever our young mother demanded. Lola smelled blood and wanted to swallow it in gulps down her gullet.

'Agents, I was supposed to join that girl in the quarry today.' She rubbed her girth, hugging the baby. 'I cannot explain the depths of my hate for these people. You've seen what I'm capable of, what I did to their goon upstairs. I want to destroy them. And I will. I will hunt them down and poison them slowly, unless you agree to lay a trap and arrest them all today. I must be the bait. It is the only way. I've thought it over a million times.'

I had no doubt she had.

'Lisa, tell us your plan,' Lola said.

With what I would later learn amounted to a wide grin in the emotionless girl, Lisa clicked her eyebrows and slightly lifted her chin toward Lola. A sign of respect. A sign of thank you.

Lisa detailed her plan. It was simple really. She said we needed to force Brad, at gunpoint to his temple, to call The Doctor and tell him she was in labor. 'The Doctor seems to travel with The Obvious Couple, so he'll bring them with him, they're so anxious to take my baby. We'll snag them all together. Got it?' We agreed we'd have my back-up agents, who were close to arriving, stakeout the hotel of The Obvious Couple and office of The Doctor – which we'd first confirm before allowing Brad to place his call – in case his accomplices somehow got tipped off. I wanted Lisa's plan to work, to capture them all together at the Appletree, for a few reasons:

Appletree was a secluded spot and civilians would not get hurt in a shoot-out.

Them driving to the premises after being beckoned by Brad would be solid evidence of their involvement.

Lisa had asked, and I agreed she deserved, to see them face-to-face, outside of the restrictions of a courtroom or prison. Or witnesses.

I later got enough details to understand what Lisa meant by The Doctor and The Obvious Couple. She also explained that Brad was not the 'Ron Smith' – Ding-Dong – I thought he was, but rather his twin brother. Obviously shocked, I had a million questions to ask of her. But at the time, I just said, 'Okay. Let's go over your plan one more time.' There was no way I was going to insert my own design into Lisa's war. I was her sudden soldier. Lola happily hoisted her gun as a crouching sniper in an apple tree in the adjoining orchard. I reluctantly reminded her not to shoot if the clan we expected was unarmed. Her left nostril twitched like she might bark, and her finger curled tighter around the trigger. I left her in the tree and hoped she'd obey, planning to back her up if she didn't.

I'd called my bureau back-up and had them meet me at Cousin Bobby's so I could hand off Brad to one team, and instruct the other team on where to lay low and hold sniper spots. I didn't mention to them Brad's failed attempt to 'flee' the back of the truck where we tied him up, cuffed; didn't mention the deal we struck with him, in private. A private deal between me, Brad, and Lisa. After removing Brad's scarf-muzzle before delivering him to the other agents – who actually followed protocol and wouldn't have gagged a prisoner – I was forced to listen to his histrionic whining about the hole in his face, which made me wish I'd left him on the bottom of the quarry. What a ball of crazy he was, vacillating between a high girl voice and a demented demon, his pitch constantly shifting as I pushed him through the field to Cousin Bobby's. When we passed a mooing cow and he looked her in the face to say, 'Big Bessie, aren't you just precious, now, Bessie,' and then shifted to a growling yell, 'I'll slice your babies into veal, bitch,' I became concerned he'd walk on an insanity defense.

It went down just as Lisa expected. The Doctor came hauling up in a brown-on-caramel El Dorado, The Obvious Couple his passengers. This Mr Obvious and his wife, the Mrs Obvious, had been holed up in a local motel, ironically – and horribly named – The Stork & Arms, waiting out the time until their bundles of stolen joy came into the world. They planned to abscond to Chile, to their chic and tree-covered mountain retreat, nestled among five vineyards and the bliss of a southern hemisphere. Blond babies would be their ultimate art in a practical castle of paintings and sculptures. Lola and I were allowed to visit the estate when a team inventoried the place. We found so much documentary evidence tying them to our crime and several others, such as high-profile art thefts, we lost count of the charges.

On the day we nabbed them, Lola pounced from the tree to kick dirt in their eyes for taking from her the chance to shoot them, for they showed up unarmed and duped.

'Check,' Lisa said, while I cuffed The Doctor.

Being a chess player myself, I wondered why she didn't say 'checkmate,' as in, 'game over', but I soon learned Lisa had more planned for The Doctor.

CHAPTER TWENTY-FOUR

Liu, he's so dramatic. I know he's told you all about his childhood scare. How he came to be what he is. I think what he did for his brother was flat-out marvelous. Genius. When he told me his story, I decided he should be my eternal best friend.

Of course, I would have handled his brother Mozi's situation much differently. But let's not dawdle on impolite criticisms. Besides, Liu should be championed for his superior pupil cones and what I suspect to be an impressive amygdala and hippocampus, along with enhanced connectivity between the two. The circuit between these brain parts in Liu is likely a superhighway with huge neuron trucks barreling back and forth with payloads of rich sensory and factual experience: memory. My theory is that Liu's heightened visual acuity mixed with a larger than normal amygdala and hippocampus is what provides for his scary recollection of details. I'd need to split his skull and dissect his eyes to be really sure – I don't trust the accuracy of MRIs – but I'm not about to perform an autopsy. On a friend.

Nevertheless, how tenacious, how calculating, how heroic Liu was for Mozi. How very cool. I flipped on Love, Admiration, and Devotion all for Liu when he told me that story. But at first, when he saved me, or rather, when he helped me save me, I didn't turn on a thing. I used him as yet another asset: Agent Liu, Asset #49.

Liu provided the distraction I'd hoped for, opened my submerged door, and helped me bag the rest of them. So, to me, on that day, he seemed rather useful. When he finished cuffing The Doctor and The Obvious Couple, he and 'Lola' – this is how I've been asked to refer to Liu's partner – drove me to the hospital in a Ford truck. Lola wedged in the middle because my width was too wide to fit behind the stick shift. How cozy the three of us were, as if a farming family on their way to shovel seed. As for an ambulance, which might have been a more proper mode of transportation under the circumstances, they didn't trust leaving me to anyone else, and I refused to go in one anyway.

The other agents detained the farmer man, Boyd, at his 'Cousin Bobby's' farmhouse to answer questions. I really liked the speech Boyd gave Brad when he pointed his rifle in his face at the quarry. I later asked Nana to embroider me a pillow with this monologue – and you know what – given her darker view of the world anyway, what with her crime writing, and given her uncontained joy at my rescue, she considered my request. She joked about using purple thread in a cursive and appliqués of fuzzy, frolicking rabbits, tumbling over forest rocks, to signify Boyd's 'run like a rabbit' line. Ultimately, however, as I knew she would, Nana used our conversation as an opportunity to teach me about proper emotional reactions to highly stressful situations. She finished the pillow with just the rabbit appliqués and 'I Love You' embroidered on the front. I love Nana. Never turn Love off for Nana.

The worst thing I ever witnessed in my life – so far – happened only four hours after I fried my jailer and ensnared his accomplices. This bloody image of Post-Incident, Hour 4, hardened my resolve to exact even more revenge. Triple revenge.

Almost as soon as they jailed The Doctor and Mr and Mrs Obvious, I was admitted to the hospital for observation. Agent Liu and Lola never left my side. I know now, there is no other place Liu would have rather been except with me. Sadly, back then, I was one of only four lost children he'd found alive – not counting Dorothy, but counting his brother. Upon entering my hospital room after gathering us Cokes and Fritos from the vending machine, he smiled apologetically. Lola paced in the doorway like a caged and bloodthirsty tiger, fending off anyone who might even begin the thought of trying to talk to me. I really liked her. My mother would love her.

'Hello there, trooper,' Agent Liu said to me.

'Hello there.'

'They say you're doing absolutely fine.'

'Yeah, I'm fine. But what about Dorothy? Can I go see her yet?'

'Dorothy is not doing well. If I brought you down there, well, you should be prepared. Her prognosis is not so good.'

'Is she going to make it?'

'Honestly, her blood pressure is very bad. She's not doing well. If only I found you both sooner.'

'Were you the only one looking for her?'

'Unfortunately, yes, just me, and my partner, of course.' He swung his head in Lola's direction. She grunted.

'That is sad, Agent Liu.'

'It's a fucking crime is what it is.' He paused, blowing out his cheeks and popping them. 'Sorry. I shouldn't swear in front of you.'

'Oh, don't worry. I just charbroiled a man. I think I can handle some rough words.'

Lola sniggered and mouthed 'charbroiled', as though loading the phrase in her internal vernacular for later use.

'Hey, could I borrow some money until my parents get here? I would really like to get Dorothy something.'

'Anything you want.' He pulled out his wallet and handed me two twenties.

Liu and a nurse helped me into a wheelchair, which I found grating and insulting. But they refused to let me walk around the hospital, even though I'd just escaped a prison and saved another girl. I suppose, in hindsight, they had a point. I was eight months pregnant, severely dehydrated, exhausted, face wounded, and I suppose, okay maybe it's true, I was physically weak. Fine.

At the gift shop, I bought Dorothy a fluffy bouquet in a delicate pink vase, a combination Nana would love.

As Liu and I got off at the second floor and walked along the corridor toward Dorothy's room, I noticed police officers on guard and who I now know as Dorothy's parents and heart-sick boyfriend – he'd apparently been on the news with the parents begging the world to find their beloved Dorothy. Dorothy was stolen three hours away from somewhere in Illinois, so they were able to drive hell-bent to her bedside in lightning time. My parents were still waiting for their plane at Logan airport in Boston. My Lenny would not be making the trip; he hates planes. I figured I'd call him after visiting Dorothy – didn't mean I didn't love him. I knew he was there for me. No hastened, blubbering reunion would change any of that.

Dorothy's parents rushed to me, expressing their gratitude and grief in sobbing hugs. I believe I can still taste Mrs Salucci's salty tears, running down my cheek and into the corner of my dry lips.

They hugged me in the hall so long and tight, keeping me from viewing Dorothy.

We were about to disconnect from our tri-person huddle, but Dorothy's scream froze us in a merged state. We darted heads in her direction, a three-headed dragon.

I must spare you at this point. What I saw was too gruesome, too sad to repeat. In broad brushstrokes, as an impressionist painting faded by age and covered in dust might reveal, I will only say, she spilled practically all of her blood and something else too and died in a raging agony twenty minutes later.

They said her preeclampsia was mild and she would have done quite well under the most minimal of care, which they said even the lowest scoring OB/Gyn would give. They also said with her untreated preeclampsia, her immeasurably high stress, and an infection she incurred while in captivity, her body was a cauldron of heat, burning up within, imploding her skin and organs, veins, and life, hers and her child's.

No, no real words can describe that moment, because what I saw was not blood, but rather the very essence of death. The death no mortal can ever really view, except if they are condemned and in their own dying minutes find themselves in a house of mirrors. But there unleashed death, unbidden and proud, swallowing the lives within. Remaining in the hall and looking into her room, I disintegrated, watching death unfurl. Dorothy's room was framed by a pulsing black. Skin bubbled in the background. The foreground held a river of red – a river, a true river of red – the whole of the room filled with this scene. Not one speck of light, no white, no angels, no hand of mercy lifted even a peg from this black frame. Someone might have whisked me away. Someone might have jumped when I smashed the vase of peonies.

Someone might have pulled me, pushed me, dragged me crying, thrashing, fighting, punching, screaming. Someone might have calmed me with a quick shot to my thigh. Someone, anyone, everyone might have done these things. I'm not sure.

I woke up eight hours later with bruises and a hoarse voice and a patch of stitches on my ankle from a glass shard I'm told bounced off the floor during my outburst at death. Beside my bed stood my mother, holding my hand; behind her stood my father, looking over her shoulder, tears staining his face. Agent Liu and Lola crossed each other as marching guards in the doorway, scaring anyone who might even begin to think about approaching my room.

Perhaps I only imagine Dorothy's final death throes, I don't know. I just know the first image and her scream are for me, an eternity.

This is why you don't turn on your Love switch unless absolutely necessary.

CHAPTER TWENTY-FIVE

The Trial

I knew enough about *mens rea* to be dangerous. Although she is a civil trial and government enforcement attorney, my mother kept her criminal law Bar Exam book. The one chapter on criminal intent or *mens rea*, a culpable state of mind, fascinated me. I read it when I was fourteen and again when I was fifteen and again when I was sixteen, after the whole ordeal. I was obsessed with *Law & Order* and true crime documentaries. For a death sentence to stick, or my fallback, the life sentence without parole, I'd make damn sure there was no doubt in the minds of jurors that The Doctor – the only one who got a trial – had *mens rea*. As with my captor, my revenge plan for this villain had triple layers of insurance. The receptionist took a plea. The Obvious Couple, a plea. Brad? Brad is another story, so let me not get ahead of myself just yet.

If you're a legal scholar reading this, you may be confused why the federal government didn't try The Doctor in a federal trial and why it was Indiana who got the spoils of war. I don't know the details, really, but some sort of exchange was made between Liu, the Feds, and Indiana, which allowed Indiana, the one we thought most committed to throwing criminals in a dirty hole, to hold the golden keys to damnation.

As the months ticked closer to trial, The Doctor became especially villainous; he's the only one who wouldn't accept the prosecution's onerous plea deals or try Brad's road to continual judgment, and thus the only one who insisted on a trial by his peers. *What peers?* I kept thinking. *How could he possibly have peers? He killed Dorothy. He could have saved her. He's not human. He's not even good enough to be an animal. He's a lesser form. He's nothing. Peers?*

Since they'd block me from entering The Doctor's holding cell with a machete, I worked hard at his conviction. A conspiracy to kidnap and attempt murder – both felonies – would be easy to get, and since people died in the commission of these felonies, his offense was punishable by death. So far, so good. A death occurring in the commission of a felony is a murder attributable to all conspirators, even if they did not pull the trigger as they say, or, in my specific case, push the deceased into a box spring pool to drown and electrify, or purposefully leave a pregnant teen and her fetus to die avoidable deaths.

As anticipated, The Doctor argued that Dorothy would have died regardless of and not 'but for' the felony. A drowning rat will claw at any splinter floating in the ocean. I could not allow The Doctor's argument to go unchecked, so I prepared my testimony.

Courtrooms are actually quite similar to what you see on TV. The one in which I testified had dark wood paneling to about eight feet high on the four windowless walls. The pews for the onlookers, interested family members, courtroom junkies, media, and sketch artists were about ten rows deep. Past them and through a hip-high swinging door, were large tables, the left side for the prosecution, the right for the asshole loser defendant. At the very front was the Judge's raised bench, a seat to her side for a witness, and the court reporter in front.

The Doctor's trial took place six months after I was freed, fast-tracked really, and I'd slimmed back down to my prenatal size. On the day I was called as the star witness, I sat outside in a wooden chair, the kind with the indents for your butt cheeks, and I swung my feet, dressed in stylish leather Mary Janes. Mother refused to allow the prosecutors to dress me as some frumpy, poor castaway just to garner jurors' sympathy. She said such a show would encourage 'reverse bias' or 'reverse discrimination' and was 'lazy lawyering.' Oh, don't you worry, Mother had her claws firmly sunk in the prosecution's strategy, and she knew what she was doing. She was the best trial lawyer anyone could ever hope to have.

My black shoes matched nicely with my simple, black, cap sleeve dress, which had two straight pleats darting from the hip seam. Of course it was lined. Of course it was from Italy. Of course it cost a fortune. Mother lent me her best pair of giant diamond studs, which was the only jewelry she afforded my appearance in court, much to the discontent of one of the raggedy state female prosecutors who wanted me in a string of innocent pearls.

'Pearls? Pearls? Good Grace, woman, pearls are for insipid sorority girls and underappreciated wives. Pearls are not for my daughter. She's better than that.' Mother later told me that pearls are also for slutty idiots who don't know good fashion and only think pearls are good fashion because 'Audrey Hepburn wore them in *Breakfast at Tiffany's*.' She forced air through her nose and continued, 'But, film is film, and she's Audrey Hepburn, and that's the single instance in history when pearls were okay.'

So there I sat in the court's wooden chair, clad in a rich black dress, looking funereal but wealthy, not wearing any pearls, when they called my name to enter the court. On my way in, I passed Mrs Obvious, who had just left the stand and was being escorted out by the sheriff. The prosecution had offered her a deal in exchange for her testimony against The Doctor, and had also wanted her to dress as she would otherwise and not enter in or exit in cuffs, even though she was in state custody, serving time on her plea. The prosecutors and Mother didn't want any visual reminder to the jurors that Mrs Obvious was a criminal. The Doctor's 'peers' knew enough.

So Mrs Obvious passed me and how striking she looked in that country courtroom. She wore a pink silk blouse with a black cashmere skirt, stockings, black patent leather pumps, and, of course, pearls. Big, round, expensive pearls. Her hair had been coiffed for court and her makeup applied as if she were going to a gala. She was in her late thirties, so she was young, and, despite being a complete demon, rather beautiful, with her long, rich chestnut hair in an updo, so as to showcase her high cheek bones. Her nails were impeccable in a dark cherry, and her wedding ring must have been twelve carats. Walking with an air of indifference, her back stiff, her nose tilted, she pranced by me and sneered down, as though she'd flicked me off her shoulder-padded shoulder.

I held back the wink I wanted to give Mother, who sat behind the state prosecutor, for she was the one who predicted Mrs Obvious would do this, and she was the one who insisted on the precise timing of my entrance. Mother and I both looked to the jurors. I noted how they noted Mrs Obvious' display of superiority too. A neat man in a salmon-colored sweater mouthed 'damn' and jotted something in his juror's notepad.

Manipulating these fine details, predicting the personalities and actions of others, balling all the minutiae into a legal strategy, was the game of trial lawyers, who are no more than masters of theatrics. Producers and lead actors rolled into one. I almost got the bug to go into law myself from the whole experience, but how dreadful to spend your life in those windowless coffins they call courtrooms.

You already know the full extent of my interactions with The Doctor. I've told you, he came on three different days: once by himself when he had cold fingers, during which he said nothing; once with Mr Obvious for all of one minute, and again really said nothing; and the last time, when he violated me with the ultrasound wand for Mr and Mrs Obvious and referred to my captor as 'Ronald', That was it. I knew nothing about him, except that he caused Dorothy's death by refusing to treat her. I didn't even know what he looked like, until the day we ensnared him at the Appletree. He was drunk that day, disheveled and overweight. He wore a ratty vest over a light brown button shirt with sweat stains in the armpits. Brown corduroy pants completed his costume of brown. He looked like a log of wood. When Lola cuffed him, I noticed his fly was down. When I said 'Check' to him, he toggled his head so I could look straight into his red-veined eyes, and then he belched.

But six months later, when I passed through the swinging doors of Courtroom 2A and waltzed up to the witness stand, I found a completely transformed man. The defense had given him a pin-striped suit, a white-collared shirt, and a tasteful red tie. He could have been a politician or a banker. His face was slick-smooth and his hair waved and gelled like Superman's. Frankly, if I didn't know he was a monster, and if I allowed for rampant female hormonal fluctuations, I might have formed a crush on him. Instead, with the jurors to my left and unable to see my turned face, I provided him an ever-so-subtle wink and flicked my eyebrows, letting him know the game was on.

He stiffened, breathed in deep, and hunched his shoulders to his ears, appearing like a cat scared of the full moon.

Recall, The Doctor's defense was that Dorothy would have died regardless of and not 'but for' the felony. And I knew all this because Mother didn't let anything fly by me.

I sat in the witness chair, nodded hello to the kind but firm lady Judge Rosen, sitting higher than me in her Judge's perch. I swore on a Bible, answered the questions of who I was and where I lived and other biographical foundation points, identified The Doctor as the man who examined me, and then added the missing ingredients needed by the prosecution.

With my eyes down, I sniffled my nose in a certain way that I've found produces tears. When my eyes were wet enough, I looked to a sympathetic grandma in the jury and explained how on two occasions The Doctor told my captor: 'Dorothy would do well in a hospital. But who gives a shit. We're throwing her in the quarry as soon as she gives birth anyway.' I added a flourish on this lie by saying he chuckled like a cartoon villain whenever he said this. Then I garnished it all by saying he also said, 'Let's wait it out. Maybe she'll get better and the baby will be fine, and we'll have two babies to sell. Otherwise, we'll throw them both in the quarry as planned. We are obviously not sending her to the hospital. If she continues to decline, stop feeding her.'

The Doctor yelled, interrupting my testimony, 'That's not true. That's not true at all!'

I slunk into my chair and feigned fright, sucking my bottom lip while pleading with bulging eyes for the good judge to protect me. Tick-tock, crocodile tears did flow.

'Your Honor, it is true. It is true,' I cried.

'You will sit down and hold your tongue in this courtroom, sir!' she bellowed. 'One more outburst and I'll find you in contempt. Do you understand me?'

Silence.

'Do you understand me!'

'Yes, Ma'am, yes, Your Honor,' The Doctor said, with head bowed, sitting back down.

But then defense counsel popped up, and their table performed a Whac-A-Mole game. The Doctor popping up and down and counsel popping up. I had to suck in my cheeks and tilt my view to stare at a water stain on the court's ceiling so as not to laugh at such slapstick. I also did that eye maneuver again so the tears could continue crocking on down my pretty little face.

'Apologies, Your Honor, there will be no further interruption,' defense counsel said.

Mother told me this would happen. She said I could say anything at all up on the stand because the defense would be loath to call me a liar in front of the jurors. At most, they'd question my ability to recall details and events accurately, but they wouldn't call me a liar. Mother didn't know in advance I was actually going to lie. I didn't want her to bear that burden. I had no problem bearing it myself.

Still, I did catch her skeptical look, which turned into a smirk of pride, when I tearfully pleaded with the judge about my truthful testimony. Mother knows I don't cry, and she'd heard my account of my time in confinement a thousand times, during which I knew enough to give some vague indication that I'd heard The Doctor say certain things – but I'd never really given the details. I had wanted to keep my options open on where my story might go, make sure the tale went where the prosecution needed. So, Mother knew enough to be skeptical.

Everyone settled back down, and Judge Rosen shouted at

the prosecutor, 'Well, continue then. Go on. I want to get to a good point for a recess.' Turning to me, she said, 'You okay to continue?'

'Yes, Ma'am,' I said, in a timid but confident voice.

The prosecutor rolled around on his heels, picked up a plate and said, 'Exhibit 77.' Dorothy's Wedgwood plate.

'Yes, sir, that is the plate. The guy who delivered my food had her plate, too, in the beginning. I saw the letter "D" labeled on the front from the very start.' Lie. The prosecutor presented the note I found in the kitchen with the letter D, 'Exhibit 78.' 'Yes, that is the note. He must have delivered my meals first. But about a week before I escaped, he stopped bringing her plate when he came to my room. Sometimes, before that, I watched him through my keyhole eating off the same plate. In the bathroom garbage there were these Post-it notes with the letter "D" on them. He ate her food.' All lies. 'He must have been following The Doctor's orders to let Dorothy starve.' Most likely, a lie.

Defense counsel threw an apoplectic fit, practically cursing out objections to 'speculation' and 'lack of foundation' and blah, blah, blah, but in my side-eye inspection of the gasping jurists, I knew the damage had been done. *The bell has been rung,* I said in my subtle glance at The Doctor, who wrote notes and loudly whispered to his defenseless defense lawyer.

Checkmate, bitch.

I lied mercilessly and I sobbed on cue. Three jurists, including one man, cried. It was a disastrous day for El Doctor. *Boo-hoo. Rot in hell.* I have no remorse for my false testimony. Everything else I said was truthful, and I believed my testimony to be the truth anyway. If embellishing reality got the stiffest sentence possible and avoided the usual and despicable plea agreements, so be it. Justice would be served. Cold. On a toile-patterned Wedgwood china plate.

They dredged the quarry to find three girls and two fetuses. The surviving baby, they found living in Montana with the couple that purchased him. Their story is another legal saga. The Doctor argued most vocally about the quarry and denied being involved in the 'past murders.' He claimed that while on a week-long drug haze during one of his frequent Vegas benders, he met the receptionist through his bookie, who he was in to for a cool seventy grand – what with his gambling and cocaine addictions. The receptionist – who falsified her resume to get jobs at rural clinics around the country – linked the band together. The receptionist had actually scouted Dorothy months and months before she was taken, given that Dorothy tried to do the right thing and sought medical care as soon as she'd missed her period. The criminals let her stew in her pregnancy at home, until they snagged her, at which point, the receptionist had unfortunately moved on to my town.

Anything happening before or during Dorothy's

incarceration, however, The Doctor 'was not involved,' he claimed. 'They brought me in because they botched some prior C-sections. They might have done the surgeries themselves, I don't know, or they may have had another physician,' he told Agent Liu.

Predictably, he pled the Fifth at trial. The prosecution forensically analyzed his past patterns and records and came up with inconclusive evidence of prior involvement. As such, Judge Rosen barred mention of the bodies in the quarry, but not the fact of the quarry's existence on the property, as it had been a threat about which I testified. Good old Judge Rosen snapped at the prosecutor, 'Connect the dots and bring me a new case on the other murders.' I was not comfortable in taking my missionary fiction to this level, so I declined to connect those dots myself. I could have easily testified, 'The Doctor made reference to "the others in the quarry" and "throw them in just as we did the others".' But, I had a level of doubt as to his involvement with these other victims, and I had to trust that justice would find a way, eventually.

As it turns out, 'D', Dorothy, had been in captivity for one week longer than me. When the detectives scoured the boarding school, which Brad bought in a foreclosure auction two years prior, they found a 'lost and found' bin and a teachers' lounge. They surmised my pencil case came from the bin and Dorothy's knitting supplies and books from the lounge. They also speculated that Dorothy made my red blanket before my arrival and that my captor stole it from her. I choose to believe she knit with her fingers on fire, looping and purling with a furious intent of offering a weapon to our war chest.

Why would a captor give his victim knitting needles? Aren't they sharp? Can't they do harm? From holding Dorothy myself, I can tell you, she was weak; her arms were thinner than mine. Short too, about 5'1". But worse yet, she was riddled with pain, incapable of walking down the steps for rescue without my support. You'd think the adrenaline drummed up at being freed would supply some strength. Not so. So, no, I'm sure our captor was not concerned the needles would be used against him. Plus he was dumb.

We learned from the rough interrogation of The Obvious Couple the bizarre plan of how I had been taken as insurance in the event Dorothy and her baby did not survive, and how The Obvious Couple would raise both babies, if they both lived, as twins. In identical, lawyer-coached statements, they insisted in their separate interviews, 'We swear, we never intended for the girls to be killed. We were told they would be sent home.'

How does this reduce their culpability? The lead prosecutor said their sentence would be less than death. He showed me the law and tried to convince me that the best he could do was seek hefty sentences. I dumped his coffee in the station sink and told him to try harder. Mother urged me to give him a break.

I dumped my hot chocolate in the sink.

I told you she was soft. Even if she was right.

I suppose my tempers calm as the years roll on. Still, sometimes, only sometimes, I catch myself waiting for their release. Admittedly, I've crafted a rough plan in the back of my mind *or sketched out in a numbered itinerary and ordered progression of actions, weapons honed, assets lined.*

As for The Doctor, I was relentless, insatiable, mad with revenge. A conspiracy for justice is no aberration of the laws of Mother Nature, although it might be an aberration of a legislature's over-generalized and unworthy laws.

My mother took a leave of absence. She used up all her favors to get appointed to assist the prosecutor. CEOs she'd saved from white-collar jail who had senators for sons moved whatever mountains she pointed to blocking her way. 'I'm not about to let some government-paid first-year second-chair this case,' she said. She had the devil in her, just as I had.

I did try with her, right before trial. We were once again in her study at home; she sat in her throne chair, absorbed in forcibly editing the prosecutor's Motions *in Limine* – these are pre-trial motions both sides file in an attempt to bar certain evidence and bar certain arguments. Since it was early December, and since everything was picture perfect in our

New Hampshire home, the Christmas lights on our early-cut tree in the adjoining foyer reflected a rainbow of colors on her deeply waxed floor. The spotlight outside her window revealed a thick falling snow on the dark night. I was warmed, standing by the roaring fire in her office fireplace, waiting for her to look up from the massacre she gave those draft motions. My baby boy was snoring upstairs, his rounded belly so full of milk and his onesie so soft on his silk skin, I figured he might sleep an eternity with a burpy baby smile etched in his perfect, chubby cheeks.

I watched her. She didn't relent in marking up the pages, flipping angrily, muttering things about the prosecutor's writing, such as, 'Drivel', 'For Fucking Crying Out Loud', 'Moronic', 'Do you even know what commas are?' 'Mother of all that is, what?' 'Seriously?' And, 'I'll just have to write this from scratch, I guess.'

As she continued murder-editing, I recalled my time in the VW with Brad. I remembered how I had vowed to try with Mother. While turning toward the fire and placing my palms closer to the flames for nearer warmth, I continued my maternal observations. How she moved her Cross pen across the page, biting her lip as she read new paragraphs, X'ing whole those paragraphs, I wondered, *could I love her? Openly?*

I turned on my Love switch for Mother. And as I did, I remembered I had tried this long before. The experiment didn't end up good then, nor did I think it would end well this time. The emotion for her was too painful. A slow sweat formed on my neck, and a wave of nausea buckled my stomach. It seemed as though a hand were squeezing my heart. I continued to try, but with the trying, my muscles seized in anxiety. *When is she going to leave again for another trial and for how long? Will she ever look up to see me here, in her office? Will she give me any time away from her work? Play a game with me? Talk to me about nothing important? Joke? Tell me a joke?*

I continued to try. I continued to worry. My anxiety revealed itself in a deep breathing, and then I began to cry. In her office. In front of her. And embarrassment accompanied my love.

'Lisa, Lisa. Oh my, Lisa. What is it?' she said.

She jolted from her chair and crossed the room faster than as if I had sat my body in the well of the fireplace to burn myself. Encapsulating me, kissing my cheek, she kept repeating, 'Lisa, Lisa, Lisa.' I don't know if she remembered the time when I was eight and had tried this and reacted the same way, but I did, and I recalled how I shut it all off then, just as I was committed to do again.

So I could convey what I really felt, I chose to keep Love on for one more minute, still fretting she'd release her hold on me and return to her work.

Crying, I said, 'Mom, I do love you. I hope you know. It's just too hurtful to . . .'

'Lisa,' she said, hushing me by pressing my face into her cashmere sweater shoulder. 'Lisa, Lisa, Lisa. I am your mother. And although it breaks my heart to allow you to turn cold to me, it would be far too selfish for me to ask you to love me openly. I understand. If there's one thing I've learned in growing through raising you, is I understand. You are stronger than I could ever ask to be, and I quite like you that way. You're what I aim to be, you're my shining hope, my love. So if you need to stay strong, then you do whatever you need to do to be as strong as you can be. You've saved me, you've saved yourself, and I want you to always be just who you are. You are perfect. You are perfect. You are everything to me. Some of us have to bury our past in papers, darling. Some of us, well actually only you, are lucky enough to turn off switches. I think you're blessed. You're blessed, darling. I love you. Hush now.'

I allowed Love to encase her words in a titanium shell, locked her hug in there too, stored the whole shelled moment deep within my memory bank, and swayed with her a few more seconds in the glow of the fire. And as she pulled away to check my eyes, her hands on my biceps, I shut Love off, but kept Gratitude firmly on.

As for my actions in captivity and my testimony during the trial, I was a girl then, but I understand now how my mind worked, even if I had not yet harnessed the rationale behind my actions. My captor threatened to kill or take my child, and he meant to follow through with both threats. Because of this, he deserved to die at my hand. The others who were complicit with these threats also deserved to die, or rot in jail while being tortured. I am not ashamed for seeking revenge or for having to lie to do so. I am, however, ashamed that I failed to exact revenge more efficiently, in one act taken them all out. My assets, although wonderful, did not afford me such luxury.

Mostly, I'm ashamed of my abject disregard of time. Some days I can barely look myself in the mirror for having practiced so much for perfection, when I should have acted sooner and saved Dorothy.

CHAPTER TWENTY-SIX

CONVERTED PRISONS

Today, at age thirty-three, I sit in my lab and divert my attention from examining fingerprints by writing this story. On my driftwood desk is a picture of my son, who I labeled . . . I'm kidding, who I *named*, Vantaggio, which, if you don't know, means 'asset' in Italian. We affectionately call him Vanty. He is seventeen. He is beautiful. He, too, is a scientist, thank God *and his black butterfly angel.*

Vanty should be getting home from school soon. He'll be roaring down the driveway in the used black Audi he saved to buy – such a presence he cuts across the high school campus. I'm sure all the senior girls in his grade and the juniors below, the sophomores and the freshmen, long to nuzzle into his neck and bury their faces in his blond hair. But I don't really care how cute the rest of the world thinks he is; his after-school job is working in the lab with me, so he better get home soon and he better remember to get the mail at the end of this long driveway. No one is good enough for Vanty, anyway. And that's not me being biased. That's me keeping it real. I'm his mom. I would kill again and again and forever for him.

Above a red armchair in the corner by the decontamination chamber is a framed shard of china, which I stole before forensics bagged it for evidence. There is still a smear of *his* browned blood on this bone fragment, which I choose to believe is both his and that damn plate's blood, commingled in hell. When I got married, only three years ago and just as scheduled seventeen years ago, they asked if Lenny and I would like to register for china. I couldn't breathe from laughing so hard. Lenny, knowing I had transferred hatred of toile to all china everywhere, answered through his own laughter, 'We won't be needing any china, thank you.'

I'm looking at this framed art of crime today, thinking on the thing I need to pack in my pocket for my and Liu's visit to Brad's prison tomorrow.

After the ordeal, my parents rehired my evil-eye-curse-warding nanny, dependable Gilma. Because Vanty was born in June, I finished sophomore year – with a hired home tutor – and had the summer to cuddle with him. I know I am very lucky. I do. So many other girls have not been as fortunate. I honor them by allowing the switches that control feelings of gratitude and relief to remain open; I keep those for fear, remorse, and uncertainty sealed. And while I'm sure there is judgment and social commentary to be had about teen pregnancy, this tale is not about apologies or lessons in that regard.

My parents spent loads of money on family and personal counselors for me and for them and they supported me. I was lucky to have their unbridled love. But, I was lucky for them for other reasons too. All along, they provided Assets #34 and #35, a scientific mind and disdain, respectively. Had I not been able to divorce myself from my predicament and treat the whole event as a science problem, I would have crumbled under the weight of fear. And, had I not thought myself better than those despicable creatures, I might not have spent so many hours plotting their demise. Of those among you who call me a sociopath for my unwavering disconnection, then I ask what you would do if a man put a barrel of a gun to your baby and threatened to pull the trigger. You might welcome my demeanor and resolve. You might wish you had my science and fortitude. Sure, you'd use your assets in your own way, and I don't judge you for that, as I hope you won't judge me. After all, we all seek justice in our own ways. I seek mine without remorse.

My indelible time of torment is long over now, but my thoughts during it will never fade. I'll lock this manuscript away, for I fear with its finding might go the life sentences we did secure. The Obvious Couple, they'll be released next year, and, well, let's just say there are other safeguards in place as far as they're concerned.

There are three more things to mention. First, my husband, Lenny. Lenny has been my best friend since we were four years old. He agonized over my disappearance and pleaded with investigators to keep up the search. 'She did not run away,' he'd yell at them. He organized search parties and vigils and stayed up many nights with my parents strategizing my rescue. Lenny provided the very best asset of all: my condition, which ironically got me into the whole jam in the first place. Lenny – he's the compass to this little family of ours: me, Lenny, and Vanty. There's a few perfect lyrics in a perfect song that make me think of him. It's basically a guitar journey by Santana with a couple of lyrics sung by Everlast: *There's an angel with a hand on my head ... there's a darkness living deep in my soul ...*

There's still a darkness inside me. Every day, every minute, I battle the darkness, I fight the switches. Lenny, he's that angel with his hand on my head – leaving me to cool into some less malicious purpose. Perhaps Vanty too is a compass, but there are other things to consider with my developing Vanty. I lean most, we lean most, on Lenny for the moral road. Lenny's the one who remembers when we need to call relatives on birthdays; he's the one who handles the bills and the house maintenance and the life responsibilities. Vanty and I, it seems, are left to other requirements.

Second, my company. I am the Owner, President, CEO, Supreme Empress, and Ruler of my very own forensics consulting company. We hold contracts with law firms, police departments, corporations, wealthy barons and billionaires, and a handful of federal agencies I am not at liberty to divulge. One such agency inherited 'Lola' from the FBI, and this is how I get the good cases. As Liu has mentioned, given Lola's unconventional tactics, her obvious conflict of interest in contracting with me, and her constant status as 'underground and dark,' we need to keep her identity masked in this tale. Sometimes she brings suspects in off the grid and holds them in the basement here for questioning. I usually turn the green mixer in the company kitchen up high so as not to listen to her interrogations. I then deliver her batches of her favorite cookie, the cinnamon-and-sugar-laced snickerdoodle, and watch her swallow each cookie in one bite. One after the other.

I study crime scenes, analyze blood samples, dabble in metallurgy, defy chemical compounds, research, solve, and, as I am doing today, compare fingerprints if my lab tech calls in sick. I've testified as an expert witness for countless parties in countless trials. My building is filled with flat panel iMacs, the big ones. I recruit from MIT and Berkeley, the *summa cum laudes* only, and steal the top scientists from megacorps and governmental bodies by tempting them with high salaries and a lower-priced real estate market. I hired a very good consultant on staff as well, a former FBI agent, Roger Liu. He's about twenty-five years my senior and, besides my husband, he's my best friend in the world. His wife Sandra keeps us sane by reading us the sitcom scripts she writes in the office she shares with Roger.

I own instruments so advanced, NASA might believe my suppliers are aliens, and I develop even better ones, for which I hold several patents, on which I exact unconscionable licensing fees from those very same megacorps from whom I steal established scientists. I own my building, which I purchased with trust fund money Nana set up for me when I was born and which fully vested when I turned twenty-one. By that point, at age twenty-one, I had set my sights on this particular building for a good long five years. I had asked Mother to intervene with the banks and the state and the federal government, all of whom wanted to lay claim to this winged structure with rolling fields and an apple orchard. Quarry too. Mother did a fine job convincing my competitor buyers to hold their bloody horses.

I renovated and retrofit from the remaining shell of this former boarding school, one that presides over a field smelling of cows, and used to have a kitchen with long steel tables and a black oven. In Indiana. Yes, the very one. There are a couple of rooms on the third floors of Wings 1 and 2, which I converted into twin terrariums, at no small cost I might add. In these terrariums, I breed exotic, poisonous plants, tanked pit vipers, African tree frogs, and anything else I come across in nature that might 'leave a mark', I've labeled all of these assets 'Dorothy' and dedicated both rooms to 'Dorothy M. Salucci'.

Poisonous assets might be necessary someday, you never know. You know, if I'm ever asked to solve a crime involving their venom or such. Or, maybe if someone other than The Doctor helped to kill three girls and two unborn babies and thrown them in a quarry. Who knows . . .

The Dorothy M. Salucci Terrariums are powerful and lively, exotic, and dangerous, and only a fool would enter unprepared.

The quarry has long been dredged and drained. A team of landscapers filled the empty cavern with rocks and the top eight feet with vitamin-rich planting soil. For years, I've curated an amazing rose garden in the middle of the forest. There are lots of thorns among the tempting reds, sun-kissed yellows, blushing pinks, and special strain of blacks.

If you were to walk outside my no longer white building – now painted blue – you'd see my company sign just below a triangular window. It says, '15/33, Inc.'

And this is exactly what I'm doing right now as Vanty hauls his Audi down the dirt road far too fast for my taste. I've never switched off my Love switch for Vanty for even one millisecond, and because of this I am perennially traumatized by just about everything he does. When he plays basketball, will he suffer a concussion from all the fouling? When his best friend moved to another school, would Vanty make new friends? When he goes out with anyone other than me, if he were to eat a hot dog or a grape or a fistful of popcorn or any other lethal food, will anyone know how to perform the Heimlich – which is a recurring required course in our household, run by a paramedic I hire to come once a quarter. Can't practice this too much.

Vanty is getting out of his car, grabbing his backpack, and doing a pressed, closed-mouth smile to me, looking like a ten-year-old in my eyes, even though he is every minute of seventeen. All I want to do is kiss his creamy cheeks so as to feel once again the peachiness of his infancy, which no matter the years, no matter the lines on his face, will never fade to the feel of my mother's lips.

'Ah, Vanty, you sweet boy,' I say.

'Ma, I'm seventeen.'

'Whatever,' I say, returning to my regular, clinical self so he'll stop his forward movement away from me. 'Listen, Hal called in sick and we've got a big pile of fingerprints to clear. I'm going to need you to prep those slides for the university case. I'm not going to get to those until late tonight.'

'Yes, Mother,' he says, patting my shoulder and pecking

my cheek, as if my scientific analysis of major crimes is the most insignificant task in his easy-breezy-beautiful-cover-boy life.

If any other human in my employ so nonchalantly considered dirt samples from a murder happening on the campus of a major Ivy League university – hint, starts with an H and is in Cambridge, Massachusetts – I'd probably stare them into a trembling apology. But Vanty. Vanty has this unique quality, an asset of his own. And it's not just me, not just because I'm his forever heartbroken mother. It's with everyone he meets. He snakes you in like a charismatic megalomaniac. This one time, his little friend Franky went grocery shopping with us. They were about ten. Franky pocketed a 3 Musketeers, unbeknownst to me or Vanty. When the alarms sounded and a rent-a-guard stopped us in the parking lot, it was Vanty, not me, who controlled the situation. After much yelling by the guard and crying by Franky, the Musketeers having fallen on the tar, Vanty stepped to the scene, picked up the bar, handed it to the guard, and without a stitch of youthful sweetness and without a stitch of condescension, spoke to the cop as if he were his equal, assuming in his tone a matched intellect. The guard's nametag said, 'Todd X'.

'Todd, I'm really sorry about this. Franky here, he's my friend, and my mom and I are just trying to cheer him up. His grandma died last night and I think, Franky right, I think 3

Musketeers were her favorite? Right, Franky? What were you going to do, put this in her casket?'

Any other pre-pre-teen who'd delivered these same lines would have sounded like a total puke. But Vanty, and this is hard to illustrate, his delivery was as if he'd very simply known Todd his entire life and Todd was just another respected person in his life, just as respected as himself. Equality is what I think Vanty conveys and what he's taught me, because I study his techniques constantly. The perception of equality neutralizes and then entraps people. My theory is that this act plays to people's egos, and once played, they're sucked into Vanty's physical appearance, further satisfying their ego that someone so beautiful would take the time to talk to them.

Todd ended up paying for the candy bar.

I never could have pulled it off like Vanty – he's like melted chocolate on top of a Bundt cake, a perfect-fitting, sugary cover.

Was I mad that he lied? No. There are problems. And there are solutions. Problems and solutions. If Lenny were there, our moral compass may have been forced another way. But since he wasn't, we went with Vanty's solution. All in.

Is Vanty devious? I don't think so, but I do watch. And I worry. I think he's actually quite loving, but I want to be sure.

Vanty and I have two long-term inside jokes. And millions more short-term inside jokes. We laugh a lot, Vanty and I. Ever since he was a baby, I've sat in his room and either read to or talked with him before he coils in to his own sleep routine. I can tell Lenny listens in to our serious talks or tittering laughter by leaning his ear against the wall dividing our room from Vanty's room. Knowing this comforts Lenny, comforts me. Again, an angel with a hand on my head.

One of our long-running inside jokes is that before reading for the night, I pick an arbitrary time limit on how long I'll read and then set a vibrating timer that goes off in my pocket. 'I'll read for 21.5 minutes,' for example. When the timer goes off, I stop, playing a joke about being literal, then I close the book, which inevitably leaves a scene completely uncompleted or a thought undeveloped, or a sentence half-read, and thus, Lenny hanging. When I very first did this when Vanty was five, he cried because he was so enchanted with what was happening in the book, and he thought I was going to make him wait until the next night. And though I was only kidding about finishing my reading for the night, I was immensely relieved that my little boy felt so strongly for a story so as to cry real tears. Which meant he wasn't like me. He wouldn't be separate from the world, like me. The next time I stopped a story short because my arbitrary timer went off, he laughed at my lame joke about being literal, which is something I am often truly accused of, and so Vanty understood I was really teasing at my own expense. So he laughed. And I laughed. And we laugh every single time. I hope we still have this very personal joke going when I'm sixty and he visits with my grandchildren.

Our other long-standing inside joke is that we speak fake French when we're in public. But with Vanty, because of his disarming charisma, people actually believe he is speaking real French. Even a French woman once asked him, in broken English, what province he was from! While I do enjoy playing this con with Vanty, just for our own personal amusement and to fortify our insular life together, I have begun to worry about Vanty's heightened social abilities and whether they actually make him a man apart, separate from the world like me, but in a different way. I'm not really sure how far he can carry this skill or what it means or whether it's good or bad. With respect to Vanty, I try hard not to fall prey to my typical mode of categorizing everything and everyone in neat black and white boxes; rather, I work hard at allowing him organic growth. But now I wonder if certain aspects of him should be tamed or refined or reined in. Is it right that he reads body language like he breathes air? Is it normal that he commands a group to silence just by walking by and looking in? Did the principal just tell me last night that her 'advisory board' is made up of the PTO President, the Superintendent, and Vanty?

Despite Vanty's exceptional people skills, it is still Lenny in this trifecta of ours who remembers the family birthdays and the right Christmas presents to buy for grandparents and friends. Vanty doesn't *go to* people, they come to him. And I'm beginning to worry that this is somehow a scary, although useful, quality. Or maybe I'm just obsessing over every possible thing that might harm my precious boy someday and really, he's just perfectly fine. *Will I ever be settled and calm, easy in and out of his presence? Here he is before me, giving me that mock annoyed and loving eye roll again.*

'Get your ass inside and get my dirt slides together. And if you have any homework, you better get it done now, Mr Smartypants. We've got a lot of work to do. Oh, we're having homemade burritos for dinner – Dad's making them. So I guess you got your way again because I told him if he made those damn footballs one more time I was going to starve myself.' Vanty starts to walk away, but I stop him, not ready to release him from standing before me. 'Oh oh, and Grand Nana is coming in from Savannah tomorrow, so make sure your pit trap of a bedroom is clean,' I say, shooing him inside. 'And if you want to talk about *One Hundred Years of Solitude* tonight, let's do that. I'll read you my favorite passage for exactly 1.2 minutes.'

'Jun-a se in qua a twie,' he says in a very convincing fake French.

'Yeah, yeah, I love you too. Now go.'

I watch my beautiful, untroubled – although possibly frightening – boy glide inside 15/33 Headquarters. I begin

312

to dead head the purple wave petunias in the blue pots by the entrance so as to force away the sad tremble in my chin. *He'll be gone to college next year,* I remind myself.

To love someone so much you are heartbroken just to look at them. This, is to have a child.

* * *

I said there were three things to mention. Lenny. My company. And now, the last, and surely the least, Brad.

Vanty, Lenny, and Nana are the only ones for whom I keep the Love switch on all the time, without any moment of 'off'. For others, I'll switch on sometimes. And for others, Love is never on, only vast, unending hate and even, a distinct emotion of homicide. If it weren't for Lenny's angel touch on my head, several more people on this planet would be no more.

It's a new day at 15/33. After polishing this manuscript one last time, I lock it away, only to be opened and shared upon my death, just as Liu rolls up to our building. Liu's wife, Sandra, jumps out of the passenger side of their Ford F-150, the only vehicle Liu will drive anymore. I think he's on his fourth since I met him. Sandra is making ridiculous faces at him, asking him what best demonstrates a man's reaction to eating a 'shit burger.' As is a daily occurrence, she's working on some new sketch.

Personally, I think a man chewing a shit burger would

look like a cat does when dry-heaving a hairball, so as Sandra reaches the red kitchen door of 15/33, I show her my best impersonation of a cat hacking up a hairball. My own cat, Stewie Poe, meows disapproval at my theatrics. He's stretched in all his flabby stomach glory and reaching a lazy paw in an annoyed way because I've disturbed his first of thirty naps of the day. His gray fur sprawls from his resting body, and he looks like a ruling Pharoah in the way he lounges on the turquoise rug in front of the ocean-blue hutch – as close as he can be to his cat dish. Stewie is a real pain in my ass, jumping on my face when I sleep, loudly demanding chopped filet and white tuna fish instead of regular cat food. I've got no one to blame but me. I've always had real awe for how expertly cats expose their distaste of almost everything, how nonchalant they are in dismissing even the hand that feeds them. So, I pretty much cater to whatever Stewie wants. But I make him wear pink bells on his purple collar as my revenge.

'Hey there, girl, you ready?' Liu asks me, standing by his still-running truck.

'Yeah, yeah, I like it. Do it again,' Sandra says to me, as she passes through the kitchen doorway, approving of my shit-burger face.

'Liu, hang on, let me grab my coat,' I say, and I grab my white safari-style jacket, hanging on the red pegs by the door. As I do, I again demonstrate my hopefully comic face to Sandra.

'Perfect. That's how I'll write it then for this script. You guys don't be too cruel today,' she says as she pours herself a mug of coffee from the pot I brewed just for her. She heads into her writer's office after crouching with her mug to stroke Stewie's fat chin.

I walk backwards out the door, watching Sandra, continuing my contorting face-act for her, and hop into Liu's truck.

'She said not to be too cruel today,' I say.

Liu bounces his nose up as he swallows back a smile.

We're pretty much going to be as cruel as we can be today.

'Yeah,' I say. 'Sure.'

Liu's in his late fifties now. He's got a thick head of gray hair. He still works out like he's got some federal mission that requires him to chase kings of kidnapping through forests, so his body remains compact; his forearm muscles flex as he turns the wheel of the truck.

I know what he's thinking about, and I'm thinking it too. It was the bed of a truck, just like this truck, seventeen years ago, in which Brad slid down his scarf gag by aggressively using his tongue and teeth and tried to avoid our punishments by sucking gasoline from the tube of a spare gasoline can, down on his knees and with his hands cuffed behind his back and his legs tied to a hook. It was Lola who smelled the opened gas on the air, and Liu who ran and slapped Brad's face so hard we thought he broke his jaw. We'd been sketching out the capture of The Doctor and The Obvious Couple, standing in a circle by the hood of the truck, when, fortunately, the heavy odor rode the cold air like water down a steel slide – easy and fast. If Brad had succeeded in exiting the world, I would have had to wait until my death to trudge into hell to torture him. Thankfully, I don't have to wait.

Liu and I have made this particular trip two times in seventeen years. This is our third. We have to make this trip whenever Brad attempts to plead for clemency, beg for a shot at the parole board. Sometimes Brad needs to be reminded of what awaits him outside and how very lucky he is being tortured on the inside. Liu and I have friends in the Indiana State Prison system and also some informant-lifers for whom we may or may not have done a few favors. So we know everything. Literally everything.

We made a deal with Brad back in that truck: he allows himself to live, and we wouldn't seek death. Instead, we'd hand him over to the state for life, but under our unofficial supervision. Back then, in the heat of his capture, Brad was most distraught about the prospect of not death, but death row, a sentence he surely would have suffered: recall, all the young bodies in the quarry. When we presented the deal to Brad, a little glimmer awoke in him, a kernel of hope, just enough to make him want to live, which is exactly what we wanted. You could say Brad took a very special kind of plea deal, one Liu and I gave, and, as such, the special Indiana prison where Brad now stews was converted to my very own.

Liu doesn't take much convincing in aiding me in my enduring commitment to taunt Brad. He's been hardened ever since his brother Mozi failed at his third suicide five years ago. Sometimes I worry about Liu, and how he'll work all night on any of the cases we're hired to consult on – but then I switch off any worry emotion when I walk into his and Sandra's office and see her draping her body beside him, drawing him cartoons of his wrinkled brow. Some people accept their lot in life, go with it, persevere, and some of these people are rewarded with a good partner who props them up to climb every tree they need to climb in order to hunt and weed out every demon they seek to find.

We pull into the visitors' lot of our very own Indiana prison. After showing our IDs and approved passes and chit-chatting with our friends in the guard tower and stations, we wind our way to the visitors' room. I keep my safari jacket on and all of the pockets zipped and buttoned, concealing my present for Brad.

The visitors' room is an awful square of concrete blocks painted mint-green. Light mint-green, the most despicable and cheapest color a shoestring budgeted government can afford. Which is fine by me. I don't want the state spending my tax money on homing up the joint. Having to be surrounded by this nauseating color should be enough punishment to deter anyone from any crime, I think.

The rectangular, wired, and barred windows start ten feet up from the linoleum floor. About ten square tables fill the room. A woman in her sixties in a black handmade sweater nervously rolls a tissue in her hands, and not once does she look up at me or Liu. She looks sweet, like any grandma crocheting on a park bench. I assume she waits for a son who has severely disappointed her. Another woman, about early thirties, but with the aged and curled, cracked mouth of a sixty-year smoker, rounds her shoulders and crosses her arms at another table. She appears so tough, a criminal herself, and I swear she's planning to rip the hair out of my skull. I catch her ice-blue eyes and wonder how someone who could have been so beautiful allowed herself to throw it all away on some asshole behind bars. I want to talk to her, ask why she smokes so much, ask how someone with wise eyes cannot see. But I stop, reminding myself not to judge. *We all have our problems and devils to overcome, we all don't have the same support,* I say to myself, the same thing Nana has often said to me – teaching me perspective.

A barred door cracks open and in enters three cuffed men, followed by five guards who surround the room, guns ready at their hips.

'Oh hunny,' the black sweater woman weeps as she rises to

hug a neo-Nazi with a cross tattooed on his face. As she stands, her sweater rises, revealing the confederate flag tattooed on her lower back.

'Hey, Dad,' the ice-blue-eyed woman says to a white-haired man with the exact same glacier eyes. She too weeps, saying, 'Daddy, Daddy, Daddy,' into his shoulder, clearly wanting a return hug, which will not come because Daddy's arms are still cuffed behind his back.

Do not judge on first impressions. Always study further, I remind myself. *Everyone is a puzzle. Stereotypes are rarely fully correct.*

Brad sees me and Liu and tries to back out of the room.

'Sit down,' a guard gruffs, pushing Brad into a corner seat, far from the eavesdropping ears of Mr and Mrs Racist and Father-Daughter Blue Eyes.

Liu and I take our chairs opposite Brad and smile wide to his heavy, distressed breathing. The years have not been kind to Mr Fancy. When he was jailed, he was forty-three, so now he is sixty. He was balding gracefully back then, had that tight man-belly, but was impeccable, waxed, shaved, buffed, manicured, you name it. He belonged as some man's prized bride on South Beach. Now, Brad is a shriveled grape. He's lost some forty pounds over the years, and not due to exercise, due to unrelenting stress, which I may or may not have caused.

His orange jumpsuit falls off his skeletal frame like a

king-sized blanket on a toddler. His scalp is completely bald, but for the yellow knit hat he wears. His nails are filed, but not manicured, and his tarnished dentures reek.

'Your boyfriend knit you that hat?' I ask, mockingly acknowledging the ridiculous thing on this head.

'Still a little bitch panther.'

I place my hand on Liu's lap to prevent him from rising to strike Brad.

'Oh, Brad, it's okay. I understand you have to wear the hat. Harkin would be upset if he thought you didn't like it.'

The guard who had pushed Brad into the room laughs.

Brad turns to the guard, 'Oh tee-hee-hee, you mutton mouth.'

'Watch it, Brad. You'll sit here and listen to them as long as I damn well please. And your hat sucks. Harkin sucks at knitting. I'll tell him you said so,' the guard says as a warning and rather calmly.

Brad turns back to us, obviously squirming because the guard has him cornered.

Harkin owns Brad. He purchased him with the one grand I'd slipped through one of the guards. Harkin is an especially rough inmate, having choked three of his 'lovers' in another prison before being transferred. He's serving ten consecutive life sentences for ax-murdering all ten members of a rival bike gang, in their sleep. Killed their pets too. Weighing in at 350 pounds and standing tall at 7′1″, Harkin is the Redwood of prisoners. Therapists convinced him to knit to ease his constant irritation, and so Harkin knits, but only with yellow yarn, because that's the only yarn the state has, having confiscated a warehouse of Detroit-bound crates from an illegal import company in Gary.

Harkin is a terrible knitter. His yellow hat for Brad is so far from Brad's high-fashion days of velvet jackets and silk scarves.

'So, Brad, we hear you're trying to convince the state to give you a shot at parole again,' Liu says.

Brad stares back, only at Liu. To me he has turned sideways, leaning away in his chair, as though I am poking him with the point end of a long sword.

'You know, Brad, the deal was, you take a life sentence, no parole, and we wouldn't seek death row. You know we could have gotten death twenty times over, with all those girls you carved up, all the dead babies, everyone we found in your quarry and elsewhere. Remember our deal, Brad. Remember?'

Brad winces.

'What you want to come out of here for anyway? Aren't you comfortable?' I interject.

'Fuck you and your little bitch panther,' Brad growls to Liu while continuing to physically shy from me.

Liu and I stare back, waiting, and sure enough: 'Ha, ha, ha, you two, so funny,' he says in a high voice.

'So Brad, I hear you've taken up gardening,' I say, laying my hand on the table in a way to force him to finally look my way.

'So what's it to you, little bitch?' He sweeps the table with his eyes, still afraid to swivel in my direction and meet me eye to eye.

I unclasp one of the eight pockets on my jacket and pull out a leaf in a plastic bag.

'I heard you'd taken up gardening. When was this, about a year ago? You've got yourself a little plot in the prison's garden, eh?'

'Oh, you, so clever. Got all the goons working for you, spying on little old me.'

'I wouldn't call them goons. I'd call them friends,' I say, very seriously.

'Brad, listen up, listen close,' Liu says.

Brad stuffs himself back further into his chair.

'Anyway, you know what this is?' I say, pushing the plastic bag with the leaf toward Brad on the scratched table. The leaf is long and pointy, thin and leathery, and a deep green.

'Hmph,' Brad says, crossing and uncrossing his legs, shifting his head in his right hand, then left. Squirming. Fearful in the way the deepening lines on his face register his inner recoiling.

'Grew this myself, Brad. Went all the way to south China to snag a seed, all for you, Brad. All for you.'

Brad twitches.

'It's a special hybrid; one part oleander, some parts something else that grows in remote locations amongst grasses in Asia. One of the most fatal and poisonous plants available to man. Just one bite and your heart explodes.' I pop my lips and fan my fingers like the tops are fireworks. 'Pop,' I say and then pat my calm ticking heart.

The guard behind Brad stands erect and walks closer to his comrade, showing he doesn't want to hear this part of the conversation, but also showing he'll allow it to continue.

I lean toward Brad and whisper with a honey-dripping voice, as though I'm trying to seduce him, which I'm pretty sure is impossible anyway. 'All I need to do is grind up a leaf and slip it any time I want into your instant mashed potatoes. Could be while you're in here, or maybe, if for some impossible reason you get yourself out, when you're squeaking out an unemployed existence in the box of a shithole where you'll end up. I hear the burning pain from this hybrid is so excruciating, feels like gasoline burns your esophagus, rages in your chest, and dumps lava into your bowels, which are soon ripped open from within. And no one is going to care enough to do any investigation or toxicology on you, Brad. They'll be satisfied at calling it a heart attack. This leaf, this plant, looks a lot like the plants you grow in your garden. Easy to camouflage.'

'You bitch,' Brad spits, finally glaring up at me.

And this is the moment I came for. The moment he did not want to give me. The moment I get to remind him.

'You live at my mercy. Don't you forget it,' I say, stabbing my index finger on the bagged leaf of death.

Liu smiles. I grab the bag and replace it in one of my pockets, slowly.

Sure, I could have killed Brad a hundred thousand different ways. But killing Brad wasn't my, nor Liu's, *primary* goal. Number One on our Brad Bucket List was to insure that he, as Liu put it, 'Spend a lifetime in excruciating pain and unbearable humiliation.'

When I'd heard Brad was enthusiastic in taking up prison gardening, enrolled himself in prison horticulture classes, got out of bed early to rake and weed and seemed to smile and whistle in doing so, I gave him a year to let the pleasure of his hobby settle in. I wanted him to experience a true emotional loss. Choosing to threaten him with a poisonous leaf would enable a loss, a fear, a deathly reminder every time he entered his stupid five-foot plot of crappy roses and wildflowers and saw another green leaf. I might ratchet up the game by sending him a variety of plant life through the guards, all with scientific facts about how they might be poisonous – none of them would actually be poisonous because I wouldn't give him any weapons. And, soon enough, his pathetic garden would turn to dandelions and dirt and he'd have nothing to look forward to once again.

Some victims want their closure on justice; they seek the death penalty or give forgiveness. And I'm perfectly fine with that. Other people, like me, are willing to press on all fronts for a very long time to try to attain a true eye for an eye. For Brad, given his gruesome crimes, I could have burned him alive and pulled him from the flames in just enough time for his body to have seared but his organs to have not fatally cooked. But even this would not have equalized the delicate eye for eye balance, as far as I was concerned.

Liu nods to me as his silent question to see if I'm done. I nod back that I am, so as to allow Liu some parting words. He coughs to break the death glare I'm holding with Brad and says while standing, 'We're done here. You just sit tight and soon enough, don't worry, if you're a good boy and you stop trying for parole, which you'll never get anyway, you'll die of natural causes or Harkin will choke you. One or the other. And then your punishment in this life will end.' Liu stops to stifle a chuckle, but I tap him in the thigh and we share a knowing giggle. 'Although,' Liu continues, 'I'm pretty sure the devil has some sweet plans for you, Brad.'

'Oh, she surely does,' I say, thinking on Dorothy, on Mozi, and on all the girls and babies in the quarry who didn't survive.

* * *

Liu and I drive back to 15/33, listening to Liu's playlist of country and Ray LaMontagne, a perfect blending of the North and the South. He hums the words to the song 'Trouble', which works a sedation over me. We've known each other so long, there's no need for conversation; no need for him not to sing in my presence.

'Hey, Liu. You and Sandra should stay for dinner tonight. Lenny's making burritos again.'

'The footballs? Hell yeah. We're in.'

'Yup. And after, let's dig in on the dirt samples from the university case. No way those grains and pebbles are from Massachusetts.'

'Whatever you say, Lisa. You're the boss,' Liu says. He winks my way before returning to the medicine of LaMontagne's voice and lyrics.